STOLEN

Willow Danes

STOLEN
by
Willow Danes

©2015 Here be Dragons Publishing, LLC

Cover Design: Steven James Catizone

Published by Here Be Dragons Publishing, LLC

ISBN-13: 978-0692500828
ISBN-10: 0692500820

Also available in eBook publication

ONE

The alien warrior, naked beside her, gave a soft snore, his thickly muscled arm thrown over Summer, keeping her close as he slumbered.

When he had first captured her on Earth, she had only seen beast—his full mouth, his gleaming fangs, his inhuman ridged forehead and heavy brow. Now, lying beside him, his bare tan skin smooth and warm against her own, his eerie glowing amber eyes shut, she knew how very intelligent he was, this wild creature who had brought her to his planet. He, like all the males of his kind—the g'hir—was tall, powerfully built, fast as quicksilver.

Summer wet her lips. She could see the movement of his eyes behind his lids.

Dreaming.

She'd never get a better chance.

Escaping a seven-foot-tall alien warrior who's claimed you as his mate and taken you halfway across the galaxy is impossible.

But when it's your only chance in hell of ever seeing home again, you just tell "impossible" to fuck off.

Six days after her abduction, her heart hammering so hard she feared the sound of it would wake the warrior at her side, Summer eased out from under his heavily muscled arm and slid from his bed.

He stirred, reaching for her. She froze, crouching beside the bed, praying his vibrant eyes stayed shut, his face slack with slumber. His long, silky, red-brown hair was spread across the white pillow, his swarthy coloring a stark contrast to her own pale complexion.

When she'd first awoken to find herself captive on his ship he'd looked her over with his unnervingly brilliant alien gaze. He'd taken a lock of her pale blond hair between his large fingers, frowned at her skin, and asked if such pallor in a human meant she was sickly. Trembling before the huge warrior, thinking he'd kill her if he thought her ill, not even understanding how she was processing those growls of his as language—Summer swore she was completely healthy. He'd given a satisfied fanged smile; pleased, she knew now, that she'd be able to produce the robust, healthy offspring he wanted.

The warrior—Ar'ar—gave another soft snore and Summer straightened to standing.

Clad only in a whisper-thin nightgown, the polished tiles cold under her feet, she padded silently through his luxurious quarters. Sweet spring air drifted through the open balcony doors, the fine silk curtains fluttering in the breeze as she passed them.

The balcony of Ar'ar's rooms—the opulent living quarters of a clanfather's heir—overlooked his family's vast holdings, and the three moons of his world—Hir—lit her way. The wind stirred her long hair, momentarily blocking her vision, and impatiently Summer tucked the bright strands behind her ears to keep them out of her eyes.

She had one chance at this.

If they caught her she'd be watched constantly no matter what concessions Ar'ar—her new alien "mate"— made to his female's pleas. He was confident enough, and proud enough, that he had dismissed the honor guards his father, Mirak, tried to attach to her. Ar'ar gave a huffing, indulgent laugh as he'd waved them off at her request. After all, compared to him, Summer, even at five foot nine, was just a slip of thing.

A weak, harmless, helpless human female . . .

Using the building to help her balance, she climbed up to stand on the balcony's wall.

Eight stories above the ground of an alien world.

Summer swallowed hard. There was a reason she always insisted on having a room on the first floor of a hotel. Just glancing out the glass-wall window of her high-rise office back home left her woozy.

But there was only one way out into the hallway—and ultimately to Earth—that *wouldn't* wake the glowing-eyed fanged warrior snoozing back there. She had to get from these quarters over to the unoccupied rooms beside them. *That* door she could open without fear of waking him, then get the hell out of this monstrously large building they called a clanhall and run for freedom.

It wasn't even very far over. Twelve feet, maybe.

All she had to do was get to the next balcony.

Never mind that the only way there was a small decorative outcropping on the side of the building barely as wide as her foot . . .

Summer hardened her jaw and scooted her right foot out along that tiny space. It was a little lower than the wall she was presently perched on and that made the balance extra tricky. When her right foot was as close to the gap as she dared, she brought her left foot out and shifted her full weight onto the edge.

The ancient hall had something of the look of an adobe house but was made of far more durable material to have stood this long in a forest environment. Rough against her cheek, despite its age and exposure to the elements, the building's surface offered the barest of purchase for her fingers and caught at the fine fabric of her nightgown, as if the clanhall itself were trying to dissuade her from this insane crossing.

Sliding her bare feet along the rough, narrow edge, her body pressed to the building, she inched her way across.

The night's warm breeze rose to ruffle her hair and caress her back and brought her to sudden, shivering awareness that there was nothing behind her now but empty space and a hundred-foot plunge.

Halfway across, pressed hard against the building, her feet pointed in opposite directions, her arms splayed wide, Summer was too fucking terrified to move.

She felt dizzy but she couldn't turn her head to see her way back without falling for certain. She couldn't go back blind and she couldn't continue.

If she cried out Ar'ar would waken instantly. He would be here in a heartbeat and with the strength of one arm could have her right back on the balcony of his quarters.

She would be safe.

But she would never leave this planet again.

You have to get home, goddamn it! Remember why you have to get home!

Drawing a shaky breath, Summer forced herself to keep going. Trembling, desperate to be off the ledge, she reached out for the wall—

And missed.

Unthinking instinct made her lunge and somehow she hooked her arms over the wall's edge, slamming her chin and chest painfully against it. The ball of her left foot was on the outcropping, her right hanging free over the drop, her upper body and arms clutching the wall. She bit back a whimper as she started to slip.

Fingers scrambling along the small lip where the top edge attached, she seized on a handhold and launched herself forward, scraping her big toe painfully in the process.

Hanging from the wall at the waist, her legs dangling, she grabbed for a chair—heavily built to support a g'hir's larger body—that was just close enough. She pulled hard, twisting to bring her legs over, and landed on the balcony in a heap.

She huddled there, hugging her legs to her chest, shaking too hard to stand.

Eyes stinging just at the simple reassurance of solid wall behind her, she gazed up at the three moons the g'hir called the Sisters.

Man, they're gorgeous. I never even noticed how beautiful the moons are.

Summer wiped the perspiration from her upper lip with the back of her shaking hand.

Guess that's what not being dead will do for you.

Miraculously, her captor hadn't been awakened by her little high-wire act, but she wasn't free yet. Her legs still wobbly, Summer pushed herself upright.

The balcony door opened easily at her push and she was careful to close it behind her. It took a moment to get her bearings. She'd never been inside these quarters. Although uninhabited, the rooms were furnished. Near the balcony doors, the Sisters provided plenty of light but as she moved farther into the apartment the moons' light was scant and she banged her shin on a low table.

The heavy table made a scraping sound against the tile and Summer half bent over, her hands clenching, her lips pressed together against a groan, taking quick breaths through her nose against the pain.

When the throbbing in her shin let up a little she hobbled forward, feeling her way to the quarters' large, ornately carved door.

Summer pressed her ear to the door seam. She couldn't hear anyone out there but the door was old, and made of thick, heavy carved wood. There was no guarantee that she'd find the hall empty when she opened it.

But standing here sure ain't getting me home . . .

She wet her lips and cracked the door a sliver.

Dimmed for the night, the lumas still gave off enough illumination to reveal the deserted hallway. A quick look toward her captor's quarters showed that door remained closed. No outraged roar rose to rattle its hinges.

Still asleep!

Even at this time of night she couldn't risk using the majestic curving staircases at the front of the building. Many of Ar'ar's clanbrothers—huge, glowing-eyed, fanged warriors like him—resided here in their ancestral hall. Being the only human meant she would be recognized instantly.

Clinging to the shadows, she headed for the back staircase. It had been built centuries ago for servants' use, when this clanhall was full to bursting with their kind, before the Scourge had wiped out nearly all the females of their species, before that plague made this world home to a dying race—

The echo of approaching footfalls made her duck back into a doorway.

The females of this clan—herself included—numbered only nine but there were hundreds of males. G'hir men were huge, the females smaller, far more delicate, and the heavy sound of boots on the ancient floor meant a male was coming this way.

A warrior.

The footsteps paused. A door down the hall opened, then shut.

A quick glance showed the hall empty for the moment. She raced across to the ancient staircase, her trembling fingers skipping along the wall to keep her balance as she descended the steep stairs.

It wasn't a matter of *if* her "mate" would find her missing; it was *when*. And the real question was just how badly he'd react when he found her gone.

Probably pretty fucking badly . . .

Ar'ar bared his fangs at every male who came near her, even his own brothers. As far as he was concerned, she was *his*.

If he caught her she might very well wish she'd fallen from the ledge instead—as would anyone who assisted her escape.

'Course she knew better than to trust any of these beasts . . .

Two days of crying and pleading to be returned to Earth hadn't gotten her anywhere but then she'd wised up. Ar'ar was the Betari's heir. When she'd actually calmed down enough, she'd made a big show of interest in seeing her "new home." Ar'ar would someday be their clanfather and was proud as hell of it too so it didn't take much eye-batting to convince him to show her all around the Betari clan's settlement. She'd cooed over the buildings and stables and gardens of what the g'hir called an enclosure, so she knew her way around pretty well now.

But more importantly, she'd come up with a way *out*.

She'd also finally put her tears to good use too, three nights ago publicly sobbing to Ar'ar at the evening meal—before two hundred clanbrothers and his father in the clanhall's soaring dining room—that human women needed *alone time* and he never permitted her to go *anywhere* unescorted. Bewildered and embarrassed, Ar'ar insisted she could go wherever she wanted, even without him—provided she didn't leave the enclosure.

Similar to a village on Earth, the enclosure had been built around the well—now an ornate fountain—where the clan's ancestors had gathered to draw water. The oldest, and most important, buildings were located around that central fountain with other structures built farther out as needed. Since the plague struck, the sudden fall in population had left a number of these buildings—especially those on the outer perimeter—empty.

Beyond this settlement, for miles upon miles, lay wild forest controlled by Ar'ar's clan—and her only way out of their territory.

Well, short of trying to steal a transport ship she didn't know how to operate. Ar'ar hadn't been quite confident enough to teach her how to do *that*.

The enclosure grounds were patrolled by clanbrothers but she hadn't been able to discover how the Betari timed those rounds.

Which left getting past those watchful aliens and into the forest all about plain, dumb luck.

There weren't any guards visible from her place in the clanhall's outside doorway, so hopefully wherever they were they couldn't see her either. She broke from the clanhall and ran to the next building, concealing herself in the shadow it cast. She paused there a moment, her palms pressed to the rough stone, her blood thundering in her ears, but no warrior cried out at the sight of Ar'ar's human female roaming the grounds in her nightgown.

She winced against the stones bruising her feet as she trotted from building to building, from shadow to shadow, until, shaking, breathing hard from effort and fear, she made it to the outermost structure of the enclosure.

A family home before the plague struck, located only paces from the edge of the forest, it was here that she'd secreted a pack filled with the supplies she'd pilfered over the last few days.

Ducking inside, already yanking the nightgown off, Summer allowed herself a tight smile. With so few females, g'hir women usually dressed as girly as you could get: long embroidered gowns, sparkling jewels, elaborate hairstyles, delicate shoes.

As the heir's mate she'd been expected to dress like that every day. It was amazing really, what you could conceal under what looked a lot like an alien prom dress . . .

Getting the clothing out here, even the boots, had been easy. The clan had given her a full wardrobe, already prepared for whatever human mate Ar'ar hunted down, though the fit wasn't perfect. The shirt, pants, jacket, and boots she changed into had been intended for her to use when riding multari—Hir's equivalent of horses. The food too was a snap; it was plentiful and available to her at all hours in Ar'ar's quarters as well in the clanhall's dining room.

Summer's lip curled. As a fertile human female, capable of reproducing with the g'hir, she was precious breeding stock; they weren't about to let her go hungry.

And she knew now they sure as fuck were *never* going to let her go home.

Another change of clothing, tightly rolled, lay at the bottom but mostly the pack held food. She stuffed her nightgown inside and fastened the bag. She wouldn't need a nightie for her trek through the forest but she wasn't going to leave anything behind that might hint at the direction she'd gone either.

Evolved to be the perfect hunters, these g'hir were fucking *fast*. The males stood between six and a half and seven feet tall and were ungodly strong too. She'd learned *that* quick enough when Ar'ar had kidnapped her not fifty feet from her Uncle Lester's cabin in Brittle Bridge, North Carolina.

But they possessed a keen sense of smell too—the kind the best bloodhound ever born would envy.

Over the past three days of her "alone time" she'd managed to traverse the whole settlement, even the back stairs she'd just used. Crisscrossing this way and that, she touched everything she could, even leaving here and there bits of hair from her hairbrush that she'd secreted into her pockets. She wasn't sure just how well their sense of smell worked but she was going to do every goddamned thing she could think of to confuse it.

She'd managed to secure one of their weapons too, a small blaster lifted from the clanhall's stores when Ar'ar wasn't looking. She hadn't had a chance to try this one out but she'd wheedled her "mate" into letting her fire his blaster out at the practice range so she had a basic understanding of how it worked. The indicator showed the weapon fully charged, but just how many shots that meant or how powerful those shots were, she didn't know.

She hadn't secured a gun belt though so she slipped the weapon into the thigh pocket of her pants. Summer adjusted the fastening on her boot and stood, shouldering her pack.

Insects hummed and nocturnal birds *whooped* from the forest ahead but from the settlement there was no sign that she'd been missed yet. A few quick steps and she was under the cover of the trees, already bound for the stream at the southwest edge of the Betari settlement.

With the g'hir's inborn skills as hunters she, a human woman alone on a distant world where no one would help her, probably wouldn't have stood a chance.

But she wasn't the same person she was four years ago and nothing—not a race of alien warriors or the light years of space between here and Earth—was going to keep her from getting home.

And one thing she had that these alien fuckers *didn't* was a great-granddaddy who had once slipped a Georgia chain gang.

D'other men said it was right impossible, PawPaw would wheeze. His hair was mostly gone by then, wisps of white over a shrunken skull, his face leathery. PawPaw had even fewer teeth than hair but his eyes, pale blue like Summer's own, were alight with pride and glee. *That it were crazy to try and I tell ya I* was *crazy—crazy like a fox!*

Praying some of them fox-crazy genes had made it down four generations and right to her, Summer walked into the creek, just like PawPaw had done in the 1920s to throw off the dogs.

She headed upstream like he had too but it was hard going, much harder than she expected. The water dragged at her feet and even with the moonlight it was a struggle to see her way. The water soaked her boots, icy enough to make her grit her teeth—probably runoff from the nearby Zun Mountains. She slogged along until the shore on either side looked good and rocky then made her way to the eastern side to slide her pack off.

Then, bending and scooping, she covered herself from head down with mud.

PawPaw had been evading dogs, not g'hir, when he'd done this but what could fool a bluetick hound's sniffer might just fool an alien's too.

She coated her hair well, intent on dulling its bright platinum to the muck's dun color, better to camouflage herself from the g'hir's sharp eyes. The mud was just as miserably cold as the water, slimy too, but there was one thing to be grateful for: it was mid-spring on the g'hir homeworld; she wouldn't freeze to death out here. It had been winter in North Carolina; the Smoky Mountains were buried in white, every store in town alight with decorations for the upcoming holidays when Ar'ar had come to Earth and ripped her right out of her life—

Her nostrils flared, remembering. She'd fought that glowing-eyed demon with strength borne of terror until a shot from his blaster had knocked her out. When she'd awakened on his ship they were already light years from home. He'd cuffed her wrists together—some stupid alien courtship custom of theirs—and when he'd finally taken the restraints off he'd tried to mate with her.

But despite the heat of his amazing body, the warm male scent of him and that mating sound he made as he caressed her—a rumbling-purr that tightened her pussy and vibrated right through her clit till she was gasping with need, scarcely able to keep from grinding against him to seek release—Summer wouldn't submit to him and, to her genuine surprise, he didn't rape her.

That was the one good thing about Ar'ar. He'd taken her from Earth just as other human women had been to be mates to g'hir warriors but he *wouldn't* force her. With his size and strength she wouldn't stand a chance and as aroused as he made her, her body would betray her to pleasure if he took her as sure as the cold water raised gooseflesh on her arms now.

He'd claimed her; he brought her back to his clan— proof of his hunting prowess or some such crap. Nightly he tried to seduce her, that rumbling sound making her wild with need. His fangs flashed in annoyance every time when she, trembling with arousal, refused him, but he didn't insist on anything more than sleeping beside her.

But no plea or demand or efforts to reason with him were going to get her back to Earth either.

Ar'ar's father, Mirak, clanfather of the whole damned Betari enclosure himself, had told her in no uncertain terms that *this* world was her home—and Ar'ar her mate—no matter what she wanted.

With a hard *splat* she smeared mud on the outside of the pack too.

The capital city of Be'lyn lay due east of the Betari enclosure and she had a long haul to get there. Also contained in her bag, rolled into another set of practical clothes, was a fortune in jewels that Ar'ar had gifted her, as the Betari's future clanmother, enough to buy or bribe her way back to Earth.

Completely covered in muck, Summer shouldered her pack again and started east.

She *would* get home—and in time—no matter what.

The dried mud started to itch even before Hir's twin suns—the Brothers—rose. By midmorning it took a lot of her willpower not to scratch. The mud might be disguising her scent from the g'hir but it felt heavy and stiff in her hair and some flaked off as it dried, irritating her nostrils, bitter in her mouth. Gritty on her tongue, it was very like its peaty smell and, even through she knew she shouldn't waste the moisture, she couldn't help but spit to clear her mouth of the nasty taste.

It was hours since Ar'ar must've awakened to find the place beside him empty, since he'd gone in search of her within the confines of the Betari enclosure, realized she was nowhere to be found . . .

Summer batted at insects, slapping the biting ones, moving through the forest as fast as her leaden legs would allow. She wasn't sure if his pride would insist he come alone or if the Betari's leader would send clanbrothers with him to bring her back.

But Ar'ar *was* hunting her now.

Her stomach growled but she ignored it. She'd stopped briefly at dawn to rest and eat but she didn't want to stop again until—

One instant the cay'ik wasn't there then it was.

She gasped as dozens of spindly black legs propelled its worm-like body along the ground toward her. About the same size as Granny Delilah's dachshund, with a pale, waxy yellow body, the creature scuttled forward.

It made a scorpion look positively cuddly. With venom that paralyzed the victim even as it liquefied flesh for the cay'ik's consumption, it was one of the most deadly—and revolting—creatures on Hir.

Its black gaze fixed on her and her eyes widened as its round mouth opened to reveal rows and rows of sharp teeth. Fumbling in her pocket for the tiny blaster as the cay'ik lunged, Summer backpedaled so fast she lost her footing, landing hard on her butt.

The fall knocked the blaster from her hand and it bounced out of reach.

The cay'ik hissed and spit and Summer kicked hard just as it launched itself at her, catching the wretched thing in the face with her heel. Like quicksilver its body whipped around and the creature's mouth clamped down on her boot.

Yelping, she scraped at it hard with her other foot to dislodge it. The cay'ik flew though the air to land on its back but it was stunned only for an instant, its many legs waving for a moment before gaining purchase enough to flip it back onto its belly. Summer threw herself to the side as it jumped right at her face.

The cay'ik exploded as her blaster bolt caught it square on.

Shaking, gripping the blaster so hard her hand hurt, Summer realized a venomous bite would get her off Hir quick too and not in any way she'd intended.

But she didn't feel any pain. Liquefying flesh would hurt, right? Wiping her foot against the forest floor, she cleaned the top her right boot off quickly to judge the damage. To her astonishment—and relief—the cay'ik's teeth hadn't managed to breach the tough leather of her boot.

Green goo and a few still-twitching black legs were spread over a full square yard, some even sticking to the bark of the trees behind where the cay'ik had been.

Summer pushed her mud-caked hair out her face. "God, I hate this fucking planet!"

Her legs felt a little shaky as she got to her feet and skirted the remains. Cay'ik were fiercely protective of their large territories so she wasn't likely to come across another for hours.

And at least she knew the weapon worked, and worked pretty well at that since it had blown the cay'ik to gooey pieces. Next time she stopped she would check the blaster, see if it had any sort of power setting or something that she could adjust—

A flurry of movement made Summer gasp and sent her fumbling to raise her blaster again. Recognizing the flock of nuaran birds she gave a short relieved laugh and tucked the weapon away.

She might hate this world but it did have its beauty too. For a moment she was transfixed as the nuarans, their scarlet plumage glorious against the deep blue of Hir's sky, flew over her head, weaving through the trees, their cries echoing through the forest.

Then her smile faded.

Oh my God . . .

Those birds were *fleeing* something. Something big and loud enough to startle a whole flock into flight.

Like a mounted hunting party of g'hir warriors.

The sound of the blaster shot would have carried and with the g'hir's sense of smell and the creature's charred flesh—

Summer broke into a run.

Her breath burned in her throat as she ran, branches scratching her face, pulling at her clothing, as she pushed her way through the trees.

I have to get home! I have to!

Suddenly—so suddenly she was shocked into a clumsy halt—she was out of the woods and in a clearing. It was a lovely spot, the azure sky breathtaking, the ground flat and grassy, the sunlight sparkling on the river beyond.

And she wasn't alone.

More amazing still, she'd managed to startle him as much as he'd surprised her.

The warrior rose from his crouch beside the simple shelter to regard her in astonishment. He was very tall, like all the g'hir were, with the same alien rippled forehead and heavy brow. His blinking eyes glowed too but unlike the

Betari clanbrothers' amber color this warrior's eyes were as blue as the sky above, his hair black instead of the Betari's dark red-brown. His clothes were different too, softer in color and cut.

"By the All Mother—" His glowing gaze was wide. "You are *human*."

He was g'hir but he wasn't one of the Betari clan. He was just as alien as they but—

"Please!" Summer took a few stumbling steps toward the stranger. "Please help me!"

TWO

The warrior took quick strides toward her. He was powerfully built, his vivid blue eyes predator sharp, but his hold was gentle as he caught her by the shoulders.

"How are you here, little one?" His rippled alien brow furrowed as he took in Summer's muddied clothes, her matted hair. His quick sniff at her had his nose wrinkling instantly. "By the All Mother, what has happened to you?"

"I came through the forest, they're—"

"How are you here?" he asked again, sharper this time. He glanced in the direction she had come. "That way lie the Betari lands."

"Yes," she gasped. "I came from their enclosure."

He released her as if she burned him. "Then you belong to one of their warriors." His lip curled and he stepped back. "A human female separated from your mate by the forest; simply lost and seeking him."

"No!" Summer shook her head. "Please! I need your help!"

He gave a short huff. "You are not lost to him forever. If your mate is a warrior worth his name, he will find you swiftly." The stranger gave her a gentle push toward the woods. "Go back that way. You will soon be reunited with your mate, little human."

"He *kidnapped* me!" Summer cried, doggedly following the blue-eyed warrior as he stalked back to his campsite. "He kidnapped me and brought me here from my world!"

"Many of your kind are unsettled when you are first captured," the warrior rumbled. "Soon you will accustom yourself to him happily."

"Goddamn it, I don't have time for this!" Summer's hands clenched into fists. "Don't you understand? The bastard's right behind me!"

The warrior stopped short. "You are fleeing your mate?"

"I escaped the clanhall last night but he's tracked me. You've got to help me get out of here!"

"What do you mean—you escaped?" he demanded. "Why would you need to?" His glance went over her again. "Has your mate mistreated you?"

"You mean *other* than kidnapping me and taking me to an alien world?"

"To capture a female is our way," he growled, turning away. "You have nothing to fear from your new mate."

She grabbed his arm to stop him. "Goddamn it, I need your help! And I need it *now!*"

"If he has not mistreated you what reason have you to run away from him?"

Summer hesitated. He sighed and his expression softened a little, his hand covering hers where it rested on his arm.

"If he has been permitted to hunt a mate on your world then he is an honorable g'hir warrior," the stranger soothed. "You are a human female and highly prized. He will never harm you. Your mate will care for you and protect you, always." He gently removed her hand from his arm and indicated the forest. "Go. Return to your mate."

Her eyes stung with tears. It was so unfair! After all she'd been through: the capture, the terror, the translator chip Ar'ar implanted in her brain without her permission so she could understand the g'hir's snarling, growling language. The sickening, never-ending anxiety that Ar'ar might lose patience at any time and rape her, forcing her to breed a half-human, half-g'hir monstrosity. That she might never see home again, the desperate planning and sneaking and fear of what they would do to her if they caught her—

The warrior was frowning, his glowing blue eyes searching her face.

"Please . . ." Summer's vision blurred. "Please . . . I am *begging* you . . ."

The warrior's gaze cut toward the forest, past his own mount grazing contentedly near the treeline, and a moment later she could make it out too, a sound like distant thunder, the heavy beat of multari hooves coming this way.

His fangs suddenly flashed in a snarl and he shoved her toward his shelter. "Inside."

"No! We have to run! They'll—"

"Quiet!" he hissed, seizing her elbow to propel her toward the geodesic dome and shoving her inside.

The shelter was tall enough that she could stand comfortably but with his height the roof was only inches above his head. It was large enough to accommodate a wide pallet bed piled with furs and while things were neatly arrayed it looked as if he had occupied this camp for at least a few days.

"Whatever happens, stay here." The warrior pulled the pack from her back and tossed it into the corner of the shelter then fixed her for an instant with his furious blue gaze, his voice a tight whisper. "And for the love of the All Mother be *quiet*."

He ducked back out and yanked the fabric door shut behind him.

With only one entrance in or out there wasn't going to be an escape through the back door this time. There were fabric "windows" but they were closed. It was unpleasantly stuffy in here, much warmer than it was outside. But in his hurry he hadn't sealed the door completely; a tiny sliver was left open.

At the sound of the arriving riders, Summer knelt and eased herself down to lie flat, peering out through the tiny crack.

She had the answer to one of her questions immediately.

Ar'ar wasn't hunting her alone.

She counted no fewer than five clanbrothers riding with him, though his father, Mirak, was not among them.

The blue-eyed warrior strolled to meet them as they reined in a few paces from the treeline, the multari shifting restlessly under them. The stranger's pace was unhurried, the set of his shoulders showing him a man curious but not yet alarmed.

He inclined his head to the mounted warriors and when he spoke, his words carried to where Summer hid. "I greet you in peace, clanbrothers of the Betari enclosure."

"I know you," Ar'ar said shortly to the blue-eyed one. "You are Ke'lar, the Erah clanfather's son. You are brother to Ra'kur."

Ke'lar gave an agreeable shrug. "And I recall seeing you—and your father Council Member Mirak as well—at the wedding celebrations at the Yir enclosure this past midwinter, Ar'ar of the Betari."

"What are you doing here?" Ar'ar demanded.

"I might ask the same of you and your clanbrothers," Ke'lar replied, sounding surprised. "Since you come in such numbers and your multari show you have ridden hard."

Ar'ar's fangs bared. "We are hunting."

"Ah, then I must caution you—" Ke'lar sent a wave at the surrounding area. "In the excitement of your hunt you have mistakenly crossed the border into our lands. This territory is part of the Erah enclosure."

"Only the very farthest point of it!" Ar'ar snapped. "Why do you forest here, Ke'lar, son of the Erah?"

"I may forest within any of the Erah enclosure," Ke'lar said, an edge creeping into his voice. "Even to the very border of *our* land . . . if I wish."

There was a tense pause and Summer could see Ar'ar's hard stare on Ke'lar even from here.

"What are you hunting?" Ke'lar asked, pleasant again. "It is the wrong season to find kartlet in this area. They will not be plentiful here until the summer suns are on the wane."

Ar'ar's gaze was hooded, his mouth tight as the multari shifted beneath him. "A fugitive. A warrior who has broken with clan directive and fled Betari justice."

A fugitive? Summer frowned. Why the hell didn't Ar'ar just say his mate had run away? Was he embarrassed or something?

"A criminal?" Ke'lar asked, his tone turning grave. "The man must still be in your territory. I have been here many days and not seen another warrior—of my clan or yours—in all that time. In fact, I have not seen any clanbrother of the Betari—save yourselves—since the last winter gathering at the Yir enclosure."

Ar'ar's glance went to Ke'lar's camp, to the shelter where she hid, and Summer had to control the urge to duck away lest even that slight movement drew his attention.

Ke'lar patted the neck of the multari Ar'ar rode. "A fine mount indeed. Did you purchase him? Or was he bred from stock in your enclosure?"

"May we hunt the one we seek in your land?" Ar'ar asked bluntly.

He doesn't know I'm here! Summer's mouth parted. *He can't smell me! If he could he'd be on me like a duck on a June bug!*

"I cannot give permission for that." Ke'lar sounded a little offended and dropped his hand. "Only our clanfather can allow you onto our lands in such a great number."

"I could hardly invade your territory with only six warriors," Ar'ar said sharply. "And we do not seek to break the treaty! It is not by my wish that our clans are enemies. I only wish to have returned to me that which is . . . our own responsibility."

"I am sure my father will send a hundred warriors here"—Ke'lar spread his hands—"if a clanbrother of the Betari, a fugitive from justice, has dared breach our borders. I came here to offer the All Mother my reverence but I will return to our clanhall and relay your message to him, if you wish to wait."

For a moment Ar'ar looked as if he would argue further, but then one of his clan brothers caught his eye.

"Thank you, no," Ar'ar said but his brittle tone belied his polite words. "If we decide to ask for the Erah's assistance we will apply for aid from your clanfather ourselves."

Ke'lar took a step back. "Then may the All Mother bless your hunt and your clanbrother be brought swiftly to justice—as he deserves."

Ar'ar didn't reply, turning his mount and heading back into the forest and Betari territory, his clanbrothers following.

Summer put her face in her palm and closed her eyes, thanking God and the Buddha and Lakshmi and the g'hir's All Mother and any other deities that happened to be plugged into this far-flung side of the galaxy.

The shelter's flap opened and the blue-eyed warrior— Ke'lar—entered.

Summer scrambled to her knees. "Thank you so—"

His hand shot out, covering her mouth to silence her. Leaning very close he spoke in her ear, his whisper so low she could scarcely hear it.

"The Betari warriors have not gone far," he murmured. "Even now they watch, but they do not dare break our treaty or offend a son of the Erah clanfather on mere suspicion. If they discover you on my family's land, within my own shelter, they will take you. They will kill me and bring a clan war that will tear this part of our world apart."

It was a good thing he had his hand over her mouth or Summer would have told him she didn't give a damn about what these beasts did to each other—as long as she got back to Earth.

"Remain here," he continued, still murmuring. "Be silent. I do not know how long they will watch. I will be nearby at all times and when they have gone, I will return. Do you understand?"

She gave a nod.

He held her gaze and slowly removed his hand. He regarded her for a moment then pulled a soft pouch down from the hook on the support above. Detaching a tube, he held it to her lips.

"Water," he murmured.

Eagerly she drew on the straw, sighing silently in relief as the cold water hit the back of her parched throat.

He let her drink then opened another pouch and offered the contents to her.

It looked a bit like trail mix and she was ravenous but when she reached for it he looked utterly dismayed.

Summer paused, unsure, her hand hovering over the pouch, embarrassed to see her fingers were still covered in muck, the dirt caked under her nails.

The warrior hesitated, then with slow, deliberate movements scooped some of the food out to feed her himself. He waited while she chewed, offering the water and food again by turns.

Finally she gave a nod. She could have eaten all of it and finished off the water too but she wasn't sure how long he should stay in here with her if the Betari were still watching.

He directed her toward the bed, silently inviting her to lie down. He moved when she did and Summer realized he was probably doing it to help cover the sounds she made as she shifted about.

When she was lying down he motioned her to stillness. He adjusted the openings of the shelters air flaps. Fresh, cool air smelling sweetly of the nearby river washed away the stuffiness but he kept them low enough so that no one should be able to see inside.

He bent over her, his cheek nearly against hers, his long silky black hair spreading against the white furs beside her head.

"Rest," he whispered, his warm breath against the sensitive skin of her ear sending little shivers through her. So close to her she couldn't help breathing in his scent, warm, male, with overtones of cinnamon. "I will come for you as soon as they have gone."

They were a despicable race—these g'hir—hideous with their alien rippled foreheads and unnerving glowing eyes, their fangs and hulking brawn. Summer would never forgive what they had done to her, how Ar'ar had swooped in with the full knowledge and approval of his people to tear her from her home, her family, her whole life . . .

But this one, Ke'lar, was the first of their species to show her any real kindness, the first to show some respect for her rights and wishes. Knowing that a half-dozen warriors lurked nearby watching him, that they would kill him if they discovered that he sheltered her from them—

She touched his arm just as he was turning to leave, the light brown leather of his warrior's jacket soft under her fingers.

He stopped, his glowing blue eyes blinking down at her.

He must have read the gratitude in her eyes because he gave a faint smile and gently pressed her hand with his own for a moment. Then he left the shelter, careful to close the fabric door completely behind him this time.

Summer shifted a bit, slowly, trying to keep her movements silent. The sleeping pallet was incredibly comfortable. Wide and long, it was meant to accommodate his greater size so she had plenty of space; the pillow under her head smelled faintly of him. Outside she could hear the sound of the river, the splash of water running over the rock, the call of birds from the nearby forest.

She could hear him too—Ke'lar—moving about outside the shelter. She couldn't see him, of course, and so had no way of telling what tasks he tended to. To her ears at least, his movements seemed unhurried, perfectly at ease, as if he had dismissed the encounter with the Betari clanbrothers from his mind and had turned his attention to the simple work of maintaining his campsite.

But he was g'hir too, a hunter like the rest of them. There were times that she didn't hear him at all.

She wished he'd whistle or play music or listen to the equivalent of whatever the g'hir had for a ballgame. Now that she'd stopped moving, that she had to stay here, quiet and still, every bump and bruise, every scrape and blister, made itself known. She hurt all over. The lightest shift on the pallet made every overtaxed muscle cry out in protest and she had to press her lips together to silence a moan.

And if it hurts today, it's sure as hell going to hurt worse tomorrow. God, what I wouldn't give for a couple Advil . . .

And this was supposed to be my vacation.

At least that had been the idea. Two weeks at her uncle's cabin, some time to unwind and relax while he headed out to Florida for some sunshine, a nice quiet old-fashioned Christmas in North Carolina then back up to Virginia—

Summer let her tired eyes fall shut and found herself listening for Ke'lar again as he moved about outside the shelter. Just knowing he was nearby, that he was standing between her and capture by Ar'ar and his clan, let her breathe easily for the first time since that sunny, snow-filled afternoon a week ago when she left her uncle's cabin to head out to the woodpile . . .

Ar'ar's massive hands clamped around her upper arms, his shadowy bulk looming over her. Summer cried out, struggling against his grip—

"They have gone!" Ar'ar insisted in another's voice, his eerie alien eyes the wrong color. "You are safe!"

"Wait . . . where am—?"

Moonlight showed through the partially open window flaps but she couldn't see anything save the shadowy outline of him and his eyes, glowing blue even in this faint light.

Her memory came rushing back.

This was the warrior from another clan, Ke'lar, peering down at her. This was his shelter by the river.

In the next moment the space was filled with light as he activated a luma hanging on a hook on one of the shelter's support beams. Summer wet her lips as she pushed herself against the soft fur covers of his pallet bed to sit up.

"Jesus," she muttered, her hand going to her temple. Green-gray flakes echoed the movement and it took a moment to realize it was the dried mud from the creek, still caking her hair, that she'd covered herself with last night.

"I, uh—" She swallowed against the dryness of her throat. "I guess I fell asleep."

"Clearly."

He wasn't whispering! They should have been whispering!

Her frantic glance went to the shelter's open door, to the forest beyond. "Can't they—what about—"

"The Betari clanbrothers have retreated far enough into their own territory that even scouting as deeply as I dare into their land I cannot now detect them. And thankfully so—since your cries would have made your presence here plain."

Summer's mouth tightened at his chiding tone. "Sorry, I was dreaming. I thought you were Ar'ar."

"Again, thankfully I am not," he muttered, his tone dry. Despite his show of neighborly politeness there was plainly no love lost between the two. "But I believe you may move about without fear of discovery now."

Her sore muscles cried out in protest and she couldn't help a groan as she stood. She was still wearing her boots and the blister rubbing her right heel made her grit her teeth as she gained her feet.

At the pained sound she made, he turned to face her, startled. "What is it?"

For an instant Ke'lar's concerned expression, the fine, high cheekbones and square-jaw of his face, the intelligence in his bright blue gaze, made him, despite his rippled brow and glowing eyes, his growled language, seem . . .

Human.

"Nothing," she mumbled. "I'm fine."

His fingers went gently under her jaw to tilt her face up.

"You are injured," he growled, his focus on her swollen, bruised chin.

"Oh," Summer agreed. "Yeah, thanks to Ar'ar, I'm a mess."

He bared his fangs, his alien visage utterly savage, and she recoiled, any resemblance to the humanity she had seen a moment ago vanishing instantly.

"He did this to you?" he snarled.

"No. That's not what I meant." She gave a dismissive wave, wincing as she shifted her weight. That was one bitch of a blister on her right heel. "I did all this by myself.

Apparently, if there's one thing about escaping from an alien fortress for me *isn't*, it's graceful."

"But this—" He indicated her chin. "It is not the result of a hand strike? You are certain it is not from a blow? That it occurred during your flight from the Betari clanhall?"

"Actually, that one occurred during my *fall* from the Betari clanhall last night," Summer said, wincing as she touched the sore spot. "To get out of Ar'ar's quarters I had to climb from one balcony to the next. On the bright side I might have conquered my fear of heights. Space Mountain, here I come."

"From one balcony to the—" His brow furrowed. "How high within the Betari clanhall are your mate's quarters?"

"Don't call him that!" she flared. "He's not my mate. He's not my fucking *anything*!"

Ke'lar blinked and Summer's face heated at her outburst.

"Eight flights," she muttered.

"You—" His glowing eyes widened. "You *jumped*—at night—between balconies eight stories above the ground?"

"Actually there's some decorative carving that goes around the clanhall there. I got between them crossing on that."

His gaze ran down her body again. "You said you fell—"

"Well, I didn't fall all the way, obviously," she said impatiently. "Just from the carving to the next balcony. But I busted my chin up, my elbows too. Look." She took a step to move around him. "If you don't mind—"

"I do mind." He moved to block her way. "To have concealed you from your lawful clan—and one with long-standing enmity to my own—is a very serious matter. There are things we must discuss. Choices to be made."

"Like what?"

His eyes narrowed a bit at the suspicion in her tone. "I do not seek to trade my assistance in return for coupling with you, if that is your concern."

Summer shifted her weight since she'd been thinking precisely that. "Good, 'cause that'll happen when hell freezes over."

"Why did the Betari lie about their hunt for you?" he demanded. "Why would they seek to hide your presence within their clan?"

"I don't know. But then again, I don't really understand a lot of things your people do."

"They claimed to be hunting a fugitive." He folded his arms, a wall of muscle between her and the shelter exit. "*Did* you break clan directive?"

"If clan directive includes making a run for it instead of breeding a bunch of half-humans for them against my will, then hell yeah, I broke their damn directive. Anything else?" she asked. "Or are we good?"

His face tightened. "I find the Betari clanbrothers' deception, their attempt to conceal the presence of a human female on their enclosure, very suspect—and disturbing. It is important that I discover their reasons."

"Absolutely. You ponder that good." Summer shifted her weight again. "Are we done?"

His nostrils flared. "To assure your safety—as well as mine—we need to have these questions answered now."

"Actually, what *I* really need right now," she grumbled, pushing past him, "is to pee."

THREE

"Have you finished relieving yourself?"

"You know—" Summer began, still squatting behind the tree. The moons were waxing, their cool light bright enough to allow her to see pretty well. His g'hir vision was better, of course, but his back was turned and he was determinedly looking the other way. "The fact that you followed me over here *and* listened to me pee and even *asked* me that question is freaking weird. Even for an alien."

"I meant—" he growled, "do you require a cleansing cloth?"

Funny how a couple short years ago a conversation like this would have left her mortified.

How things change . . .

"Toilet paper? Sure, if you've got it, I'll take it."

She put her hand out and without looking at her he offered her a soft biodegradable cloth.

"Hey, this is even nicer than what the Betari stock," she commented, feeling it between her fingers. "Really, this stuff should be in the bathroom at the Ritz hotel."

"I am glad it meets your approval," he muttered, his face still turned toward the river.

When she'd finished she stood and fastened her pants, then joined him on the other side of the tree.

His glowing eyes finally turned her way. "My impression of human females was that they tended to be more fastidious than this."

"Hey, I climbed across a building, ran—covered with mud!—from an alien posse, shot a spitting centipede from hell, and wrecked my manicure. Sorry, warrior, but I'm not sure I can be called a lady by any stretch now."

"I knew that you fell." His gaze swept her. "What I do not understand is how you could have fallen in such a way so that you are so completely covered in muck."

Summer put her hands on her hips. "Oh, I liked it so much I rolled in it. Like a hog."

His brow creased.

"I used the mud to cover my scent so they couldn't track me," she said impatiently. "You know—because I was *escaping*?"

"It is very effective," he agreed. "You do not smell human at all. I detect only organic decay and fish remains."

"You know"—Summer shut her eyes briefly—"believe it or not, I was happier not knowing just how much I stink."

"You may wash in the river. In fact," he grumbled, heading that way, "if you are to spend any more time with me, I insist."

As much as she wanted to get off the planet, needed to get back home, she knew she had to sleep. Had to eat. And if the Betari couldn't cross over into Erah territory, she certainly wouldn't mind washing the muck off either.

"Why are you out in the middle of nowhere anyway, warrior?" Summer asked, following him. "Did your clanbrothers banish you to the wilderness for having too much charm or something?"

He stopped, his mouth pursed to retort, then his brow creased. "Why are you walking like that?"

"We human types call it 'limping.'" Those boots had done a number on her; she was wincing with every step.

"And gee, O great alien overlord, I don't know—maybe because my feet hurt?"

With a g'hir's shocking speed he swung her into his arms.

"What the hell are you doing?" she cried, struggling at finding herself cradled in his arms—not that it did any good. His grip was warrior strong, his long strides carrying her to the river faster than she could have jogged there. "Put me down!"

"I intend to." He spoke as if he were trying not to breathe while he carried her. "The Betari clanbrothers have retreated into their own territory for the moment but they may return at any time. We cannot afford to dally about till the suns rise simply because your feet are tired."

He was already wading into the river, water sloshing around his legs as he bent down to place her, sitting, on a large smooth rock there.

"Tired! Are you fucking kid—!"

With the swift movements his kind were capable of, he unfastened both her boots, already pulling the right one off before she could finish her protest. It felt like sandpaper being scraped against her injuries to have the leather yanked across them like that.

He stopped instantly at her whimper.

"Wait . . ." His frown deepened. "How much do they pain you?"

Without waiting for an answer, his touch gentled but even such care couldn't stop her from gritting her teeth as he eased the boot off.

He stared at her bare foot for an instant then with doubled gentleness removed her other boot and tossed both to the nearby shore.

His alien square-jawed features were softened by the moonlight, his eyes luminous as he bent, gently cupping her heel to examine one foot then the other.

"Little one . . . why did you not tell me?"

She couldn't see the abrasions, cuts, and blisters as clearly as he could—not with his alien acuity—but she bet her feet probably looked as bad as they felt. The cool air and blessed freedom from the pressure and rubbing of her footwear was pure heaven though.

"You are badly blistered, the soles of your feet have many cuts." His touch hovered over one spot lightly. "Some of these are showing the early signs of infection." He looked up at her. "This is the result of your journey through the Betari territory?"

"I got out of the clanhall barefoot, probably cut the bottoms up a bit then. And then there was the fourteen-hour walk without socks in ill-fitting boots . . . Wading through creek water teeming with bacteria probably didn't help any either but there was nothing I could do. I didn't steal myself any medical supplies," she admitted. "I didn't even think of it before I left and I sure as hell wasn't going back."

"What about—" He hesitated, his vibrant gaze meeting hers seriously. "Do you have other hurts? Other wounds I have not seen?"

"Bruises, cuts, scrapes on my arms and upper back. My feet are probably the worst of it."

He gave a huff. "I have supplies to treat your injuries at the shelter."

"You might want to hold off on the Band-Aids till I can get some of this muck off," she said, indicating her matted hair. "I don't think I can stand this crap on me a minute longer."

"The water of this river is safe for you to wash in," he agreed. "Wait here. I will return soon."

He was gone before she could say anything more. Scooting forward on the rock, she carefully lowered her hurting feet into the cool water. It stung like hellfire at first but she'd been expecting that and once she withstood the initial shock the chill felt fantastic. Summer, her hands behind her, leaned back and let her head fall back in relief.

The splashing of his boots alerted her to his return.

"I have brought cleansing lotion and a cloth for you to dry yourself." He placed them beside her on the rock. "After you have bathed I will carry you back to the shelter and then tend your wounds there but I am here if you have need of me."

Summer heaved a sigh and began unfastening the filthy shirt she wore. "Peep all you want, warrior. Just keep it in your pants, okay?"

He scowled. "It is not my intention to 'peep' at you," he said shortly and turned his back to her.

Summer kept one eye on him as she finished opening her shirt. G'hir females wore short halters to support their breasts but she hadn't put one in her pack. Since she'd originally thought to disappear right after the morning meal, she'd mistakenly assumed that her breakout from the enclosure would happen at a time when she was wearing day clothes. Her nighttime escape left her without a halter or bra but a suspicious glance his way showed that—true to his word—he wasn't even trying to peek. She eased off her mud-encrusted pants and carefully stepped into the water, trying unsuccessfully to hold back a groan.

"Are you all right?" Ke'lar asked over his shoulder, but he didn't look at her.

"Yeah," she said, wincing. "Just hurts when I walk."

The last thing she needed was yet another bruise and she took a few steps deeper into the river, cautious about her footing. The water was cold but not fast moving. She wasn't worried about getting swept away by the current.

Anyway, he'd probably just jump in after her and haul her out with one burly arm if she did.

A half-dozen paces in she found a little depression where the riverbed fell away and the water was deeper, a little pool she could lower her body into by halfway bending her knees. She dipped down, spreading her arms out for a moment in the water till she was submerged to her neck.

She put her face in the water, rubbing at the dried mud with her palms, then tilted her head back. It was a weird but welcome feeling to have the mud soften and float from her hair. Summer used the pads of her fingers—she'd broken a couple of her nails off short since last night—to scrub at her scalp, loosening the dirt and muck there.

When her hair was good and drenched she waded back to grab the cleanser. She lathered her hair, rinsing the long strands and lathering again. She washed her face and body of the dirt and sweat and scrubbed off the mud caked behind her ears.

She washed her lower body and legs and, gingerly, her heels and feet too. Then she waded back to the depression to rinse. For a few moments she just relaxed there, letting herself float, letting the cool water soothe her aches and bug bites, letting the river's currents carry away some of the terror she'd known since her abduction . . .

"Are you all right?" he asked again, his tone urgent. "You are not moving."

The warrior still wasn't looking at her but his sharper g'hir hearing would let him listen for her movements, even above the gentle sound of the slow-moving water. He shifted his weight restlessly, his upper body already half turned her way.

Summer sighed. *Break over.*

"I'm fine," she said aloud. "I'm going to be dunking my head so don't panic if you call out to me and I don't answer immediately."

"I would not 'panic' in any case," he grumbled, folding his arms and firmly turning away

She dipped her head back to rinse, the strands of her hair billowing out around her, feeling so much lighter and cleaner.

In fact, Summer felt cleaner than she had since Ar'ar had first put his meaty hands on her.

As wonderful as it felt here, the water was starting to get chilly and she was shivering a bit when she stood and headed back to the rock. She grabbed the large drying cloth and stood behind him to towel dry her hair.

"I have another set of clothes in my pack." She'd wrapped the drying cloth around her body and retook her place on the rock. She shook out her shirt, stiff with dirt and sweat. "But since I'm wet anyway I should wash these. Just give me a minute."

"I will wash them after your injuries have been treated."

"I'm right here. I can do it."

He huffed an annoyed sigh and started to turn toward her, then caught himself. "May I look at you now?"

"I'm wearing the towel if that's what you mean."

Apparently that satisfied him because he turned to face her. "Leave the clothes. I will—"

Ke'lar broke off, his vibrant blue eyes blinking down at her and his mouth parted, the white tips of his fangs just visible between his full lips.

"What?" she asked then realized this was the first time he'd actually seen her not covered in gray-green muck. With the moons' light and his superior g'hir sight—able to detect color even when moonlight blanched her vision to black and white—he could see her perfectly.

He dropped his gaze and reached for the cleanser.

"I will tend the clothes later," he said gruffly. "Come here so that I may wash your feet."

"I just washed them," she objected, scooting a little away from him.

"And then walked here from where you bathed," he pointed out. "I will be quick."

"Fine," she grumbled. She was sore and stiff but it was hard to be too mad—it was thanks to him that she'd gotten this bath at all.

And that she wasn't back at the Betari clanhall right now.

His touch was soothing as he bathed her feet, a tender gentleness surprising in a man so big.

Summer's brow creased. Ar'ar had never physically injured her, hadn't even left her with a bruise, not even when he'd "captured" and restrained her, but his touch lacked any warmth to it, any caring behind the dutiful attempts at coupling—

"Have I hurt you?" Ke'lar asked at her frown. "I apologize. I did not intend to."

"No." She shook her head, relaxing her brow. "No, you didn't."

He bent to gather her into his arms. "You must tell me immediately if I do."

But his hold was as careful as if he bore one of their precious few g'hir young as he carried her back to his shelter. He ducked inside and leaned down to place her on the sleeping pallet as if she weighed nothing at all. Apparently before he had returned to the river with the cleansing lotion and towel he'd taken the time to shake the furs clean of the mud that had flaked off while she'd rested here.

He settled her on the pallet sitting up, then adjusted the light so it would shine more directly on her. He had a case of medical supplies in hand and knelt in front of her, already lifting the lid.

"I will begin with the abrasions and bruises on your face. I have a mild oral analgesic suitable to human physiology."

Summer rubbed at her sore shoulder. "I'll take a handful, thanks."

A frown touched his rippled brow. "That would be far too high a dose for your body weight."

"I'm kidding," she assured, putting out her hand for the medication. "I'll take whatever you've got. And something for the damn bug bites too, if there is anything."

"I have salve for that."

He gave her a single pill and handed her the water pouch to wash it down. For each cut and blister he applied a sterilizing ointment and then a sealant to protect and cushion the flesh even as it sped healing. Summer sighed in relief as the salve took away the miserable itch from the bites.

"I do not even know your namesound," he commented, his fingers gentle on her cheek. His glowing gaze met hers and he inclined his head to her. "I am Ke'lar, of the Erah enclosure."

"Yeah, I heard Ar'ar call you that. I'm Summer."

"Summer . . ." He applied healing salve to her shoulder, cradling her arm in his large hand. "Did they give you that namesound because your hair is as bright as the sun in that season?"

She gave a short, surprised laugh. "No, I was born bald. The blond happened later. Lucky thing too, they probably would have named me Marilyn instead." At his puzzled glance she explained, "After Marilyn Monroe, the actress. A human female very famous for having blond hair."

He tilted his head. "You would not have liked that namesound? It is pleasant enough."

She gave another laugh. "Not really, too many expectations on me—to be this blond *and* named Marilyn. But to answer your question they named me Summer 'cause I came two weeks late—my birthday is June twenty-first. That was the summer solstice the year I was born, the first day of summer. Well, at least in the region of Earth I'm from."

"You do not have a second name? The other human females seem to have a second clan name, as well."

"My full name is Summer Elizabeth Mills. I was Summer Elizabeth Baker for a brief stint there but it's Mills again."

Ke'lar's brow furrowed. "Were you adopted into another clan?"

"I'm divorced." He looked at her blankly and she sighed. "Okay, 'Summer' we already covered. My middle name is to honor my grandmother, Elizabeth. My family name is Mills but when I married I took my husband's family name, Baker."

He blinked. "You have a human mate, Summer?"

"Oh, hell no! Not anymore anyway, and thank God that's over with! Dean is some piece of work—as Uncle Lester says. Dean actually manages to make Ar'ar look good in comparison and Ar'ar is a kidnapping alien monst—"

Ke'lar's luminous gaze met hers and she broke off, her face heating.

"Sorry," she mumbled.

"A salve will aid the healing here," he said, indicating the ugly purplish bruise on her shin.

He took his time, thoroughly examining and treating even the smallest scrape. And she had dozens of them. On her face from the branches, on her arms and elbows and shoulders where she'd caught herself against the balcony, and other injuries that she couldn't begin to say where she'd picked up.

"You do not like my kind," he said finally, applying a bandage seal to the blister on the back of her right heel. "The g'hir."

Despite his mild tone, his gentle touch, her nostrils flared. "I didn't get a chance to like—or not like—your kind! I was at my uncle's house, just heading out to the shed for firewood, and then a humongous *demon* full of teeth and glowing eyes was coming at me and roaring. I was screaming, running for the house, and something hit me hard in the back. When I woke up I was fucking *handcuffed*! And when I *begged* to go home he explained how he and I were going to breed new g'hir! That's why he took me away from—away from home! To breed with him!"

His expression was shuttered. "Other human women have found g'hir mates pleasing to them."

"But you aren't sorry, are you?" Summer narrowed her gaze. "For what he did to me. For what your kind is doing to other human women. None of you are."

"You are our last hope," he said, but he didn't meet her eyes. "In all our searching only human women have proved compatible mates. You are our only chance of survival."

"If the cost of your survival is the brutal exploitation of another species," she gritted out, "what the hell makes you think you even *deserve* to survive?"

"What would humans do?" His eyes flashed blue fire. "If faced with this choice? Would you breed with another species like my kind or watch your own become extinct?"

"Oh, I'm not playing all high and mighty on you. Based on stuff like, I don't know—the Holocaust—I'm sure we humans would be just as uncivilized, just as selfish and brutal, as you g'hir are. But that doesn't make it right and I'd have a lot more respect for *your kind* if you'd just admit what you're doing is wrong."

His face was stormy. "No human female has ever been mistreated on Hir. You are honored, cherished, coveted—"

"Never mistreated—?" Her face went hot. "What the fuck would *you* know about it?"

"My brother's mate, Jenna, is human," he growled. "She loves Ra'kur and their daughter. She is happy and content living with my clan."

"Jenna?" The name came like a punch in the stomach. "Wait, you don't mean—Jenna McNally? Jesus, I *know* her! We were best friends as kids. We hung out every summer, whenever she and her grandfather came up from Asheville. We traded friendship bracelets when we were twelve. I don't believe this! I mean . . . I haven't seen her since I moved to Alexandria, not since before I—" She shook her head. "And when Uncle Lester told me last year that Jenna disappeared . . . I mean she was always so level-headed, so responsible, I *knew* she wouldn't have just up and left. I—

we all—thought . . . She's *here*? Holy hell, everybody back home thinks she's rotting out the woods somewhere!"

Summer's whole body went cold.

And I've been gone a week already! What will they think—what would anybody *think—with the house door unlocked, holiday cards on the table, the lights and TV on, and me nowhere to be found . . .*

Oh my God, if they think I'm dead —

"You have become very pale." He was frowning. "Do you feel ill? Or faint?"

"No." Summer swallowed hard. "I'm—homesick. I just want to get back as quickly as I can."

"I understand."

Her gaze snapped to his. "You—you do? You mean . . . you'll help me? You'll help me get back to Earth?"

"And force my clan into a war with the Betari?" He shook his head. "No, little one, I am taking you back to your mate."

Four

"*What?*"

"Ar'ar captured you in accordance with our customs and laws." Ke'lar's mouth was tight. "By your own word he has not mistreated you. You must be returned to him."

Summer's hands clenched. "You call kidnapping me, keeping me prisoner, not mistreating me?"

"Prisoner?" His bright eyes were alert. "How were you held prisoner?"

"How about not letting me go back to Earth?" she cried. "I wasn't even allowed to leave the enclosure!"

He turned away, focused on gathering and repacking the medical supplies back into their case.

"Ar'ar would not wish to risk one so precious. Keeping you safely at the Betari enclosure would be prudent," he said evenly. "You are a great temptation to unmated males. Likely even those within his own clan have coveted you for themselves but they at least are held sway under enclosure loyalty and clan directive. And there have been assaults on human women by the Purists—"

"Purists?" Summer stared. "Who the hell are the Purists?"

He met her gaze, surprised. "Did the Betari never speak of them to you?" At her headshake, he frowned. "The Purists are g'hir who have united in their disapproval of this new breeding with humans. They seek to end all such matings and purge our world of the human influence and offspring."

"No," she breathed. "Nobody said anything to me about that at all."

Why am I so offended by that anyway?

The g'hir were huge, hulking, fanged alien beasts with rippled foreheads. The very idea of reproducing with Ar'ar was repugnant, but that some of their people should feel the same way about humans, the same way about *her*—

"Likely the Betari did not wish to worry you with talk of them." He sealed the case and stood, holding it between his hands. "Their enclosure is well protected, you were safe there, in your home clanhall. I am actually surprised you were able to escape."

"You can hardly call it my home *and* say I escaped from it in the same breath." Her fingers clenched in the soft fur of the covers. "So that's it, huh? You aren't going to do anything about this? You're just going to patch me up and send me right back to Ar'ar?"

"There is nothing to be done," he growled sharply. "Not without breaking g'hir law. Not without causing a blood-soaked rift between two clans who have been at peace since the Scourge. Ar'ar captured you. You are his now."

Summer felt her nostrils flare. "I'm not *anybody's* but *mine*! And I want to return to Earth!"

"Then tell Ar'ar you wish to go home!" Ke'lar snarled. "Tell *him* of your decision to abjure a g'hir mate and return to your homeworld."

"I *have* told him! I've told anybody who would fucking listen!"

He gave an impatient huff and his voice fell to a grumble as he began packing the foodstuffs within the shelter. "You have only a moon's cycle of time with Ar'ar before your Day of Choosing. On that day announce that you wish to return to your own world. Your memory will be wiped of our world, of us. He must let you return then."

"No, he won't! Who do you think relays that 'choosing' crap to people *outside* the enclosure? A Council member! And guess who the Betari's clanfather is? Council member Mirak! He's already told me that it doesn't matter what I say, he's going to go out there and tell everyone I chose Ar'ar!"

That stopped him cold, his face shocked. "He cannot. It would break the All Mother's sacred decree. It would be an offense to the Goddess and violate Hir law. Even Mirak would not dare!"

"Oh, really? Have you met the son of a bitch?"

She could see from his expression that not only had he met the Betari clanfather, he was sifting through what the man was capable of, what he might do to ensure the continuation of his own bloodline . . .

Summer folded her arms. "Yeah, probably starting to see the reason for the whole 'escape' thing, now, huh?"

"I cannot deny that they lied to me as to what they sought," he allowed. "I still cannot fathom why they would not admit they sought the mate of Ar'ar . . ."

"Maybe because they're a bunch of kidnapping, lying sleezebags."

He studied her for a moment then gave a reluctant nod. "Very well. You have persuaded me."

Summer blinked. "You mean you'll—"

"I will take you to the Erah clanhall," he interrupted. "There you may make your decision known to our clanfather. *He* will see to it your choice is heard by the Ruling Council. You need only wait until the moon's cycle ends and then you will be returned to your world."

Summer's hands clenched into fists. *Jesus, what does it take to get through to this guy?*

"I shouldn't have to wait at all! It's my choice—my *life*—and I don't have another—what, three weeks?—for this bullshit! I have to be back in Brittle Bridge in seven days!"

"*Brittle* Bridge?"

She waved her hand impatiently. "It's the town—territory—where I come from."

"Why?" he asked, frowning. "Why seven days? What demands you return within that time?"

Summer pressed her lips together and a heaviness seemed to settle over him.

"You do not trust me enough to say."

"Look at it this way—" she began with a toss of her head. "I trust you a hell of a lot more than I've ever trusted any g'hir." Her throat tightened. "Just believe me when I say I *have* to get back there in seven days. No matter what it takes."

"I will take you to the Erah clanhall," he promised. "I will see to it that you can make your plea to my father."

"But—will he help me get home? Get home in time?"

"I do not know," Ke'lar said quietly. "My father is a good man, a fair and compassionate ruler. I know he will do what is right."

It sure wasn't much, but at least it was something. At least he wasn't sending her back to Ar'ar.

Still—

"How long will it take us to get to the Erah clanhall? I don't have a lot of time."

He considered. "Three days, at least."

"Three days! Isn't there a faster way?"

He shook his head. "I cannot allow the Betari proof of your presence in our territory, not until we have reached the stronghold of our clanhall, not until we have spoken to my father. We must go deeper into Erah lands first to avoid the places where our territories touch those of the Betari, then we will head south to the clanhall. To do this—to keep you safely from their sight—will add a day to our travels. I have only one mount and she must carry the supplies of the camp, as well as us. We can only push her so hard for so long. She will need the nights to rest." He glanced toward the shelter's opening, to the moonlight brightening the landscape beyond. "It is late but I think she will be able to carry us a few hours tonight. The sooner we are away from the border of their lands, the safer we will be."

Sure wasn't what she'd hoped for, but riding with him on a multari was going to be a hell of a lot faster than trying to get anywhere alone on foot. And there was a chance, maybe even a good one, that she could convince Ke'lar's father to intervene on her behalf, to get her home in time . . .

"Okay." She gave a nod. "What can I do to help?"

"Stay out of my way," he said bluntly. "I can break camp faster if I work alone. I will begin by saddling the multari and getting her ready to load our supplies." He glanced at her. "You said you had other clothes. You can get dressed."

Summer's face went hot. She'd almost forgotten that she was still sitting here in just a towel.

"Right," she mumbled. "Uh, my boots and my other clothes are still out on that rock—"

"I will tend to your clothes but you should not wear the boots until the medpatches have had some time to repair the injuries to your feet. " He started pulling things from where they hung about the shelter, pulling packs and supplies together. "We will likely travel hours before I judge it is safe to rest in any case."

He offered her the pack she'd brought with her, still covered with dried mud. "Empty this and I will clean it as well."

She reached out to take the bag but he kept hold of it and, confused, she met his eyes.

"Do not underestimate the risks we take," he growled. "The enmity between our clans is ancient and runs very deep. Despite the treaty that forbids their trespass into Erah territory I do not trust the Betari not to breach our borders in search of you. If we do not reach the Erah clanhall and the protection of my clanbrothers—if they find you with me, the Betari will be incensed; they will accuse me—and with good cause—of stealing you. It will give them every right by law to invade our territory, exact revenge, and take you back by force."

Summer's mouth tightened. "I don't suppose anyone will even stop to consider that I might have a say in this."

A flash of . . . *something* passed over his features, gone so fast that she, who had so little experience with their species, couldn't begin to discern it.

"They must not find us," he continued. "And if we are to succeed, if we are to reach the Erah clanhall, you must vow to follow my orders at all times. You must obey me instantly, without question."

"Like a slave? Like a good g'hir mate?"

"Like one who is wholly unfamiliar with the wilderness of Hir," he said, annoyed. "If a fethon slithers within inches of you I cannot take the time to formally ask that you hold still before I shoot it. If I ask you to stop, you will stop. If I say run, you will run. Are we agreed? Or shall we pass the night here so that you may think on it till morning?"

She wanted to argue, she really did, but Summer was practical enough to admit that she'd been lucky as hell when she'd run into the cay'ik. If she'd missed, or just wounded it, she'd be a cay'ik snack right now. Like it or not, this was an alien warrior who knew his own world very well. He knew the way—and the dangers—and he was willing to risk his life to take her to his family's clanhall, the safest way he knew how.

All she had to do, for once in her life, was shut the hell up, follow the rules, and they would both come out of this fine.

Man, we are so screwed . . .

"Sure." She gave a nod. "Fine. As far as I'm concerned, you're the Jungle Jim of Hir."

Clearly he caught the sarcasm, even if he didn't get the reference. His jaw tightened.

Suddenly she sobered. There was a countdown happening and just talking here was wasting precious time.

"Yes," she said, solemn now. "You lead, I'll follow. I'll do whatever you say. Just get me to the Erah clanhall. Help me get home."

"I will bring you safely to the clanhall and to my father," he said, plainly unwilling to promise more. His gaze swept over her. "Get dressed. We depart as soon as I finish breaking camp."

FIVE

"What are you doing?" Summer demanded as Ke'lar brought the multari to a halt and slid from the saddle behind her. "Why are we stopping?"

Not that the past couple hours had been fun—or comfortable either. They rode double, a tight fit on the g'hir saddle, she in front, her back pressed to the warmth of his body, his thighs pressed to the back of hers. The saddle had a handhold at the front that—since the multari stood at least eighteen hands high and the only light was courtesy of the Sister moons—Summer gripped white-knuckled as they sped over the gently hilly terrain of the westernmost Erah land. But Ke'lar wasn't content to trust her safety to her own efforts, his massive arm encircling her waist to keep her securely on the beast, the reins held easily in one hand as they rode.

His greater height had her head resting in the curve of his shoulder and neck as they rode, his cheek against her temple, his skin smooth and free of stubble despite the late hour. G'hir males, despite their thick hair and heavy eyebrows, didn't grow beards.

Her back felt cold without him behind her—g'hir body temperature was naturally higher than a human's—and she shivered a bit with the chill. Her boots were somewhere in the packs but he'd found her some of his own soft foot coverings—too big of course—to keep her feet warm as they dangled over the multari's sides.

He took the beast's reins in hand and started to lead her at a walk. "We are far enough into the Erah territory now. The Betari would be foolish to venture this far into our lands, even to seek a stolen female."

"I thought the whole point was to get to your clanhall *quick*. We should be riding like a bat out of hell!"

He gave her a quick, confused look and Summer sighed inwardly. Ar'ar had attached the translator chip to the language center of her brain when he'd first her brought her onto his ship. Since then she'd learned the thing did some peculiar and unexpected things when translating English idioms onto the g'hir side of things.

"I mean," she began before he could ask what a flying mammal would be doing in the human underworld, "we should continue to travel as fast as we can. Between her speed and your night vision we were making seriously good time."

"Pushing our only multari beyond her capabilities will only leave us walking the entire way rather than part of it—and shouldering our own supplies as well."

"Wait, you're kidding, right? You're going to *walk* her? For how long?"

"Beya is growing fatigued carrying so much weight. She is not young. We cannot ride her to exhaustion."

"You really care about this thing, don't you?" she blurted.

His gaze snapped to her from his place leading the multari. "That surprises you?"

"I don't know." She tucked her hair behind her ears—again. Dozens of girly hair accessories back in the dressing room they gave her at the Betari clanhall and she hadn't even grabbed a clip to hold her hair back. "Yeah, I guess so."

His nostrils flared. "Truly, you do think the g'hir monsters if you believe us incapable of attachment."

"Look, I didn't mean . . . I'm sure your people have feelings, anyway."

"How observant of you," he grumbled then indicated the multari with a g'hir's nod and his tone softened. "Beya came to me as a filly, a gift from my father when I reached nine summers, with clumsy legs too long for her body and a playful heart." He stroked the animal's nose with the palm of his hand and she tossed her head a bit as if to encourage him to continue. "I trained her myself, rising early to feed and water her. She was my sole companion on the many long and lonely ventures into the wilderness needed to earn my place as a warrior. But that was twenty years ago. She has this summer left . . . perhaps one more." His voice was fond but heavy too, his touch gentle on the mount's nose. "And then I, like so many of our warriors, will walk alone."

"Why haven't you gone to Earth then?" Summer demanded. "Captured yourself a human woman like Ar'ar did?"

He turned his face away, leading the multari again. "Very few are selected for the competitions. Even fewer win the chance to journey to your world to hunt a mate."

"I thought—"

He made a huffing sound, a bitter g'hir chuckle. "What? That any male who wished it was provided with the location of your homeworld? That we would let loose millions upon millions of warriors to hunt there unchecked?"

"Why haven't you?" she demanded. "You could. I've seen your people's technology for myself, up close and personal. My world wouldn't stand a chance against you."

"You—human females—our last and only chance of survival," he said grimly. "To invade your world—we would bring you to the brink of destruction as readily as those who unleashed the Scourge upon us have."

"The Zerar." That story—of how their enemies created and introduced the plague called the Scourge, the disease that had killed nine of ten of the g'hir female population in a matter of weeks, while leaving the males alive—she'd heard during her time with the Betari.

"How old were you, Ke'lar? When the plague came here?"

"Five summers," he said, without looking back, without breaking stride. "I do not remember a time when Hir was not a graveyard, when mine was not a race looking into the face of its own extinction."

"I'm sorry." Her throat was tight, recalling the Betari enclosure's monument, the thousands of remembrance stones sparkling under the suns to honor their lost females, women, girls, babies . . . "I'm sorry for what the Zerar did to your people."

He didn't reply. She shifted in the saddle uncomfortably, the unspoken retort hanging in the air—that if she were truly sorry, truly cared about the survival of their kind, she would accept Ar'ar as her mate and provide the g'hir with the children they needed so badly.

"So you seem young and healthy," she said, her throat tight. "Fast enough to catch yourself a human woman for certain."

"I would gladly hunt a mate from your world if I could. I would lay down my life for her. Bleed myself dry for her happiness."

"Her happiness?" she scoffed. "You know, I don't understand you at all, Ke'lar. How can you claim to feel any respect for women—for our rights and wishes—if you'd hunt us like animals?"

His fangs flashed in the moonlight. "I would give a day's blood to the Goddess in thanks for the chance. I would have treasured her, my human mate, with every breath." He turned his face away, walking again. "But I will never be permitted to compete. I will never be among those who journey to your world."

"Why not?"

The reins in his hand were slack and Summer realized Beya, her big head lowered to be level with Ke'lar's, was not being led at all but walking contentedly with him.

"A number of reasons," he said, just when she had begun to think he wouldn't answer her at all. "I am the second of our clanfather's sons. My brother Ra'kur has his Jenna to lead when he becomes clanfather. My mate would have little chance of becoming a clanmother. I will not be chosen when other clans lack a female to lead. I am a second son but had the plague not come . . ." His voice was tight. "I love my brother. We have always been best friends as well as brothers and no one knows me better but—may the All Mother forgive me—I . . . envy him."

"Because he will lead the clan? Because you want to be clanfather?"

Ke'lar gave a short huffing laugh. "If you knew me better you would not ask that. A clanfather must be the perfect balance of the All Mother's sky children: powerful as the Brothers' morning rise with the coolness of mind of the Sister moons."

Summer glanced at his shoulders, the breadth of his back, the astonishing strength of his body. "And you don't think you're powerful?"

"I am too much of the Brothers, with too much sunfire in my essence," he said easily. "And not nearly enough moon. I am told I take after my mother in that way but I could not say. My father loved her greatly but from what I have been told of her, she, like me, would follow her fire and go her own way. Ra'kur was once like me, one who also always chafed against the rules. That is the fire that sent him into the stars and ultimately to find your world. My fire sent me to forest. Perhaps it simply suits my nature better. That way I have no one to argue with but Beya"—he threw Summer a smile—"and out of pity she lets me win. But since he found his Jenna, Ra'kur has found his balance, the moonlight to his fire. It is best for all that Ra'kur will be clanfather and in that I am content."

"Was that why Ar'ar got to go to Earth but not you? Because he's the heir?"

"The Betari are a powerful clan and wield great influence. Mirak would do whatever was necessary to ensure that their enclosure has a clanmother."

"What will they do?" she wondered suddenly. "Now that I've run off?"

"I do not know. To publicly forswear a mate—as you intend to abjure Ar'ar when we reach the Erah clanhall—is shaming to him. Even more so to a proud man, the heir of a powerful enclosure." By the light of the Sisters his shoulders were tense. "His father may demand compensation from the Council for the loss of a potential clanmother by our interference."

Her hold tightened on the saddle, her heart thumping in her chest. "Wait—you don't mean Ar'ar will get a crack at another human woman? If he can't have me he gets to go back to Earth and grab some other woman?"

"You are jealous?" Ke'lar was looking back at her, his glowing blue eyes cool in the moonlight. "That your mate might seek another female?"

She grimaced. "God no! But that means—I'm saving myself but condemning another woman to take my place here."

He gave a shrug. "Human females have shown themselves just as happy as g'hir women to be claimed by a strong mate. Ra'kur's mate is loved and happy, content to live at our enclosure."

Summer shook her head. "I still can't believe Jenna's *here*. I can't believe she's—she's—"

"Mate to my brother? Mate to an alien monster?"

"Hey! I didn't say—!"

"You did," he growled sharply. "Not a few short hours ago while I tended your injuries."

"I was talking about Ar'ar," she grumbled. "In case you didn't notice, he's kind of a dick."

Apparently *that* made it through the translation matrix just fine because he burst out in a g'hir's huffing laugh.

He looked back at her, his luminous eyes crinkled with humor, and Summer, for the first time in a week, laughed too.

"I hope," he began when their laughter had faded, leaving both of them still smiling, "you will find that we are not all like Ar'ar."

"I—Thanks," she mumbled. "For helping me. I started to say it before . . . but I didn't get a chance to finish. Thank you for helping me get home."

"Do not thank me." He turned to lead the multari again. "I am not sure that it will be enough. No matter what I do."

SIX

Summer was drooping in the saddle, their conversation having ebbed to silence as the night wore on. At their last stop to rest he'd given her a blanket to wrap around her shoulders against the chill and with one hand she held it closed over her chest. As she gripped the saddle's horn with her other hand, Beya's swaying walk, the late hour, and the dark and quiet left her struggling to keep her eyes open.

"Come." The sound of Ke'lar's growl at her side jarred her fully awake. "We will make camp here."

"Here?" She looked around sleepily as he tied Beya off to a nearby tree limb. It didn't look any different to her than any other stretch of land they'd covered that night. The moons were lower in the sky, the trees softly rustling with the cool, sweet breeze. "Why here?"

"The ground is higher and there is fresh water nearby."

She frowned. "Have you been here before? How do you know there's water nearby?"

"I can smell it," he said, surprised.

"Right," she murmured. "I forgot you g'hir are all half bloodhound."

His large hands went to her waist, effortlessly helping her down from the multari, but her legs felt wobbly and her feet were asleep from so long in the saddle. She had to grab his shoulders just to keep herself upright.

"You are not accustomed to riding," he growled, helping her keep her balance. "I should have stopped earlier."

"I'm fine." But a step away from him still had her legs struggling to work properly.

"Here," he said, encircling her waist and drawing her arm around his shoulder, his body very warm against her side. "Walking a bit will help."

She had to rely on him a lot for support as they started, he moving with careful slowness for a g'hir, she stiff and limping a bit.

"Man, I'm glad that painkiller hasn't worn off yet." Her feet were tingling as the blood started moving through them again and it was hardly a fun feeling. "I'm not looking forward to when it does."

"I have more in the pack," he assured. "I will try to make the journey as comfortable as possible for you. There will be a healer at the Erah clanhall who can better tend you. I regret greatly that I did not bring a comm unit. If I could call for assistance a ground transport would have you there within the hour."

"Why don't you have a comm unit anyway?" She frowned. "Isn't it dangerous to be out in the wilderness without a way to call for help?"

"I would not be much of a warrior if I needed to call for help and I did not think to be concerned with any but myself." He gave a huffing chuckle. "I certainly did not expect to share this foresting with a human female."

His tone was friendly, respectful, not at all seductive, but Summer—suddenly aware of the heat of his body beside hers, the warm scent of him, male with a bit of cinnamon—felt her face go hot.

"I'm good, thanks," she mumbled and stepped away. "The walking is helping so I should probably move around on my own a bit."

Ke'lar gave a nod. "I will have the shelter in place shortly."

Summer moved about and stretched, trying to work the kinks out, but it couldn't have been more than a few minutes before he had the geodesic dome set up and was carrying the packs in.

He opened the flap to the shelter to invite her in. He already had a heater set up that both lit and warmed the space and had arranged the pallet bed, thick with furs, along the side of the shelter.

"Are you hungry?" he asked, already setting out the water pouches, pulling foodstuffs out.

"Not yet." They'd eaten some dried meat that reminded her a lot of beef jerky—except it couldn't possibly be beef—as well as nuts and dried fruit before they set out and again when they'd stopped to rest earlier. But at his size he must need something like five times the calories she did. "And anyway I think I'm too tired to eat."

"The bed is ready." He indicated the pallet. "I must tend to Beya."

"Right," she murmured.

His brow creased. "What is the matter?"

"Well, to state the obvious . . . there's only one bed."

"I have no intention of trying to couple with you," he growled, his gaze on the supplies he was unpacking and organizing. "I will sleep outside."

"Okay," she managed in a rush of embarrassment and annoyance. "No, that's fine."

He sought her gaze, confused. "Would you feel safer if I slept inside the shelter instead?"

"I don't care where you . . . Look, it doesn't matter. You can sleep in here if you want," she said shortly. "You might as well share the pallet for all the difference it makes."

His brow furrowed for an instant, and then he gave a short huff and stood.

"Beya needs to be watered and we need fresh water as well." He grabbed a few pouches of food, obviously intending to munch as he worked, then lowered the heater's light to minimum. "Go to sleep. I will be nearby if you have need of me."

He did not want to sleep.

Sitting inside the shelter now, Ke'lar did not even think he could, though his body cried out for rest at this late hour.

He simply could not stop looking at her. She was asleep, resting easy on the pallet bed he had prepared for her, her arm thrown wide beside her face, her bright hair covering the pillow. Her delicate face was turned toward him, her skin smooth, her full mouth so rounded and pink.

He had seen only two other human women before and they were beautiful.

But she . . . *she* was exquisite.

Summer . . .

She was very like that season, soft and golden, sweet smelling.

And mate to the heir of an ancient enemy clan.

But one she is fleeing.

She must hate Ar'ar very much to risk her life to escape him. And be very brave to journey through the forests of an unfamiliar world, alone.

Ke'lar breathed her scent in. It was intoxicating; that had to be it. He had his faults, had often struggled with the rules, but he had never endangered his enclosure by his acts, never shown himself as anything other than an honorable man, as one worthy to be called a warrior.

His clan's feud with the Betari had been a long and bloody one, the reasons for it buried in antiquity. Generations of animosity would unexpectedly blaze into conflict. Only the Scourge, the need for unification against a common enemy, had brought about their treaty.

Just to take and conceal her—the mate of the Betari heir—was justification enough to draw his enclosure into a war with the Betari that could see the destruction of both clans.

Nor could he count on the sanction of his own clan for what he had done. There were few crimes more abhorrent to his kind than to steal a female from her mate, from her clan, especially in the wake of the plague.

Ke'lar knew himself innocent of any crime. He had not stolen her but there were many—including his own father— who were not likely to see things that way. Just concealing her from her clan might earn him banishment from his own.

But . . .

She had taken food and drink from his hand yesterday when he had first hidden her in his shelter. Not as formally done as it should be, certainly, and at first he himself had not realized the significance of what he was doing.

But Summer was human. Would she even know the meaning behind the ritual; that a warrior could provide for his mate and that she would trust him to?

He wished he had asked Jenna more about their customs. When his brother's mate had first arrived on Hir, he had been so eager to learn all he could of that distant planet that he had pestered her often.

But the news from the selection committee that he would not even be permitted to compete, that he would never journey to that world and had no hope of hunting a mate there, had discouraged him so that he ceased his badgering.

Was he a fool to hope that it was not a g'hir mate but Ar'ar himself that Summer found undesirable?

She did not seem afraid of *him*. She had asked his help, accepted his touch as he treated her injuries. She spoke easily with him, laughed with him.

Perhaps . . .

Ke'lar edged a little closer to her.

She said she did not mind if he slept here, if he shared the bed with her. Had she meant it as an invitation? He had so little experience with females, and less still with human ones, he did not wish to offend her or, worse, frighten her.

Ke'lar shifted the covers just enough to ease himself into the bed beside her.

She did not wake. She was cool against him—a human's body temperature was naturally lower—and he trembled with desire to feel her curves, his penis already hard as he fitted his body to hers, lubricating in anticipation of mating. He bent his head to where her neck met her shoulder, breathing in her scent deeply. Instinctively a rumble-purr of desire sounded in his chest and she, still asleep, responded with a moan, turning toward him. He could scent her instant arousal.

Her bright hair was silky against his cheek, the blood thundering in his ears as she softened against him.

He groaned, wanting so much to stoke that heat in her, ease her to wakefulness and pleasure . . .

Her offer to let him sleep beside her may have been an invitation to mate . . . or not. He had to know she wanted this as much as he did.

That meant it could not be now; it could not be tonight.

As much as he wanted her . . .

He had seen her fear of Ar'ar, witnessed for himself the injuries and suffering she had endured to flee him.

I must wait. I must be sure.

He was trembling with the effort it took to hold back but a mate bonding could not be undone. With slow, deep breaths, he quieted the rumble-purr of his arousal and with it she quieted too. He would find the strength to be patient, to draw her to him slowly, to learn how she needed him to court her . . . how a human would court her.

It might cost him everything to win her.

He cradled her against him, contentment blossoming in his chest just to hold her.

You are worth that and more . . .

SEVEN

"Summer?"

Her name was soft thunder rumbling in her ear and she became aware of many things at once: the wonderful comfort of a bed in the morning, a large hand gentle on her shoulder, the light streaming into the shelter, the astonishing blue of his glowing eyes—

"Man . . ." Her lids felt heavy and she fought the urge to burrow beneath the covers. "I feel like I just laid down."

"I am sorry to wake you," Ke'lar said, his tone regretful, his hand tracing her shoulder as he pulled his hand away. "But the suns rose hours ago and we have much territory to cover to cross the Te River before nightfall. "

"'Kay." Summer passed her hand over her face, trying to wipe away the last vestiges of sleep, and sniffed appreciatively in the direction of the shelter's open flap. "God, whatever that is cooking out there smells amazing."

"I am glad you think so." He leaned back on his heels. "For it is our morning meal. It is nearly ready but I thought you would wish to wash and dress before we ate." He tilted his head. "I can allow you a few more minutes' rest if you prefer to eat first."

"Better not," she sighed, pushing herself up to sitting. Who would have thought a pallet bed on the ground would be so damned comfortable? "If I close my eyes for a second I'm just going to fall asleep again."

"Here." He offered her a simple glazed cup, steam curling over it. "Jenna says this is much like what humans call cof."

"Cof?" she wondered, taking the warm cup from him and peering at the dark liquid inside. "I think you mean 'coffee'? Actually"—she gave it a sniff—"this isn't . . ." She took a sip and raised her eyebrows ". . . bad at all."

"Jenna vows she could not live on Hir without it." Ke'lar gave a faint smile. "I have not acquired a taste for this beverage but she gifted me some when I left the clanhall."

"I'm glad she did," she said, sipping again. Okay, it wasn't Kona coffee for heaven's sake, more like what you'd get at Denny's at three in the morning, and she preferred cream and sugar but it was welcome all the same. "Thanks, it really helps." She threw the blankets off. "Just give me a minute and I'll get dressed."

"I will tend to our meal," he said and ducked out.

Man, that got him outta here quick.

It didn't look like he'd slept in here either. Frowning, she took another sip of the drink then set the cup down and eased her way up off the pallet. As expected she was sore all over, but a quick inventory showed their advanced g'hir medicine had worked magic; her bruises were faded to almost nothing, her scrapes and blisters gone.

She'd slept in the shirt but it wasn't as rumpled as she thought it would be. Granny Jones, a Southern belle if there ever was one, always said that a lady never set out of the house no matter what the day or time without her hair neat and a least a little lipstick. Summer's mouth curved into a wry smile. Granny would probably have paused during the escape to touch up her face powder but Summer didn't even have a brush or comb; sneaking those hadn't been a priority.

Neither was make-up. She didn't even have lip balm with her.

She pulled on the trousers then ran her hands through her hair, not that it did much good against the many tangles.

Damn it, who cares how I look out here anyway?

She'd used Ke'lar's too-big soft foot coverings last night when her feet hurt too much to don her own shoes but she'd been riding, not walking, then. They kept her feet warm enough but flopped comically whenever she walked and Ke'lar's fangs flashed in a smile when he saw her emerge from the shelter.

"Sorry," she mumbled, embarrassed at being so clumsy. "I didn't see my boots and I didn't want to just go riffling through your stuff looking for them."

"There is no need," he said, bending to retrieve a bundle of shaped skins. "I have made you new ones."

She blinked. "Excuse me?"

"I have made new boots for you."

"Wait—you *made* boots for me?" He jerked his chin toward her—a g'hir's nod—and her eyebrows rose. "When did you have time to do that? And why?"

"After this morning's hunting. As to why—" He sent a glance at her feet. "You cannot wear the others without suffering pain and clearly my foot coverings will not suit." He extended the boots toward her. "These are of simple design; they will be easy to adjust for your comfort but you must put them on for me to be sure they fit. If they do not, I can alter them."

"Uh, okay," she managed, taking the pair from him. They were beautifully made, a deep brown, created from skins that made them look a lot like the sheepskin boots she wore at home in the winter but made without a hard sole, like moccasins.

Balancing on one foot, she pulled on one then the other and using the leather straps secured them to the carved buttons. She took a few experimental steps. They were soft, warm, and extremely comfortable to walk in.

His glowing gaze met hers. "Do they fit?"

"They're perfect," she said honestly. "They're amazing." She gave a laugh. "I can't believe you just made these for me! Where did you learn boot-making, Ke'lar?"

"It is one of the skills a warrior learns."

"Like fighting? Like hunting?"

Her throat tightened. *Like capturing women?*

Ke'lar indicated the spit and the meat roasting there. "And cooking."

Her stomach chose that moment to growl and her face heated when he gave a huffing laugh.

"It will be ready shortly," he promised.

"Well, then." She brushed her hands on the sides of her trousers. "I best hurry and wash up. Which way to the water? I want to take my new boots for a test drive."

"Come." He swung a small pack over his shoulder and indicated a thicket of trees about a football field away. "It is not far."

"I just needed you to point the way," she said, turning in that direction. "I'll be back a few."

In an instant he was in front of her, blocking her way. She gasped at his speed.

I'll never get used to how goddamn fast they are!

"You are my responsibility, Summer." His glowing blue gaze was earnest, his growl caveman brash. "Mine to protect now."

"What are you going to protect me from?" she asked, her face heating. "The fish?"

"I vowed to bring you safely to the Erah clanhall so that you may make your appeal to my father." His nostrils flared a bit, his booted feet planted firmly. "I cannot honor my vow if I do not keep you safe."

"Damn it, I don't need you to—!" Summer threw her hands out in frustration. "You know what? Fine, whatever. I'm hungry." She gave a flourishing mocking wave in the direction of the trees. "Lay on, Macduff."

He didn't budge, his alien brow furrowed. "'Macduff'?"

"It's a line from a human play called *Macbeth*." The sweet morning breeze lifted her hair, blowing a few strands into her eyes, and impatiently she pushed her hair back. "It means 'Let's go already.'"

His glowing gaze was still puzzled but he jerked his chin toward her again then led the way, she behind him. He walked his clan's land with the easy confidence of one well accustomed to life outdoors on Hir, his g'hir physiology giving him a smooth, catlike gait despite his size.

The stream Ke'lar led her to was heavily shaded, the water moving placidly between the rocky banks. The water wasn't deep, maybe three or four feet at the center, the kind of creek that growing up back in Brittle Bridge she and her friends might have splashed in to escape the heat of July.

She might even have taken it for a creek back home, with the sunlight dappling across the water, except that ursh trees, their limbs heavy with fernlike gray-green leaves, overhung the banks on either side and a bright nuaran bird that hopped on one of those branches, its glowing eyes darting her way before it flew away, belied any resemblance to North Carolina—or Earth for that matter.

Ke'lar stopped and held up his hand in silent order for her to pause. His body was tense, his hand at the blaster he wore on his hip. He shifted his weight, pivoting as his glowing gaze swept the area. He took a few quick sniffs.

Her glance darted about; she couldn't detect any but themselves here but his senses were far keener than hers.

"This place is secure," he confirmed. "We are alone." He gave another light sniff. "There have been no others save myself here for weeks."

"Weeks?" Summer muttered. "Jeez, what a nose." She indicated the creek water. "Is it safe to drink?"

"It is safe to rinse your mouth with," he cautioned. "I have filtered the water we will drink." He handed over the sack. "Here. There is cleanser and a cloth for your face, other things for your comfort."

"Thanks," she said, taking the bag and hoping he would give her at least a little privacy.

"I will be back in a few minutes," he said. "Call out if you have need of me."

He left then, apparently confident she wouldn't fall in and drown in the creek if he took his eyes off her for a second.

Not wanting to get her clothes wet or ruin her new boots, Summer was careful to kneel where the bank was dry but she could still reach the water. She cleaned her teeth and used a corner of the cloth to clean her face so she wouldn't get her shirt soaked either.

She groomed herself as best she could and was already heading back toward the camp, the bag swung over her shoulder, making another half-hearted attempt at getting the knots out of her hair with her fingers as she walked, when he returned.

"Always does this without a load of conditioner," she said with a self-conscious laugh and gave up. "I'm probably just making it worse."

"The fault is mine." He held up an intricately carved wooden comb, his grip on it gentle, almost cradling. "I meant to include it in your pack."

"Wow." It was hand carved, the wood a natural deep, vibrant red, the decoration lovely even in its alienness. "It's beautiful. It looks more like art than something you use on your hair."

"It was my mother's." Ke'lar held it out to her. "I gift it to you and hope it will serve to make you feel welcome on Erah lands."

"Oh." Her cheeks warmed. "Well, thanks. It's such a rat's nest, I'm probably just going to wind up tearing half my hair out."

She reached for the comb but before her fingers closed around it he moved with a smooth g'hir quickness, taking up position behind her.

"It is not as bad as you say," he assured her, his body warm at her back as he took the strands between his fingers.

He deftly worked at the knots out, his alien dexterity allowing him to untangle them without so much as a tug.

"You are fair enough to be born of the Yir clan," he rumbled, his voice like soft thunder in her ear. "Some of them have hair this bright."

"I uh—" She cleared her throat. The brush of his fingers over the nape of her neck sent tingles running through her body. His gentle coaxing had some of the strands tamed already, the comb and his fingers sliding through her hair. "I didn't know g'hir could be blond. I've only seen the Betari clan." She looked back at Ke'lar. His hair was so dark it reflected blue in the sunlight. "And you."

He blinked and paused in his task. "The Betari did not let you see any not of their clan? How is that possible? You should have been taken to the medical center at Be'lyn City, at the very least, for a health evaluation."

"Well, I wasn't," she said shortly, facing away again. "Ar'ar kidnapped me, he imprisoned me at the enclosure, and Mirak made it clear I'd never leave it again."

"I am sorry, Summer." His hand smoothed her hair, his touch soothing, his rumble soft in her ear. "It was not supposed to be this way."

"Really?" she asked, her throat tight. "How was it supposed to be then?"

"You were to be treated with all honor, cherished, respected—"

Her nostrils flared as she faced him and he dropped his hands at her glare.

"I'm a goddamn hunting prize, Ke'lar! A pelt on a floor, a head mounted on a wall. As long as I'm able to breed that's *all* the g'hir care about."

"That is not so! The Betari should never have treated you this way, never made you doubt your worth." His face worked for a moment. "Never made you fear us."

"Oh, don't worry. It'll take a hell of a lot more to break *me*." Summer lifted her chin. "And I'm not afraid of the g'hir."

"No." His blue gaze was raw, the comb clenched in his hand. "You simply hate us."

"After what they did to me? What the fuck do you expect?"

"I am g'hir," he rumbled, searching her eyes. "Do you hate me as well, Summer?"

"*You?*" She pushed her hair behind her ears. "That's not—Look, you've got to understand. Ar'ar—"

His fangs bared. "I am not Ar'ar!"

"I *know* that, goddamn it!"

"Do you?" he demanded. "Do you truly know me to be a different man?"

Summer threw her hands out in frustration. "You said yourself that you'd take a human mate if you had half a chance! That doesn't make you much different, does it?"

His blue eyes flashed. "I will *never* treat a mate as Ar'ar has! The arrogance! The ingratitude! I would never have let anyone—"

He broke off and looked away, his grip tight on the comb.

"Look—" She wet her lips. "Ke'lar, I really appreciate all that you've—"

"By the All Mother, please do not thank me," he interrupted, shutting his eyes for a moment. "These wrongs done you, Summer, I cannot ever set to right." He offered her the comb and she took it from his hand. "The Betari sought to deny you a Day of Choosing, they kept you isolated, prevented you from receiving even the most basic medical evaluation by an impartial healer. They have acted unconscionably." He took a step back, his voice hoarse. "And you have every right to hate my kind."

EIGHT

"What's wrong with her?" Summer asked, holding her hand up against the pelting rain as Ke'lar dismounted from his place behind her, keeping hold of the reins, his brow furrowed as he hurried to stand before the nervous animal.

He didn't answer, stroking Beya's long nose to soothe her, searching her rolling eyes. It occurred to Summer then how much of Ke'lar's life had been spent in silence out here, how much of it in quiet communication with this creature.

The day had started clear enough, then clouded over. A few drops here and there had turned into a downpour.

"The storm is worsening." His face was grim. "We must seek shelter."

"It's just a little rain!"

It was a ridiculous way of describing this cloudburst. The skies had darkened terrifyingly and the wind was picking up fast but—

"We can ride through this! We have to!" she insisted. "You said we need to get to the other side of the river before nightfall. How much farther is it?"

"Too far." He shook his head. "We will not make it in time to cross."

"How can you be sure?"

"I am not," he said. "Beya is sure."

She wiped the water out of her eyes. "So we ride faster. We ride real fast and we can get across the river, right?"

Ke'lar glanced in that direction, his long blue-black hair lifted by the wind, his grip tight on the reins, Beya shifting nervously beneath her.

"Right?" Summer prompted, her legs dangling on either side of the multari's powerful back. There were only two stirrups and Ke'lar used them as he rode, leaving her feet hanging. It didn't take long for that to get pretty uncomfortable and they'd been riding for hours but she wasn't about to give up.

"No." His glowing gaze met hers then, and he had to raise his voice over the sound of the storm. "If she has become this agitated we will not have time to cross the river safely before the waters rise. If they rise too quickly we will be caught in the valley."

"Wait, are we talking flooding here? But—" They weren't even in sight of the river yet. "How bad? The bridge will still be there. We could still cross."

He shook his head. "There is no bridge."

"No bridge!" she exclaimed. "How the hell were we going to get across if there's no damn bridge?"

"I would swim carrying you, then return for Beya and our supplies."

"You were going to *swim* it?" Summer squinted against the rain. "Twice—no, three times?"

"If the storm had not come I would not doubt my ability to get you safely across but—" He shook his head and mounted behind Beya again, turning the multari. "We must make for the mountains."

"No!" Summer cried, trying to catch the reins for the all the good it did her. Ke'lar had four times her strength. "That's the wrong direction! We have to get to the clanhall as fast as we can!"

"What we must do is reach higher ground—and quickly," he said grimly. "Once the storm has passed we will take the mountain pass to the south and reach the clanhall that way."

"But—how much longer will it take to get to the clanhall if we do that?"

Ke'lar's arm went around her, holding her firmly against him. "It does not matter if the alternative is not getting there at all."

He kicked the multari and the beast took off at such a speed that Summer was clutching the saddle, her head bent to protect her face from the pelting rain as Beya galloped toward the mountains.

Summer never knew rain could *hurt*.

But this rain sure as hell did and this wasn't a storm—it was a goddamned hurricane.

Ke'lar's arm was like steel around her middle as he fought to control the multari one-handed. Summer didn't know how he could even see where they were going. She was forced to ride curled forward in the saddle, her head bent to her shoulder, trying with her other arm to protect her face against the pounding rain, utterly blinded by the downpour. She ached from holding this position so long but she didn't dare shift. It was all she could do against the wind to hold on.

She was shivering, the new boots he'd given her heavy with sopped up water. He'd thrown a blanket around her shoulders when the rain had started getting bad but the sodden fabric did nothing to keep her warm and her teeth had been chattering so long her jaw hurt.

Summer screamed as a flash and instant loud crack electrified the air. Her cry was swallowed up by the storm and her ears were ringing. The stench of ozone and charred wood mixed with the dampness and mud made her choke. The tree beside them swayed, then there was a loud crack and a *whoosh* as the tree fell, nearly crushing them beneath it.

Ke'lar strained to keep the beast from bolting as the terrified multari spun away, her huge body trembling beneath them.

He swung down from the multari and Summer gasped as the freezing rain pounded against her unprotected back. He yelled something to her but his words were carried off by the wind. Nearly blinded by the darkness and the rain, Summer reached out, fumbling for him.

His fingers caught hers, strong and steady as ever. He pressed her hand for a moment, then let go. Holding her palm above her eyes and squinting against the rain, Summer saw Ke'lar take the multari's reins and bend his body against the storm. A moment later Beya started forward again, the terrified animal moving as if by her master's will alone.

It went on like that, Summer huddled over the saddle, her fingers cramping from gripping the wet leather, Ke'lar, his shoulder to the wind, pulling on the reins to keep the multari moving.

They were ascending again, although slowly. From the rocky path they rode upon, the swaying trees revealed the valley beneath, the water swelling the already turbulent river. Summer had seen flash floods on TV, seen the devastation a wall of water could do. The valley was flooding fast and if Ke'lar hadn't insisted they turn toward the mountains they too would have been swept away with it.

I would have been out here alone if I hadn't stumbled into his campsite. I'd be dead . . .

Ke'lar yanked Beya's reins hard, urging the animal to the right. A glance to the left showed why—the path had narrowed as they climbed and there was a drop sharp enough to make Summer swallow hard.

The beast stopped moving as Ke'lar's arm went around Summer's middle. He hauled her down from the saddle as if it were effortless.

"I can't see!" she cried, thankful at least to feel firm rocky path beneath her feet as he pulled her along. She stumbled on legs that felt wooden from the long ride and his hold tightened, his strength all that was keeping her upright. "Where are we going?"

The howling wind took his answer, the rain and wind so heavy they had to lean into it to move at all. Ke'lar gripped her waist tightly and she knew if he let her go she'd be lost here in a nightmare of lightning and never-ending water.

Summer had to fight to take every step, blindly clutching at him, wondering in a jolt of panic if a person could actually drown standing up.

Suddenly they were out of the rain. She passed her hand over her forehead to clear the water from her eyes. The damp smell made her nose crinkle, the dirt soft and powdery under her new—now soaked—boots.

"Oh my God," she panted, wiping her nose with the back of her hand. "I never thought I'd be so happy to be in a freaking cave."

His bright glance went over her. "Are you all right?"

"Soaked, freezing, but yeah. You?"

"Also pleased to have shelter, even here." His eyes narrowed as his gaze turned to the furthest reaches of the cavern. "If it proves unoccupied."

"Considering the alternative," she offered with a glance at the wall of water at the cave entrance, "I'm willing to share."

"I am not," he growled, pulling a luma from his belt to reveal the rock walls, the ceiling rising high above them. The cave extended many meters into total darkness. "Wait here."

"You got it. Not big on bats, personally. I bet on Hir they have glowing eyes too. Do me a favor, 'kay?" Summer, trembling a bit with cold and exhaustion, wrapped her arms around herself. "Don't find any bats."

"I do not think we have that creature on our world." Ke'lar advanced into the cave, his blaster in hand as he explored.

She watched him go, his movements lithe, catlike, until the light he carried vanished and he was swallowed up by the darkness, leaving her alone in the gloomy, chilly cavern of an alien world. He moved silently, of course, a true g'hir warrior, but that was hardly reassuring. She'd feel a hell of a lot less creeped out if she could see or hear him.

What if they *weren't* alone in here?

Crap, maybe I just should have gone with him and screw whatever Hir's equivalent of bats is . . .

Summer chewed her lip. Should she call out to him? Go after him? She didn't even have a luma and her blaster was in her pack back on the multari. Her glance darted around, seeking a rock she could take along to defend herself if she had to go in search of him.

"Are you okay?" she demanded at first sight of his light as he finally emerged from the cave's depths to join her near the entrance. "You were gone so long!"

He gave a short huff of disbelief as he joined her near the cave's entrance. "A few minutes at most. Not long enough to distress you."

"Sorry, we humans have something called a horror movie." Summer pushed her hair back behind her ears. "And trust me—being the braless blonde in the wet shirt is *always* fatal."

Ke'lar's vibrant gaze dipped to her breasts for an instant, to her nipples taut and apparent under the soaked material.

Summer's face went hot. Why the hell had she been talking about her boobs anyway? She might as well have just pointed at them.

"This cave ends many meters from here," he growled, looking back toward the darkness of the cave. "But there is no chance we would become disoriented or lost and we are alone here, thank the All Mother." He holstered his blaster. "You are shivering, little one. I will set the heater to maximum when I return."

"When you—?" The cave opening showed nothing but gray rain and bursts of lightning. "You can't go back out into that!"

"Our supplies are out there." He raised black eyebrows. "I think you will want to have food, a bed, as well as warmth tonight, will you not?"

"I'd rather have you not dead." She folded her arms. "You are *not* going back out there. We'll just suck it up till the storm passes."

"I must find shelter for Beya as well," he reminded with a gesture toward the downpour. "I will not leave her in this."

Summer shifted her feet. Leaving that poor creature out in that kind of weather wasn't just cruel, it was criminal.

"Can't you just bring her in here? This place is huge."

"A smaller cavern would make Beya feel more secure. There are other caves nearby. I will find one to house her, settle her there, and return as soon as I am able."

She had barely started to warm up a bit but she gave a reluctant nod. "Okay, but I'm going with you."

"No, you will not," he growled. "I cannot tend to a skittish multari and guard your safety as well. Going back with me endangers us both. You will remain here, where you are safe."

"Oh, yeah, nothing safer than two people trapped by a storm, miles from any help and with no comm, deciding to split up," Summer snapped. "You know, you g'hir could learn a lot from watching a few human horror movies."

He bared his fangs. "Our agreement was that you obey me during this journey. You stay here."

"You're crazy!" she burst out. "It's a goddamn tempest out there *and* it's getting dark. How will you even find your way back here?"

He offered her the luma. "You will guide me."

Summer glared but he met her look for look.

"Thirty minutes," she warned, her own voice almost a g'hir growl, the luma's bright beam illuminating the floor as she snatched the light from him. "You have thirty minutes to get back here. I'm already soaked, hungry, and cranky so you sure don't want see how ticked off I'll be to have to come after you."

"I imagine that is true." He gave a human-style nod. "I will return as soon as I am able."

"Good," she grumbled as he went out, ducking his head against the gale. "I'm timing you!" she called after him.

He probably hadn't heard that last part, not with the storm.

Fuming, Summer sat on a rock by the cave opening and pointed the luma toward the entrance, wondering if in all this rain he'd even be able to see the light at all. It also occurred to her then that, without a watch or a phone or even one of the g'hir timepieces, she didn't have a way of timing *anything*.

"Not now, damn it," Summer muttered, wiping impatiently at her eyes. "He's coming back. Jeez, Ke'lar's the kind of man that would probably—"

But Ke'lar's not a man.

That wasn't fair, not really. He wasn't human, of course, but he was male through and through—stubbornness and all. He was honorable too, maybe not *human* honorable, but still it counted for something. He was willing to help her, willing to risk himself and his clan to make sure that her rights—at least the warped, screwed up g'hir version of her rights—were protected.

Summer shifted her weight to a more comfortable position, trying to settle in for the wait, trying to keep her mind from what she would do if he didn't come back.

It made sense just to sit tight if he didn't; just let whatever happened to him out there happen. *He* was the one who insisted he go alone. This was his planet and he was an alien warrior, part of the same race and culture that had torn her from her home without a thought.

It was freezing and she was soaked through, her belly empty, but with the cave clear of predators and herself safely out of the storm she would survive till it passed.

God knows I won't die of thirst. Just stick my hand out there anytime I'm feeling a bit parched.

Summer pushed her hair back behind her ears again, startled to find the strands half dry already. She stood and went to the entrance, trying to peer through the curtain of rain, but of course she couldn't see a goddamned thing out there.

How long has it been?

Her hand was beginning to cramp from holding the luma and she changed her grip, careful to keep the light shining outward for him even as she made her way back to the rock to sit again.

It was a cyclone out there. He might have gotten lost.

Or hurt.

The paths were slick even for a sure-footed-as-a-mountain-goat g'hir warrior.

Summer crossed her legs, her foot tapping on the dirt floor.

Five minutes. I'll give him five more minutes . . .

They'd changed direction in the storm so many times she wasn't even sure which way the clanhall lay from here. She might be in the Erah's territory but it was vast. Besides, it wasn't as if she could stroll into the Erah clanhall by herself. She might run into another of their clanbrothers while wandering around their lands but that didn't mean that man would keep Ke'lar's promise to her. Any other Erah clanbrother would probably just return her right to Ar'ar to keep the peace between their clans, so if she thought about it, it only made sense that she'd be worried about—

"Oh, thank *God*!"

Summer was on her feet instantly as Ke'lar, loaded down with supplies, appeared at the cave's entrance. He brought a spray of water with him, soaking her anew as he ducked inside. He gave a startled grunt as she flung her arms around his neck in a hug.

Ke'lar was solid muscle against her and with her cheek pressed to his chest she could feel the strong rhythm of his heart. He was really warm too, despite the rain and the chill, with that amazing male scent of his—

Summer's mouth popped open at the realization she was positively clinging to him. Her cheeks burning, she instantly let go and stepped back to scowl at him.

"Where the hell have you been?" she demanded.

His vibrant eyes blinked down at her, rivets of water running down from his rippled forehead and beside his nose, his black hair plastered to his head. "Housing Beya and getting our supplies."

"Damn it, I know *where*—" *Guess I can stop pointing the damn light!* "Anyhow . . . I'm glad you're okay."

He shook the hair out of his eyes. "Did you worry for me?"

"No," she said instantly. "I knew you were fine."

"I was greatly concerned for you," he rumbled. "I feared you would come to harm while I was away from you, that I would not be at hand when you needed me." His full mouth curved into a smile, his eyes warm. "I thank the All Mother you are safe, Summer."

"Oh," she murmured. "Well, I'm . . . fine. I uh—" She tore her gaze from those earnest blue eyes and indicated the packs he carried. "Lemme give you a hand."

"I am more than capable of carrying such a light load," he growled, pulling back in offense. "I am strong. I have trained for such things for many years."

"Look, I'm not disparaging your warrior-ness here. I'm just being polite by offering to help, okay?" Summer folded her arms. "But if you don't want my help, fine by me."

He searched her face for a moment and his expression softened again. "If this is a human way of being gracious"—he inclined his head, a little guardedly—"I thank you for it."

"Well—" Summer cleared her throat. "I guess . . . you're welcome."

He swung a pack—the tiniest of them—off from his shoulder and offered the strap to her. "You may take this one."

It was a water pouch, smaller than her J.Crew leather handbag, and Summer bit the inside of her cheek to keep back a smile.

"Sure." It was lighter than her bag—usually crammed full of crap—was too. "Happy to."

He set down the rest of the packs, sending a quick glance about. "Was there any difficulty during my absence?"

"Nope. Just me, sitting on a rock, with a flashlight, in a cave."

"This is not the foresting I hoped to provide you." Ke'lar gave her a wry smile. "It was to be starlight and roasting meat, not cavern walls and emergency supplies."

"Oh, I really wish you hadn't said 'roasting meat.'" Summer mock-sighed. "I'm starving."

"I will have a meal prepared for you shortly." He sat on his heels, already increasing the speed of his organizing and unpacking. "But I must assemble the shelter first."

"You're going to set up the shelter in here?" Summer indicated the cavern ceiling and walls. "What for? We've got a roof and walls. We really don't need it."

"It will be easier keep a smaller insulated space warm than a large one that will leak heat." He glanced at her. "I think you would prefer warmth to the chill of a cavern."

"Well, you're right about that." She studied him for a moment as he laid out the equipment and supplies with practiced movements. "Need any help?"

"I am more than capable of accomplishing this task," he said without looking up.

"I did it again, didn't I?"

Now he did look at her, his glowing eyes puzzled. "Did what?"

"Offended you."

"Yes," he growled shortly, two of the shelter's thin supports held in his strong hands. "One of a warrior's tasks is to quickly"—he connected the supports to each other—"provide protection and shelter for those under his care."

"Again—" Summer retook her place on the rock, since it looked like she would just get in the way if she tried to jump in and help. "I didn't mean to. I was just trying to show some camaraderie, show that I'm part of the team."

His vibrant gaze met hers. "This is how humans create affiliation outside one's clan?"

She gave a half shrug. "I guess you could say that. You know, lend a helping hand—raise a barn, join in a taffy pull, give somebody stranded with a dead battery a jump-start. Humans like cooperating for a common goal."

"That is true of g'hir as well. It is the bedrock of our enclosures." His glance quickly went over the pieces of the shelter he had already laid out. "Those two," he said with a wave at the thin metal supports near her feet. "Connect them."

"Uh, okay . . ." It took her a while fiddling at it. He probably could have had the whole shelter built in the time it took her to get them connected. "How's that?"

"Adequate," he rumbled, holding his hand out for it.

"Never had a lesson in my life." At his baffled look she gave a laugh. "I was joking."

He offered a polite smile, though of course he wouldn't have heard that before.

"How long did it take you to learn to do all this?" she asked. "Be a warrior, I mean."

"Too long," he rumbled with a huffed laugh of his own. "Training begins in the form of play as soon as a male child can walk but he is not named a warrior until he has hunted for himself for a year. I began my year when I was seventeen summers."

"But you just have to feed yourself?"

"It is not as simple as it sounds, to feed oneself, to survive only on your own skills for an entire year," he said wryly. "Nor as easy."

"Why would you even do that?" she asked. "G'hir technology is tons more advanced than humans'. You can open wormholes in space and jump between solar systems in the blink of an eye. I saw a Betari warrior gored by a tarn come back from the medical center at Be'lyn City the very next day walking around like nothing had happened. You have medical knowledge that's astounding." She shook her head. "You wouldn't catch me spending a year alone in the wilderness, and my culture is centuries behind yours."

He gave a faint smile. "Females need not earn the right to have a mate in any case, only males must."

"Decree from the All Mother, right? Ar'ar said something like that. Not," she added, thinking of that first terrifying day of captivity on his ship, "that I was paying much attention at the time."

He stood and it looked like that was all the help he was interested in getting from her since he seemed intent on assembling the shelter alone now.

Crap, I wonder if it sounded like I was disparaging their Goddess or something . . .

She cleared her throat. "So, to be named a warrior by your clan you have to . . . what?" she asked, hoping to smooth over any blunder by getting back to the topic. "Live off the land entirely for a whole year?"

"From one winter gathering to the next," he agreed. "If you are successful you rejoin the clanhall as a warrior."

"What if you aren't?" she wondered. "Successful, I mean?"

He shrugged. "You die."

Summer blinked. "You're kidding."

He met her gaze, looking completely serious. "Only the strongest must be permitted to take a mate. Especially now."

"To breed healthy daughters and repopulate Hir. Yeah, Ar'ar—and his father—had a lot to say on that subject too." She stood. "I don't suppose there's any chance my other clothes are still dry."

"Yes," he said, offering her the pack she'd brought from the Betari enclosure.

She took it from him, shifting her weight, and his posture stiffened.

"I will not look at you while you disrobe," he said gruffly, turning back to his work. When she didn't move, he indicated the rear of the cavern. "There is ample privacy to be had here; you will not lose your way."

"Thanks," she mumbled, her face warm as she grabbed the luma. She wasn't sure which would be worse—that he'd try to look at her . . . or that he wouldn't.

The luma gave off plenty of light and while the cave was chilly it wasn't nearly as spooky back here as she feared it would be. She put the luma down, angling it so it would provide her enough illumination as she sorted through the bag.

Ke'lar had been a perfect gentleman—no "accidental" brushes against her breasts, no gropes at her butt, no implying that after all he'd done for her she would owe him big.

But sometimes, when she turned her head quickly enough to catch his unguarded gaze on her, she thought she detected heat in those glowing blue eyes . . .

Stop being an idiot!

Even if he was interested—and in their many hours together he hadn't shown a bit of it—the last thing she needed when she was busy escaping her alien warrior captor was to get something going with his alien warrior *enemy*.

It wasn't like g'hir felt things the same way humans did. Half the time when she was trying to express herself—even to Ke'lar—she had the suspicion that these people couldn't even fathom how her mind worked.

Certainly she didn't understand them at all.

They revered a creator Goddess, their All Mother, but hunted women like animals. They stole women from Earth but fawned over them on Hir. They had mind-bogglingly advanced technology but the men spent years training as if everybody might suddenly have to pack up and move to the Bronze Age.

Despite that genetic aberration of human DNA in g'hir that made breeding with humans possible, Summer considered them an entirely different species. Their physical appearance was frightening, their customs bizarre and barbaric, their whole view of life was just . . .

Alien.

She had gotten the damp things off, dried herself with the towel he'd thoughtfully packed in there for her, had the dry pants on, and was just finished buttoning her shirt when she noticed them.

Black smudges. Far too uniformly placed to be natural . . .

Summer picked up the luma and moved closer, shining her light over the cavern walls, her eyes widening as she took them in.

"Ke'lar," she cried. "Come here!"

He was there in a rush of movement, at her side so quickly she nearly dropped the light. His blaster was already in hand, his glowing gaze scanning for the threat; a flicker of confusion crossed his features when none was evident.

"Did you see these?" She clasped him by the hand and drew him nearer, her luma lighting the wall to show him.

"Cave drawings," he murmured.

Summer shone the light on them. The drawings continued at about the same level above the floor but it was impossible to tell if they had been done by one group living at the same time or completed over the generations, if the pictures were part of a story or even a ceremony. "People lived here?"

"The g'hir did once live in caves," he agreed. "Before we ventured into the forests to live, before we formed the enclosures."

"These are amazing. They're just . . . beautiful. I wonder how old they are."

"Tens of thousands of years." His fangs flashed in a smile. "It has been very long since my kind occupied caves. We have missed our hosts by millennia."

Many of the drawings showed humanoids carrying weapons, showed them beside beasts being hunted, showed some that were family groupings. There were dozens of handprints too; marks left by those longing to connect through time, to be remembered, somehow.

Like any humans did.

"I cannot believe I did not see these," he rumbled, delighted. "They are extraordinary."

Ke'lar stretched toward the marks left by his ancestors. His glowing eyes shone with awe, his face softened with wonder as he traced the simple figures with his fingers, every line of his face and masculine form beautiful by the luma's light . . .

"Funny how something could be right in front of you," she murmured, "and you can't see it at all."

He sent her a wry glance. "I came back here searching out danger, not anthropological finds."

"I didn't—" She shook her head and gave a quick smile. "Never mind. Humans did that too, you know. Lived in caves, made cave drawings like these—images of people and animals. They did handprints too. I saw some reproductions of them at the Museum of Natural History."

He indicated the wall. "Our drawings are like the humans', Summer?"

On this wall both beasts and two-legged figures had fangs but—

"Yeah," she murmured, fitting her hand to the print left by a g'hir who must have stood here millennia ago. "Yeah, they're a lot alike . . ."

NINE

He had already set up the shelter to face the cave's entrance and Summer scrambled gratefully into the geodesic dome. The heater had warmed the inside enough that the door flap could be left open but still allow them to sit inside comfortably.

The storm didn't seem to have let up at all and Summer chewed her lip for a moment. "With this rain, and the runoff, the river is going to be impassable, isn't it?"

"There are passages through the mountains," he assured as he finished assembling their simple meal. "We will bypass the river and reach the clanhall from the north."

"But it will take longer," she said for him.

"Perhaps whatever draws you home—"

He broke off when Summer dropped her gaze, her lips pressed together.

"Now that the valley has flooded," he continued after a moment, offering her a plate, "the high pass is the only way to reach the clanhall. There is no choice but to take it, even if that way is longer."

"How much longer?"

His eyes met hers. "I cannot say for certain. A day, perhaps two."

"Oh, that's just fucking great," she muttered. "It doesn't give me a lot of time to convince your father to help me get home."

"The journey from Hir to your world will not take long."

"Yeah." She gave a wry smile. "Too bad you can't open a wormhole to take us from here to the clanhall."

"I would need a ship," he reminded, smiling a little too. "One cannot open a wormhole with a multari."

"I didn't even ask—is she okay? Did you find a place for her?"

"Beya is comfortably housed in a small cavern not far from this one. She was not happy that I left her to come here." His glowing eyes crinkled. "I think she is jealous of you."

"You're kidding, right?" Summer's eyebrows rose. "Why would she be jealous? And how can you even tell if a multari is jealous anyway?"

He gave a short huff. "She has feelings just as you and I do. Of course she feels jealousy. As to how"—his broad shoulders lifted in a shrug—"when you spend as much time with one as I have with her you come to understand a being, even when she cannot speak."

Summer took a bite of the food he'd prepared and blinked.

His brow furrowed. "Is there something wrong?"

"Wrong?" she got out, already spooning up more of the stew. "This is fantastic!"

He gave a half shrug. "It is not my best . . ."

She gave a laugh. "Well, now I want to know what your best is."

"I will hunt a kartlet." His chest puffed up a bit. "I will roast it for you over an open flame, and season it. Then," he added with a g'hir chin jerk, "you sample my best cooking."

Summer dropped her gaze and offered her own half shrug. "I make a real good lemon pie."

"What is that?" he asked, his eyes bright and curious.

"It's a dessert . . . from Earth." Her bit her lip. "Jeez, *obviously* it's from Earth. It's my Granny Crawford's secret recipe. I'm the only one she taught how to make it. Probably on account of being the only one bugging her to learn it. It's all from scratch, even the lemon curd. Everybody loves it," she mumbled, suddenly feeling silly for having bragged on it at all.

"Then I am sure it warrants their esteem," he rumbled.

Despite his claim that it was nothing more than emergency rations, dinner was delicious, and he seemed very pleased that she took seconds.

"What is 'bloodhound'?"

Summer blinked at his sudden question—and that he'd said the English word. "What?"

"You said I—that the g'hir—are half 'bloodhound.' I do not know what 'bloodhound' is."

"Oh." She *had* said that. "It's a dog."

"*'Dog'?*"

"A dog is a domesticated animal, a canine. Bloodhounds are a breed of dog well known for having an amazing sense of smell."

"Because the g'hir have a more acute sense of smell than humans." He tilted his head. "You equate me with this 'dog' creature."

If she tuned out the translation in her head and just listened with her ears Ke'lar's speech sounded just like a bunch of snarls and growls.

His brow furrowed. "You are smiling. Why is this funny?"

It was actually *really* funny but she didn't think he'd get the joke.

She shook her head. "Don't worry, even if I did equate you with a dog you should take it as a compliment. A lot of humans love them like family."

He was silent for a moment. "I should like to see a dog someday. To taste lemon pie."

"Maybe you will."

"Perhaps." He was already busying himself by gathering the remains of their dinner. "I will clear this away, then leave you so you may sleep."

"*Leave* me? Where are you going?" She glanced toward the shelter opening. "You're not sleeping outside?"

"We are still within the cavern," he reminded with a raised eyebrow. "I will not drown."

"Well, Jesus, I know *that*. I didn't mean, were you going to go sleep out in the rain! I meant there's no reason for you to sleep on dirt in some miserable, damp—Look, it's warm in here and—" She gestured to the pallet, as comfortable as anything she'd ever slept on. "This is your bed. You should get to sleep in it."

He frowned a little. "I do not wish my presence to make you uncomfortable."

"It doesn't. I mean—you don't. It's fine." She cleared her throat. "You can sleep in here. You should get as much rest as you can, right?"

"It would be more comfortable." He gave a shrug. "And if it does not discomfort you to have me here . . ."

"Nope," she said firmly. "Won't bother me at all."

Ke'lar went to check on Beya one last time for the night and Summer had just gotten under the covers when he returned. He was soaked again but threw her a smile when he ducked into the shelter.

"She okay?"

He nodded, grabbing a cloth to rub his hair with. He'd left his boots outside so as not to track mud into the shelter.

"She was asleep when I entered the cavern," he said with a huffed chuckle, already unfastening the jacket of his warrior's clothes. The jacket served as shirt too and his chest was bare beneath it, the muscles of his broad back evident as he turned to hang the damp garment. "Apparently I disturbed her."

She's not the only one . . .

Summer shifted under the furs, wondering why she'd ever thought having him sleep in here—and share the bed— was a great idea.

"I offered her some grain," he said, already undoing his trousers. "But she would not eat. I think," he continued, stepping out of them and hanging them as well, "she is simply too tired."

He turned to her then, unabashedly bare.

Holy cow, that All Mother does some seriously good work . . .

His skin was darker than hers all over, a natural color, not a tan. His shoulders were broad and his muscled chest had only fine hairs. On either side of his abdomen, the muscles of his groin created a vee and the planes of his perfect stomach flexed as he knelt beside the pallet.

He was beautifully male, with cock and balls very like a human. The skin was darker there, veins visible beneath the skin, and resting on his muscled thighs, his penis was long and thick already. She was surprised by the longing to touch him; with a few strokes of her hand she could have him standing—

"Summer?"

His brow was creased a bit. G'hir didn't have the same concept—or really any concept—of modesty as humans did.

Likely, he really was wondering why her face had gone all pink, why she couldn't look at him . . .

Why she couldn't *stop* looking at him . . .

He knelt at the pallet's side, his vibrant gaze catching hers. "Do you want for anything, little one?"

"Excuse me?" she got out.

He indicated the luma. "Before I lower the light."

The luma's light played over the flatness of his abdomen; he was so close she could feel the warmth of him, could breathe in the cinnamon scent of him.

His brow creased again and she realized he was still waiting for her to answer.

"We should get some sleep," she mumbled. "Right?"

He gave a human-style nod. "That would be best."

He lowered the illumination but not to total darkness, and she suddenly thought that he had done that out of consideration for her. He would be able to see well in far less light than she.

Unfortunately, that had her able to see every curve and plane of his beautiful body as he joined her on the pallet.

Dismayed, Summer realized that when she was alone in it the pallet seemed huge but there wasn't a whole lot of space left when you added a nearly seven-foot-tall warrior to it.

She realized too how thin her nightgown was. His skin brushed against her bare leg as he settled beside her and it was impossible to ignore his warmth, his scent . . .

"I would never hurt you, little one," he rumbled softly, his face inches from hers. "You have nothing to fear from me."

Startled, she met his gaze. "I know that. I'm not afraid of you."

"I can hear your heart." In the next moment his warm, broad palm rested on her breastbone. "It is going very fast." He searched her eyes. "Your breathing has quickened as well."

In fact, this close he ought to be able to scent her arousal too.

Thank God at least he thinks I'm scared instead of—

"Perhaps," he suggested, taking his hand away, his fingers lightly brushing her skin as he did, "if we talked, you might be reassured. Perhaps become calm enough to sleep."

Gotta do something.

He settled beside her, his warmth and male scent making her long to be closer still.

"Tell me of your world," he urged. "Tell me of Earth."

She cleared her throat. "I don't know what to say. Earth's not like Hir. We have so many different cultures on my world, so many different religions and languages and traditions . . . it's not an easy question to answer."

He turned to lie on his side, facing her, his head propped up on his elbow. "Then tell me of your home there."

"Well . . . I grew up in Brittle Bridge—that's a town in North Carolina—but I moved to northern Virginia when I went to college. My parents died when I was in school there." She wet her lips. "That was awful. Mom had breast cancer and we really thought she was going to make it but . . . anyway I think it was just too much for my dad. They say people don't really die of a broken heart but I know that's not true 'cause he did. I buried both my parents in eighteen months and I was a mess. That's probably why I took up with Dean so quick."

"Your human mate."

"I guess you could call him that but he was no kind of husband, really. We got divorced the week before I graduated from college. He wanted a fun girl, someone up for anything . . . I was such a mess when my mom got sick, when I lost her and dad too, that I graduated a year late—" She shook her head. "Anyway, Dean and I met at a party the night I got back to school and I had had *way* too much Smirnoff." She gave an embarrassed smile. "Between the vodka and the platinum blond hair, I think I just gave him a bad impression of who I really am."

"And who are you?" he rumbled, his eyes glowing blue even in the faint light of the shelter.

She blinked. "That's not an easy question to answer."

He gave a quick smile. "But if you know who you are not . . ."

"Then that just leaves who I am?" she asked wryly.

Ke'lar shrugged. "It is a place to begin."

"Well," she began slowly after a moment. "I guess you could say I'm pretty responsible, but then again I've had to be. I'm twenty-six and a lot of women my age are still clubbing while I'm the coupon-clipping, money in the cookie-jar *and* in a high yield CD type. I guess that has a lot to do with losing my parents when I did. My parents left me some money, not a lot, and I wasn't about to squander what I had especially since . . ." Summer shifted on the pallet. "Well, since everyone else could go home to mom and dad if they ran into trouble but I had to rely on myself." She passed her hand over her eyes. "I sure couldn't count on Dean for anything."

"You have great courage," he growled. "To head into the Hir forests alone and untrained."

She gave an embarrassed shrug. "I had a blaster."

"I have been meaning to ask . . . Did you have a destination when you fled their land?"

She hesitated, but really, what difference did it make? "The capital. I knew if I headed east from Betari territory I'd eventually hit Be'lyn City."

His black eyebrows shot up. "You were going to the capital?"

"Yes," she said, a little annoyed that he made idea sound ludicrous.

"*You*—a human female"—his voice rose—"were going to go alone and unprotected—into Be'lyn City?"

Her eyes narrowed. "Typical dumb blond thing to do, huh?"

"I do not understand what your hair shade has to do with any of this," he growled with a dismissive glance at it. "And your high intelligence is unquestionable but—the recklessness of it! Why would you go there?"

"Where the hell else *could* I go?" she demanded. "Besides, it's a big city and in my experience if there's something that you're looking for that's tough to find—say, transport off the planet—a big city is a good place to find that."

"And that was your plan? To wander the city alone, seeking help?"

"I can take care of myself! You know," Summer said, turning and leaning on her elbow as he was, "you guys go on and on about how g'hir are honorable warriors—"

"Not all of us!" he burst out, flinging his hand out in an uncharacteristic show of frustration. "Did you think a city full of males from a dying race would let a beautiful human female just *walk by* without seeking to capture her? If you had even reached the capital! You would have to cross Erah land and Arnaru lands before you came to the city outskirts. And with no resources—"

"What the hell happened to thinking I'm brilliant and brave? Those are resources. Besides, I have a truckload of stubbornness and a backpack full of jewels!"

"You—?" He shook his head a little. "What do you mean—what jewels?"

"The jewels the Betari gave me as the next clanmother."

"*What?*"

"Well, I had to have something to bribe or buy my way back to Earth! It's not like they take Visa."

He stared. "You are a thief!"

"You can't steal what people *give* you!" she threw back. "They insisted I take them! Swore up and down that they were mine!"

"I do not think using the riches of a hundred generations of Betari clanmothers to flee their enclosure was what they intended!"

"Oh, well, oops." She gave an exaggerated shrug. "Maybe next time they kidnap someone they'll explain the terms in writing."

"This is an affront to their enclosure." He passed his hand over his face. "Now they will say I have stolen you *and* their heirlooms."

"Stolen me?" she asked. "What are you talking about?"

His face flushed with annoyance but then he met her eyes and his expression eased. "There are traditions, forms that must be observed to prevent war—"

"I guess your clans really hate each other, huh?"

"An ancient rivalry," he grumbled. "And a pointless one, since we are all dying out." He shook his head again. "The jewels must be returned to the Betari."

"But not me?"

"Of course not," he growled, sounding surprised. "I would never return you to them."

He actually seemed to mean that.

"I'm not sure I was going to make it to the city anyway," she mumbled. "I mean I figured I could do ten miles a day easy, maybe fifteen if I pushed it. Turns out I was figuring it with paved roads in mind. I really underestimated how hard it was to travel through uncut forest. I'm sure I didn't have enough food. I didn't really know how to find water—I can't smell it like you can. And now, with the storm—"

"Then it is fortunate the Goddess brought me to that riverside," he said with a faint smile.

She hesitated. She shouldn't even care but . . . "What were you really doing way out there anyway, Ke'lar?"

"Foresting."

"Yeah . . . you may not have noticed but I'm *human*," Summer said dryly. "I don't really know what you mean when you say that. It seems a bit like a mix of what humans call 'camping' and exploring but from just the way you guys say the word I know it's more."

He regarded her thoughtfully. "It is a difficult concept to express in words. It is something instinctive to g'hir, something we understand from earliest childhood. To forest does mean to travel, to explore the land as our ancestors did, but it *is* more," he agreed. "It is a sacred journey as well. A way of opening oneself to the lifeforce that is Hir, that is our All Mother."

"So you weren't . . . Look, I'm just going to say it— Were you out there to spy on the Betari?"

He gave a short huff, a surprised g'hir chuckle. "No. I confess it did not even occur to me. I care little for enclosure politics. I only sought a solitary place."

"Why?" He was silent for several moments and she raised her eyebrows. "Is this some kind of secret g'hir thing humans shouldn't ask about?"

"I sought to commune with Hir," he said reluctantly. "With the All Mother, the giver of all life. I was praying to Her."

"For something? Or because you've done something you were sorry for?" She covered her eyes with her hand and flopped onto her back. "Never mind. I can't believe I even asked you that. It's none of my business anyway."

"The answer is both," he said quietly after a moment. "I went to ask the Goddess for something but also to loose my anger upon Her."

"Your anger?" She frowned at him in surprise. Ke'lar seemed like the most even-tempered person she'd ever met, g'hir *or* human. "Why are you angry with your Goddess?"

His throat worked for a moment. "Because she had long ignored my pleas, denied me that which I have longed to have. I begged the Goddess to let me go to your world that I might find a mate," he rumbled quietly. "When I knew for certain there was no hope that I would ever make that journey, I could not bear even the company of my clanbrothers. I forested for weeks, alone, raging at Her . . . *hating* Her . . . before I came to that place by the river. I looked into the night sky, to the Sisters looking down so coldly on me, I watched the Brother suns rise, demanding to know why our Mother would have had me be born at all only to suffer. But I was a fool. I will forever beg Her forgiveness, offer up my gratitude."

"A fool?" she asked. "Why do you say that?"

"Because She brought me something more precious than I could ever imagine." His blue eyes glowed in the dimness as they met hers. "You."

TEN

"Me?" she breathed.

"You cannot say you have not noticed." His bright gaze was raw. "I cannot hide my feelings for you any more than I can stop my heart from beating."

Her own heart was hammering in her chest as his fingers lightly brushed her forehead, tracing the curve of her cheek to run down the tender skin of her throat.

"When you emerged from the forest I thought the Goddess had sent you to me." He swallowed and his words suddenly came out in a rush. "It sounds foolish, I know. And I know too you do not feel the same for me but if someday you thought perhaps you could . . ."

Shyly, he leaned closer, his breath mingling with hers, to brush his nose up one side of hers, and down the other—a g'hir's kiss.

"My sweet one . . ." His breath mingled with hers, his voice lowered, a soft mating purr rising in his chest to vibrate through her, right to her clit. "My Summer . . ."

"Ke'lar—" Her head was spinning from the heat he sent rushing through her; that rumble-purr of his had made her breasts heavy, her center so tight she was clenching her hand, the nails biting into her palm, to keep from reaching for him. "Oh, goddamn it . . ."

A look of embarrassment, of shame, crossed his face.

"Forgive me," he mumbled. "I forgot for a moment how the g'hir have wronged you, of what you think of my kind." His expression was wretched, his mating purr fading.

"You have asked my protection, nothing more. I should have never spoken of my feelings for you. I vow I will not again . . ."

He began to draw away but with a low moan Summer brought her mouth to his, her arms winding around his neck to pull him close.

He froze, uncertain, because he would never have kissed like this. G'hir didn't touch mouths like humans did.

But he let her kiss him now, his full mouth softening against hers. He caught his breath when she sought to part his lips, yielding easily as she deepened the kiss, and she shuddered with wanting to feel the sharpness of his fangs against her tongue.

He sighed, accepting all that she offered. His touch on her was gentle but he was rock hard against her thigh. His mouth had the sweetest spicy taste to it and he pressed closer, eager for more. His fingers threaded through her hair as he experimented in the ways of a human kiss, lightly flicking his tongue to the corner of her mouth then running along the inside of her upper lip.

He brushed his nose to hers and his lips traced her cheek and throat as he fit his body to hers, his skin warm and smooth, the broad muscles of his back under her fingers. Ke'lar pressed his face to the spot where her neck and shoulder met, pausing there to breathe in her scent, and the rumble deepened in his chest, thrumming through her, rising to tighten her nipples.

She wore nothing but the nightgown and Summer slid her leg over him, wrapping around his hip to press his hard cock, already lubricating in readiness, to her entrance.

A fine tremble ran along his body and suddenly he was no longer docile, yielding to her, but the hunter he was bred to be. His hands moved with a g'hir's speed to free her of her nightdress and in a heartbeat she lay bare beneath him. His eyes were blue fire as he drank in the sight of her, open and ready for him.

His fangs flashed and his touch turned slow, deliberate, possessive. His knuckles traced from the hollow of her throat to her breastbone. Then lightly, with just the pad of his finger, he brushed against her nipple and she gasped as shocks exploded along every nerve of her body.

"You cannot know how many times I have stopped myself from touching you," he rumbled hoarsely, cupping her breast, his thumb tracing the peak.

"God!" she got out.

His fingers ran the length of her body, over her ribs and belly to rest against the lips of her pussy.

"How I have ached for you . . ."

His rumble-purr sent tingles of pleasure racing between her thighs to vibrate her clit. Her mouth parted as he found her sensitive nub but he simply held it captive between his warm fingers, his gaze burning into hers, watching her reaction.

He bent closer, his breath hot on her throat. "How I longed to have you ache for me . . ."

His fangs nipped her then, lightly, just at the base of her neck, and simultaneously, with a single flick of his thumb against her clit, he had her coming so hard she whimpered, her nails digging into his shoulders.

He slid two fingers inside her and her pussy pulsed around them with her climax. Rumbling, he withdrew his fingers to take position over her, the tip of his cock gleaming with moisture.

His purr had her arousal soaring again instantly and having him there, hot against her opening, was driving her wild. She arched against him, desperate to have him inside her.

He made a sound then, a strangled gasp at the sensation as the very tip of his cock dipped between her lips.

"I have not—" he gasped. "I have never—"

"I know." Summer shifted beneath him, her hands going to his hips to press him forward, lifting her body so the head of his cock slipped inside. "It's all right."

"Summer . . ." His whole body was taut, trembling with the effort to hold still. "You must be sure—"

"Please," she begged.

She pressed harder, urging him on, mad with it. He was big but she was slippery from her climax and he surrendered, groaning with pleasure as he slid into her, in a heartbeat fully sheathed inside.

He resisted for just an instant as Summer urged him to pull back then into her again and his eyes widened as he caught the rhythm. It was glorious to watch him as he moved inside her, abandoning himself to it.

He balanced effortlessly on one arm, cupping her buttock to hold her still for him, every thrust and withdrawl of his cock brushing her clit.

"Say—" he rumbled hoarsely, his voice deep and hungry, the combination of his strokes and rumbling-purr soaking her pussy, bringing her to the brink again. "Say you are mine."

"I'm . . ."

His glowing gaze held hers, his cock hot and slick as he rocked inside her. "You are mine."

"—yours! God, please . . .!"

His fangs bared, his rumble-purr tightening her center to aching as he thrust deep and hard and then she was coming again.

Her pleasure took the last of Ke'lar control. His growl rose to a roar and then his rhythm broke and he shuddered, pulsing hot inside her as he came.

He was shaking, his head hanging, their bodies slick against each other. He shifted then, still filling her, his cock still rock hard as he caged her face with his arms.

"And I am yours . . . " He brushed his nose to hers. "My beloved. My Summer . . . "

Her eyes stung at the sincerity, the reverence, in his eyes. Only one other in her life had ever looked at her as if she were the whole world—

But Ke'lar was g'hir, not human, and once was not nearly enough to sate him. He was still hard inside her. His rumbling purr rose to hum through her and then nothing in the universe existed but them. Summer curled against him, gasping in renewed pleasure as his strokes started again.

Eleven

Ke'lar was aware of her before he was fully awake, as he would be aware of her, seeking her presence, every moment till the end of his existence.

The scent of her sex filled the shelter, inviting forth his mating purr, stirring him again to full arousal, his penis already lubricating for more coupling. Her rounded buttocks were pressed to his hips, his body curled around the softness of her.

His fingers brushed the tips of her breasts, the sweetness of her taut pink nipples. She was already responding, pressing back against him in irresistible invitation.

Ke'lar's hand rested on her hip for a moment to hold her steady, feeling the bone beneath her skin, the warm, slight roundness of her belly as he placed his penis between the lips of her opening. Sure now that his purr had readied her, he slid into her taut slick center.

He held there, inside her, and moved his hand lower, from her belly to the soft, golden hair of her mound. His fingers came to rest at the apex of her opening, her lips held open by his sheathed cock.

His thumb pressed there, to that sensitive spot of human female anatomy. In the night of coupling he had learned how to heighten and extend her arousal by softening or deepening his purr, just how hard to bite so that he deepened her pleasure without causing pain, how the lightest touch just *here*—

Summer moaned, the walls of her sex contracting around his penis as she came. Her back arched to press herself closer as he started to thrust. He kept his fingers between her lips, at that sweet, tiny nub as he rocked inside her, his eyes closing at the pleasure of it.

She was gasping, her head flung back, the strands of her bright silky hair brushing his skin, the scent of her spiraling arousal urging him on to plunge faster. She was nearing another climax and he lowered the vibration of his purr to keep her just at the peak for a moment more . . .

Then she was contracting around him hard, her release demanding his own, and he bared his fangs as he pulsed inside her.

He collapsed beside her, his breath still quick as he withdrew, laughing softly at the sheer delight of loving her.

My Summer . . .

She rolled toward him, her eyes opened, and she gave him a joyous, sleepy smile.

My mate . . .

Nice way to wake up . . .

Ke'lar's glowing eyes were soft, his black hair curtaining his face as he smiled down at her.

"What time is it?" she asked. They were still naked, that was for sure. His body was warm against hers, curled around her.

He traced the skin of her cheek. "I do not know." He gave a quiet, huffing chuckle. "We did not sleep until very late."

"I could sleep more," she mumbled, her eyes already falling shut again.

"Then sleep, little one." He drew her closer into his embrace as he settled against her. "Sleep as long as you wish."

His head was cradled against her neck, his mouth warm and moist against her throat, the silkiness of his hair spread over her arm and shoulder. There was nothing but the sound of their breathing, the sweet feel of Ke'lar against her.

"We should get up," she murmured, but made no move to do so. She had never been so comfortable, so content in her life.

"No, let us stay here," he rumbled, his breath hot on her skin.

"You mean just live in this cave—like ancient humans and g'hir?"

She felt him smile against her neck.

"We will be far more comfortable than they ever were. We have our shelter and a heater and our bed. We will delight in each other." He snuggled closer. "I will hunt for you, and we will make our home here until the snow brings the next gathering . . ."

An image of shops bright with holiday lights, of snow blanketing Brittle Bridge's Main Street, flashed through her mind, jolting her awake.

Through the shelter's opening, through the cave entrance, the sky was as vibrant blue as Ke'lar's eyes.

"The rain," she whispered. "It's stopped. When did it stop?"

"Hmm," he rumbled, moving closer. "Hours ago."

Oh God, what did I do?

This—she and Ke'lar—wasn't supposed to happen, this was never supposed to happen. What about home, what about—

So I just . . . what? Forgot?

Guilt slashed her heart and Summer disengaged from Ke'lar's embrace, and sat up, clutching the fur covers to her chest.

Sunshine filled the cave entrance, birdsong drifted in on the sweet air . . .

What the fuck time is it anyway?

"We should go."

"What is the matter?" He propped himself up, his rippled brow creased. "Your heart is racing."

She avoided his gaze and ran her hand through her hair. "How long before we can get packed up and out of here?"

He pushed himself up to kneeling, as comfortable with being bare as ever, his black silky hair in disarray from their lovemaking, his beautiful cock resting on his muscular thighs.

"Little one? What is it?" He searched her face. "You are greatly distressed."

"I'm fine," she mumbled, already reaching for her clothes. "How quick can we get going?"

His brow furrowed as she climbed over him to yank her trousers on, her fingers flying to fasten the shirt. Thankfully her new boots had finally dried and she pulled them on, quickly tying them closed.

"Come on," she urged, her throat tight. "We need to go."

He blinked up at her but took his own clothes in one broad hand and stood to dress.

"How long?" she asked as soon as he'd finished fastening his boots. "It must be near midday."

"We should eat—"

"Can't we eat on the way?" she interrupted.

His brow furrowed but he jerked his chin in a g'hir nod. "I must break camp and saddle Beya. It is better I carry the supplies down to her than bring her here."

"Can I help?"

"If you wish to leave swiftly, it is quicker if I do this alone."

"Okay," she said, heading out of the shelter and into the chill of the cave.

Waiting while he disassembled and packed everything had her practically dancing back and forth between the sunny, rocky path outside and the chill of the cave. It wasn't as if he were taking a long time—he was a model of warrior efficiency—but it left her with nothing to do and no way to speed things up.

"Wait here," he said, hefting their supplies. "When I have saddled her I will return for you."

"That'll just waste time," she said impatiently. "This is your clan's territory, there's not going to be some Zerar horde hiding behind a bush waiting to attack us. I'm going with you."

Clearly this was the perfect way *not* to motivate an alien warrior because Ke'lar's jaw hardened and he stopped dead, instantly transforming into an unmovable wall of muscle and male stubbornness.

"You are my responsibility," he growled. "I could not call myself a warrior if I neglected your safety so."

Summer had to force herself to slow even breaths.

Eyes on the prize here. The point is to get to the clanhall as fast as possible, not to debate g'hir cultural ideals.

"Fine," she bit out, folding her arms. "Go. I'll wait here."

His gaze narrowed a bit as if judging the sincerity of her word.

"Seriously. Go." She sat down on the rock she'd perched on while waiting for him only last night. "I'll be right here."

After a moment he inclined his head. "I will return as quickly as I am able."

Summer chewed her lip as he started on the path down to where he'd housed Beya.

It was Wednesday, at least back in Brittle Bridge. She only had until Sunday afternoon to get home . . .

It was another two days to the clanhall. That left her a little over a day to convince the clanfather of the Erah to disregard g'hir cultural traditions, to incur the greater enmity of a rival clan

Dammit, where is he already?

She was on her feet, about to go after him, but, as if he somehow sensed she was on the verge of breaking her word, he chose that moment to return. She was past him in an instant, heading down the rocky path toward where Beya waited patiently, already saddled and loaded down with their supplies.

Before she could get to the beast's side to mount up, he loosed the reins from the tree and began to lead Beya.

"We're walking?" Summer asked, frowning. "The path is wide enough to ride, isn't it?"

"We can eat as we travel," he said. "But she must be fed and watered before she is ridden. There is a creek not far from here. She will drink and I will fill our water pouches."

It was on the tip of her tongue to object. Then her gaze met Beya's and she read patience, deep loyalty, and weariness in that animal's glowing gaze.

"Yeah," she murmured. "Okay."

Summer took the opportunity—since they were stuck waiting on the multari anyway—to eat some of the jerky-stuff Ke'lar offered her and splash some water on her face. Beya dipped her heavy head and drank deeply when they reached the creek but wasn't nearly as interested in her feed.

"Which way is the clanhall from here?"

He pointed. That way the valley curved to the left, and the river far below led in that direction.

"So which way is faster?" she asked, as Ke'lar stroked Beya's nose, coaxing her to eat. "The mountains or doubling back to go through the valley?"

"The valley is the shortest distance but we will continue on through the mountain pass."

"Why? You said yourself that if we do that it'll add a whole other day." She indicated the blue sky, the fluffy clouds. "I'm pretty sure it's not going to rain today. It doesn't even look flooded down here."

"Travel through the valley will be far worse than it seems from here." He gave up trying to feed the multari and offered a g'hir's nod toward the verdant land below. "The ground has absorbed some of the rain but not much yet. There will be places Beya may sink to her knees in the mud."

The sweet spring air lifted her hair as Summer turned her face toward where the river curved at the base of the snow-capped mountain. "On Earth, settlements—especially old ones—were always built near a river or sea. The Betari clanhall was built near water. Yours was too, right?

He shot her a puzzled look. "It was."

"Well, let's use the river then," she said briskly. "That would be the fastest. We could sail there, couldn't we?"

"We could," he agreed, stowing the animal's feed. "If we had a boat, which we do not."

"Well, there must be one on the river," she pointed out. "We'll hitch a ride. You're the clanfather's son and this is urgent, that would put any boat at your disposal."

"Do you see one?" he demanded with a wave toward the river.

"No," she admitted grudgingly. There wasn't a boat in sight. "But there are fishermen that use the river all the time, aren't there?"

"Yes, and who would have sought a safe place to moor during the storm. The river will still have the runoff of the storm and they too are wisely waiting till the river is less treacherous." He stopped walking, Beya shifting beside him. "But perhaps you would prefer that we camp at the river's edge and wait there until a boat appears to carry us to the clanhall instead."

"It would be faster, wouldn't it? The river should take us practically to the front door."

"*If* there were a boat at hand, and *if* they were willing to abandon their own work to cater to us, then yes, that would be the swiftest way to the clanhall," he growled. "If a boat sturdy enough to navigate the swift currents were to magically appear, we would reach my father by nightfall. But—as you can see—there are no boats and there are unlikely to be any for at least a day or two."

Summer gritted her teeth. "It sounds like you think it's a stupid idea."

"It *sounds* as if you do not trust my judgment as a warrior," he growled sharply. "It sounds as if you do not trust me to protect you."

"This isn't about trusting you! It's—" She broke off, her hands clenching.

"What is it?" he rumbled, frustration plain in his face. "What distresses you so?"

"Nothing," she insisted. "I just need to get the clanhall as fast as I can."

She tried to push past him but he caught her gently by the wrist.

"Will you not let me share this burden?" he asked and offered a faint smile. "Surely I have proved I am strong enough to carry anything for you?"

She stayed stubbornly silent and he cupped her cheek in his warm broad palm, serious. "I know you are afraid. I vow there is no need for it."

Summer's hands wrapped around her middle. "There is."

"You do not fear Ar'ar? He has no claim on you any longer."

"I think he would disagree with you on that," she muttered.

"It does not matter what he thinks." He gave a short huff, a derisive laugh. "You are my mate now."

"Wait—What?" Her head came up sharply. "Ke'lar, what did you say?"

"You are mine," he repeated. At her stare, his alien brow furrowed. "We are mate-bonded."

Her mouth parted. "Oh, God . . . I didn't even think . . ."

She'd forgotten about that aspect of g'hir males. Of the powerful instinctive bonding males experienced during sex. Something about their physiology left a male permanently imprinted on his mate.

Like Ke'lar was now imprinted on her.

Summer wet her lips. "Ke'lar . . ."

"You have nothing to fear, my mate." He took her hand in his. "You will be happy here—on Hir—with me. I will protect you; provide for you—" He gave a gentle smile, his blue eyes so loving it broke her heart. "I will cherish this honor always."

"Listen to me," she said, tightening her grip on his hand. "I can't stay here, Ke'lar. I *can't*, even if I"—she swallowed hard—"even if I wanted to. I have to go back to Earth."

"Summer, we are mate-bonded." He blinked down at her. "You know I cannot live on your world."

"I do know that." She swallowed hard. "And I'm sorry."

"No, you cannot mean this." He shook his head. "You cannot mean you still intend to return to your world, not after—"

"I *have* to."

"Why?" he demanded, his voice echoing the anguish in his eyes. "Why can you not remain here with me?"

"Ke'lar . . ." She closed her eyes briefly. "I just can't."

"Even now?" he asked tightly. "Even after I have bound myself to you you do not trust me?"

"Ar'ar—"

"You are not Ar'ar's mate!" he snarled, his fangs bared. "You are mine!"

"I have to go back." Her eyes stung. "I *have* to."

"Tell me why!"

"I can't." She blinked the tears back. "I'm sorry."

His glowing eyes were raw. "Perhaps you do not love me as I do you but I know you feel something for me. What is it that demands you must return to your world? Will you not give me at least that much? Do you—" His voice was strained. "Do you understand what it will be for me to be parted from you, from a mate I have bonded to?"

Summer looked away.

"Wait . . ." he whispered. "This is more than fear. I see guilt in your face too . . ."

She raised her gaze to his. His breath caught and she knew he'd read the truth in her eyes.

"It is not something that draws you back . . ." The color had drained from his face. "It is some*one*. There is another there—back on your world . . . one you love deeply."

"This is my fault." Summer closed her eyes briefly. "I shouldn't have let that happen last night, this morning, not when I'm leaving—"

His breath exploded in a rush and he stepped back as if she'd slapped him.

"I'm sorry, Ke'lar." She reached for him but with g'hir quickness he eluded her grasp. "I'm so sorry . . ."

He was facing away from her, his lips white as if he were remaining standing by will alone.

Summer pressed her hand hard to her mouth. There was nothing she could say to him, nothing she could do to make this right.

"I will keep my vow. I will take you to the clanhall," he rumbled tightly. "I will give you over to my father." Ke'lar took Beya's reins in hand again. "You will be returned to your world . . . and the one who awaits you there."

Twelve

The suns were nearly set when Ke'lar slid off the saddle again, leaving a rush of cool evening air against Summer's back where a moment ago the warmth of his body had been.

They rode double for long stretches of time but there were few words exchanged between them. There was no comfort she could offer him now that he knew the truth of what drew her back to Earth. Small talk was impossible and he was a warrior well accustomed to solitude.

But they weren't making great time either, despite their focus on the journey.

Even when Ke'lar pushed the animal to a run he did not force her to it for long, but Summer knew he wasn't purposefully delaying their journey; even she noticed that Beya was tiring quicker than she had the last time they had ridden her. They had been going since the suns were at their zenith and during the course of the day Beya's galloping had dwindled to trotting and frequently simply walking.

"Is she all right?" Summer asked. The multari was still breathing hard even though she hadn't run for long at all this time. "She sounds like she's wheezing a little."

"The rain yesterday, the chill last night, and this journey have worn on her," he growled. "When we reach the clanhall's stables I can rub her down, cover her with a heated blanket, and let her rest. In a few days she will be strong again."

"Should I get down? That'll make it easier on her and we're only at a walk anyway."

He glanced back at Summer; he'd been avoiding looking at her since this morning.

"I think that would be a kindness to her," he rumbled.

Of course it meant that Ke'lar was going to have to help her get off the multari, since the thing was roughly the size of a damn Clydesdale. Summer's hands rested on his shoulders as his hands went to her waist to help her off. For just an instant it seemed as if he held her against him, then ducking his head, he let her go.

"It'll be dark soon," Summer commented, wincing a bit as they started walking. Spending that long in the saddle, even with the frequent breaks, left her sore and aching.

"We have reached the other side of the river," he said. "Walking through the night means we will be at the clanhall by morning."

Summer glanced at Beya. She was breathing easier, that was for certain, but still—

"I'm not sure an all-night walk is a great idea, Ke'lar."

He kept going, his gaze on the path ahead. "It is your wish that we reach the clanhall quickly."

"I know, but we've been on the go for almost nine hours. I'm not sure Beya is up to it. I know I'm sure as hell not going to able to manage a ten-hour walk. She's exhausted and I'm getting that way fast."

"You are too tired to continue?" He stopped, frowning around at her. "You would have us make camp and spend the night here?"

"I'm a human woman, not a g'hir warrior, Ke'lar. You're the one that's indestructible, not me."

He shifted his weight, his eyes aglow in the twilight.

"If we let her rest for a few hours," he rumbled finally with a measuring look at the multari, "she may be able to carry us the rest of the way. That would make up for the time that we lose if we make camp tonight."

"Sounds good to me." Summer rubbed her hand over her face. "I don't suppose you can smell any water nearby?"

"There is a creek ahead. I intended to let Beya drink before we continued but if she were to rest for a few hours as well she would be the better for it."

"Her and me both," Summer said. "How far to the water?"

"Just beyond that tela tree."

"Which one is that?"

He pointed to a tree in the distance. "The one with the red flowers."

"I can't see colors in this low light," she reminded.

That startled him. "You cannot?"

"I don't have g'hir eyes either, Ke'lar. I have human ones—you know, the kind that need a certain light level for the cones to work? And I'm going to be stumbling around in the dark pretty soon here so I'd be grateful if you could hand me the luma."

"Is this night-blindness typical of humans?" he asked curiously. "What can you see now?"

"I can see your expression but your face is in shades of gray and black. Except I can see that your eyes are blue because they glow. "

"Will the Sisters' light not let you see?"

"I'll see *better* in bright moonlight but it'll be a cool light. No color."

"How did your ancestors hunt at night?"

"We didn't. Before electric lights people pretty much stayed indoors if they could at night. Though humans are a greater danger to each other than any wild animal probably ever was."

He slowed his pace to match hers. "How could your species survive if they could not hunt at night?"

"We had a meeting and decided to go in the whole hunt-during-the-day direction."

He gave an annoyed huff at her tart reply. "Come, if you wish to make camp. We should not stroll here talking."

"I'm only strolling because I'm trying not to fall on my face in the dark. And, hey," she grumbled, nearly twisting her ankle in a furrow she'd mistaken for firm field, "feel free to hand over the luma—which you clearly don't need—anytime, Ke'lar."

With a blast of light he activated it and offered it to her.

"Thanks," she said, gratefully using its beam to pick her way across the field as he led them to the water.

He had Beya unloaded and the shelter built in a few spare minutes while Summer rinsed her face and hands in the creek. It was a testament to how practiced he was at this that he could do it so swiftly, so silently.

One accustomed to a solitary life indeed.

She waited inside the geodesic dome—already toasty warm since he'd already set the portable heater running—while he fed and watered the multari.

She offered a wry smile when he ducked inside. "I wanted to get dinner for us but I don't know where you've stashed everything," she said with a wave at their supplies. "I was afraid digging through all of it would just make a mess."

"It will be dried fruit and meat again," he warned, quickly shifting through the supplies to the right sack. "You must be tired of it."

"Oh, I don't mind." She gave a grin. "Hell, I'm hungry enough to eat my own cooking."

"You will not have to, little one," he assured, returning her smile. "There is plenty of food still. And I would hunt for you if there were not."

"Right," she said, taking the simple meal he offered. He handed her a pouch of fresh water too. "The famous g'hir eyesight. Without the luma I'd be lost if I took two steps away from the shelter, you know, so you're not getting it back until morning."

"I will not need it," he replied easily. "Unless we decide to shelter in another cave."

"I think it's safe to say we won't need to tonight," she said with a nod toward the shelter door and the clear, star-filled sky.

"You fled the Betari enclosure at night," he commented, settling beside her with his own meal. "And with no luma. Were you not afraid?"

"Hell, yeah, I was. I intended to leave during the day but then I realized that whenever Ar'ar wasn't with me the other Betari clanbrothers were keeping an eye on me. The only time everyone assumed I really didn't need extra guarding was at night when Ar'ar was right next to me. But afraid?" She gave a humorless laugh. "There's a whole running theme in horror movies where the dumb blonde takes off alone through the woods at night."

"I do not know what 'horror movies' is."

"Oh, right . . . Well, a movie is like a holotale, only two dimensional. And a horror movie is designed to scare you. The good ones keep you from being able to sleep—or shower." She laughed at his perplexed look. "Never mind. But they usually take place somewhere remote or at night. Humans find both of those pretty scary."

"Do humans have an instinctive fear of the dark then? Because you cannot see well?"

"Maybe we evolved that way. I'm guessing that the humans who were afraid of the dark didn't leave the cave at night and didn't wind up getting eaten. And here I am—" She struck a mock dramatic pose. "The proud product of many humans who did not get eaten."

He gave a huffing laugh. "And the g'hir who could see at night could hunt better. So I suppose I am the descendant of many well-fed g'hir."

"Have you ever wondered how it's possible for humans and g'hir to reproduce?"

His gaze met hers and her face went hot. Clearly neither one of them had forgotten just how well humans and g'hir could mate—

"I mean," she blundered on, "we're different species. From different sides of the galaxy. It shouldn't be possible for us to reproduce."

"G'hir have human DNA," he reminded. "It became part of our genome untold millennia ago."

"But you shouldn't have human DNA at all," she argued. "How the hell would a human have gotten all the way out here in the first place? We didn't have space travel then. *Your* people didn't even have space travel then."

"I do not know," he said quietly. "I believe it is a gift from the All Mother, bestowed long ago, to give us hope now." He dropped his gaze. "To give others hope."

"Ke'lar—" Her throat tightened at the anguish in his face. "I didn't—I never meant to hurt you—"

She reached for him, sure he would pull away, turn away from her touch, but he closed his brilliant eyes and gave an achingly soft purr of contentment. He leaned into her, pressing his cheek against her palm.

"My Summer . . ."

In the next moment his arms were around her and he was gathering her against the broadness of his chest, wrapping his warmth and strength around her.

"I do not regret what the All Mother granted me." His rumble was like fierce thunder. "I am grateful for what I have had even if it is fated I must lose you to another. Every moment with you has been precious. I know you were never truly mine at all, little one . . ." His voice caught. "But I will always be yours."

He cradled her, her cheek pressed against his chest; she could feel the strong beat of his heart. She could almost feel that other—so very precious—heart, a half a galaxy away, beating too . . .

"Emma," she whispered hoarsely. "My daughter's name is Emma."

THIRTEEN

Ke'lar went still. "What?" He drew back to regard her, his brilliant eyes wide. "What did you say?"

"I have a little girl, Emma, back on Earth." Her tears overflowed. "She's three. Well, three and a half actually."

"You—" He shook his head as if he sought to clear it, as if his ears were buzzing. "You have a child?"

"That's why I ran away from Ar'ar. That's why your father has to get me to Earth, why I can't stay with you. I have to get back to my baby. My baby needs me."

"She is the one you love," he breathed. "This is the source of your guilt? Not—not—"

"No, it's not another man." She wiped at her face with the back of her hand. "And mommy guilt comes with the job. But being on the other side of the galaxy without even a cell phone, raises it to a whole new level."

"A child—a daughter . . ." He searched her eyes. "By the Goddess, little one, why did you not tell me?"

"Are you kidding? I couldn't tell anyone! Females are so rare here, any daughter, even a fully human adopted one, would give Ar'ar—*and* the Betari—so much status that he could never just let her be! As my mate Hir law gives Ar'ar a legal claim as her guardian. What if he found her, forced her to live with the Betari too, kept her imprisoned in their enclosure—"

"Ar'ar should never have brought you to Hir! Should never have captured you at all. No female with offspring is to be taken. If you already have a child then . . ." His gaze snapped to hers, his eyes wild. "Your child—Emma—Where is she? Is she—?"

Summer shook her head. "She's safe. She wasn't with me when Ar'ar kidnapped me. She's with her father."

His lips tightened. "Your human mate."

"*Ex*-mate—and thank you very much, State of Virginia." Summer bit her lip. "But Emma is only visiting him for two weeks. And nine of those fourteen days are already gone. He's bringing her for Christmas but if Dean brings her back to Brittle Bridge and I'm not there—if people find the house empty, they're going to think that—" She shook her head. "Oh, hell, I don't know *what* they'll think! That I'm dead, that I've starting doing drugs—I don't know! But what I *do* know is that if I'm not there Dean'll call Social Services and dump Emma with them. He'll tell them I'm nowhere to be found, that I've run off, that I'm an unfit mother—"

His brow furrowed. "But . . . surely if you were to return after the Choosing Day—"

"With no memory of where I was for a month?" she cried. "They won't let me go back to Earth unless they wipe my memory of Hir, of everything from the moment I stepped out of the house! I won't have an explanation of where I've been, why no one has seen me, why I didn't even take my cell. I haven't even called Dean to find out how Emma is and that's—look, that's just not like me. I still have the rest of this moon cycle before the Day of Choosing comes and I can't wait that long. Unless your father intervenes and helps me get home I'll get back two weeks after Dean is going to drop Emma off."

"And he—Dean—will search for you?"

She gave a short bitter laugh. "Actually, first he'll search for my wallet and relieve me of any cash I have, then he'll call Social Services and tell them I ran off." Summer shook her head, not bothering to check her tears. "Don't you understand? The courts could take Emma away from me. It might be years before I get her back—or never."

"I will go," Ke'lar promised swiftly. "I will go to Earth and find your child. I will bring her to you. I will appeal to the Council myself, apprise them of the urgency—"

"Ke'lar!" she cried. "You're an almost seven-foot-tall alien! You can't go running around the southeastern part the United States, hoping to find one little girl—even if your government allowed it—and we both know they aren't going to let you go." Summer passed her hand over her eyes. "Look, it comes down to this—if I'm not there when Dean comes back he'll probably hand her over to the state. I have four days left to get back to Earth."

His frown deepened. "Surely he would not surrender his child? He would care for her, protect her—"

"Yeah, you don't know my ex. He was a lousy husband but he's been an even worse father. He wasn't even there when she was born and since then he's hardly seen Emma at all. The only thing he seems to make time for is to bitch every month about sending support for her—not that it adds up to much. I even had my attorney draw up papers for him to waive his rights just so if anything happened to me Emma wouldn't wind up being raised by someone who'd treat her like a burden. Well—" She ran her hands through her hair. "At least until she was old enough to be treated like a *servant*. The only reason he's got Emma now is 'cause his mother begged me to send her. He's got visitation but he never uses it so I couldn't really object. And God love her, Dean's momma is a real good woman with a jerk for a son. All Dean is really doing is picking Emma up and driving her back to mooch off his mom for two weeks, while Emma sees her grandmother."

"He is not fit to be a father," Ke'lar snarled. "He does not deserve all he has been given."

Summer sighed. "You sure won't get any argument from me."

"I wish you had told me." He closed his eyes briefly. "I wish you had trusted me."

"I *am* trusting you, Ke'lar, with the most precious thing in my life—I'm trusting you with my baby girl." She caught her hands in his. "You have to help me. You have to convince your father to send me home."

"I cannot live on Earth with you." His gaze was raw. "And I cannot live without you. There must be another way."

"She's my baby." Her vision blurred. "And goddamn it, choosing between you is killing me."

"I thought"—his throat worked for a moment—"there was another male that you loved."

"No," she murmured, taking his face in her hands. She brushed her nose to his in a g'hir's kiss. "There's no one but you."

His eyes softened and he wrapped his arms around her, drawing her close. "Summer . . ."

He tilted his head, bringing his mouth to hers, his tongue flicking against the sensitive spot at the corner of her mouth. The cinnamon-sweet taste of him was delicious; his soft purr sent heat racing between her legs. This time, though, it was she who unfastened his clothing, who knelt above him, allowing him to enjoy the sight as she removed her own clothes.

He cupped her buttocks, ready to lift her onto his hard cock, when she put her hands to his shoulders to stop him.

"Wait—" She offered a quick smile. "My turn."

He was ready, eager to be inside her, but he yielded, letting her push him back to lie down upon the pallet. He was all muscle and warm skin, his penis jutting upward, a gleam of moisture at the tip.

"Put your arms up," she said, her voice husky. "Over your head."

"Why?" he rumbled, looking perplexed even as he complied.

Her fingers traced the sinew of his hips and his cock twitched in response, his eyes like blue fire.

"Because now," she murmured, "I want to capture you."

His mouth parted as she slid her hand around his shaft, feeling it grow more taut, the lubrication increasing as she stroked.

His glowing eyes widened as she bent to press her mouth against the tip of his shaft, groaning as she ran her tongue along the luscious sweet wetness there.

His rumble went deeper than she'd ever heard it when she took him into her mouth, her hand stroking the length. With the heat of his cock in her mouth and his purr vibrating her clit she groaned, wondering just how long she could do this before her own need grew out of control.

His muscles were quivering, his hungry rumble making her tremble with need. She pressed her tongue to the underside of his shaft and suddenly the sweet taste of his seed burst into her mouth, leaving his body quaking.

"I did not . . . know," he gasped, "you could . . . do that."

She laughed, licking his candy sweet taste from her lips as she straddled his hips. "Like it?"

"Yes," he growled fiercely.

His cock was still hard, his rumbling deep, and she shivered as he traced the outline of her body with the tips of his fingers.

"Let me pleasure you the same way," he murmured.

"I don't know," she teased, a little breathless. "Those fangs look awful sharp."

"You have fangs too." He half sat up and she gasped as the wet heat of his mouth closed around her nipple. "Dainty little human ones."

It was a moment before she could think clearly enough to answer as he kissed his way to the other breast.

"Those are called 'canines' and they aren't really—oh!" she breathed as his fingers brushed her clit, the moisture there making it easy for him to stroke her.

"I love to see you find your pleasure," he rumbled. "I have never imagined anything so arousing."

He lay back and clasped her by the hips. He lowered her slowly, till his cock filled her completely.

His hands rested on her thighs, his fingers stroking in rhythm as he rocked beneath her, his glowing eyes blue fire as he watched her. Suddenly her climax hit and his fingers tightened reflexively as he pulsed inside her.

She collapsed atop him, too spent for the moment even to roll off.

His arms encircled her, holding her. "There will never be another but you, my mate, my sweet Summer . . ."

Summer stirred and reached out, only to find the place beside her on the pallet empty.

She blinked, rubbing at her eyes. From the light filtering through the shelter she knew it was very early morning but she didn't hear Ke'lar moving about outside.

It was very quiet.

Too quiet.

Her heart in her throat and trying to make as little noise as possible, Summer reached for her clothes and dressed swiftly. She hesitated for a moment, listening, at the shelter's exit, then pushed it open and stepped outside.

The suns had not yet risen over the Zun Mountains; the air was cool and fog swirled through the valley, blanketing everything in an otherworldly mist.

She was alone.

Her glance darted about the field, the mist-shrouded trees, but there was no sign of him.

"Ke'lar?" she whispered.

Summer wrapped her arms around herself at the answering silence.

Would he do that? Would he just go off and leave her in the middle of nowhere?

Like hell he would. Something's wrong.

Not that it was much protection, really, but it was hard to take even those few tentative steps away from the shelter.

Summer raised her voice. "Ke'lar?"

She heard it then, male, g'hir for certain, off to her right in the same direction as the stream—a groan of one in great pain . . .

"Ke'lar!"

She ran that way, trying to watch her footing, cursing herself for leaving the blaster back at the shelter, considering and discarding the idea of going back for it.

He was slumped over but she couldn't see him clearly. There was a shape there in the fog but like nothing familiar at all.

A few more stumbling steps and the sight came clear.

"Oh, no. Ke'lar—"

He was kneeling at the multari's side, his hand gently stroking her nose. Beya's long neck was stretched out along the ground, her legs tucked under her where she lay, her face peaceful, her glowing eyes closed forever . . .

G'hir couldn't cry but the grief etched into his face showed he felt loss as deeply as any human. Summer knelt beside him on the cold, damp ground. She wrapped her arms around him and trembling, Ke'lar clung to her. A wail rose in his throat till it echoed through the small grove.

"I'm sorry." Summer rocked him as he keened for Beya. Any thought of how this might delay them, how badly they needed the multari to reach the clanhall, vanished in the face of his pain. "I'm so sorry . . ."

She stayed there with him, holding him against her, and he clung to her. In time his keen quieted but he did not let her go.

"I do not remember her. My mother," he murmured finally, his eyes on the multari who had been his companion for so many years. "I ought to, I was five summers when she died; old enough to have some memory of her but I have none. They say it was the trauma, that when the Scourge tore through our enclosure my mind blocked the horror of it. But I do not remember much before that time either. It is as if I were born into a world already broken, with no recall of a time when my kind was not a dying race. . . ."

"I'm sorry." Summer stroked his silky hair, wishing she could say more, wishing she had some great comfort to offer.

"No child so young should be without her mother," he said hoarsely. "We cannot let your child know such terrible grief. We cannot leave her unprotected. You are right, my

Summer. No matter what the cost, you must return to your world."

Fourteen

Ke'lar shouldered most of the supplies on their trek to the clanhall, although he allowed her to carry some small portion of them. Summer waited respectfully as Ke'lar returned the animal who had been his companion and comfort for so long to the g'hir's All Mother.

His face was ragged with grief but he sent her a grateful look when Summer took his hand.

"We will be there by the evening meal," he promised, with a glance at the suns.

"Only because I walk so freaking slow." She raised her eyebrows. "We could just leave everything here and you could carry me on your back."

He shook his head. "This foresting has been one full of surprises and—difficulties. It is a few hours' walk to the clanhall but I will not leave our supplies here, and risk finding shelter and food—should we need them—to chance. Carrying you and the supplies both will tire me. I may need to protect you and I will not gamble with your safety."

"Protect me from what?" she asked with a worried glance at the forest around them.

His fangs showed for an instant as if warning the universe at large not to dare threaten her. "From anything."

"We're in your clan's territory," she reminded. "We should be pretty safe here."

"I am a g'hir warrior, you are my mate. I cannot tolerate danger to you." His hand cradled hers. "But you are human, I do not expect you to understand."

"Hey, I have a kid, remember?" she pointed out. "You want to see some serious mama-bear action—threaten a human female's baby."

He stopped, his glowing eyes serious. "You must tell them."

"About Emma?" Her jaw hardened. "No fucking way."

"When the decision was made to take women from your world it was decided that no female who had already borne offspring be taken from her young. Ar'ar has broken this directive. They will allow you to return to Earth. They must."

"Or instead," she began sharply, "the Council—that Mirak practically *runs*—will give their clan a slap on the wrist instead and decide that Ar'ar has a right to get 'his' daughter. That's the law too, isn't it?"

"A child belongs to the mother and the mother's mate. Emma is not Ar'ar's daughter," Ke'lar said quietly. "She is mine."

Summer swallowed hard. "What will your clanfather do? What will the Erah do if they find out they can add not just one female but two to their enclosure?"

"I am not saying they will be pleased to let you go," he growled softly. "But they will obey the law. My clan *will* respect your choice."

"The choice I get to make after one moon cycle with you, right?" she asked hoarsely. "To obey the law your clan could only let me go home after my Day of Choosing—a full moon cycle from our first coupling, right? Twenty-seven days from now."

He passed his hand over his face. "Yes."

"That just resets the clock. That has me getting home a month after Dean brings Emma back."

"And so I must not claim you for my mate," he said, his shoulders falling. He regarded her gravely for a moment, then gave her hand a gentle tug. "We will plead your case to my father. He too has great influence with the Council."

"What if that doesn't work? What if your father won't help?"

"Emma—"

"No," she said firmly. "I won't risk them knowing about her. For all I know Mirak will arrange a military raid to find her."

His glowing blue eyes were steady. "Then we must trust that the All Mother will soften my father's heart to your cause."

They walked in silence, hand in hand, each absorbed with their own thoughts when Summer slowly became aware of something she hadn't seen in days.

Summer blinked. "Hey, this is a road! An actual road!"

It was dirt road, granted, but a wide cleared space. The kind of road she'd thought would enable her to cover ten miles a day when she'd first escaped the Betari clanhall.

"It is the southern road of our territory and will lead us to my clan's enclosure. I have walked it many times. But come," he said, leading her instead through the trees, toward the river and to a shaded spot there. In the distance was a village-like cluster of buildings and towering over them a structure that could only be the Erah clanhall.

Her way home.

Ke'lar glanced about the place and gave a nod of approval, already shrugging off his pack. "This will do."

"Why are we stopping here?" she asked, and her eyebrows shot up as his clothes started coming off. "And uh, what are you doing?" Her gaze traced his naked form, her breath quickening. "I mean, not that I mind . . ."

Her tone was husky but the expression he turned on her was serious.

"They will smell me on you, and you on me," he reminded. "They will know we have mated."

"Oh," she murmured.

His jaw worked for a moment. "We must convince my father to return you to Earth. If I claim you, you must remain on Hir until your Choosing Day, so I cannot do so. The only way for you to be returned to Earth is to publicly accuse the Betari of threatening you, of denying your right to choose, and then asking my father to take up your cause. You must enter the Erah clanhall as Ar'ar's mate to do that."

"I see." She shifted her weight. "I didn't realize how much that was going to bother me."

"To proclaim yourself his mate and then forswear him?"

"No," she said softly. "To pretend like you don't mean anything to me."

"It will take all my strength to do this." His face was ragged. "To stand by and not declare you mine. But if you are to forswear Ar'ar and do it in the Erah clanhall, you must be seen as one of the Betari, not one of my clan. You cannot be seen to favor me as an alternate to Ar'ar. We must wash and change here before we encounter any of my clanbrothers and we must not touch again."

Her throat tightened. "You mean never?"

Ke'lar met her gaze and in his eyes she saw something of what this was costing him. "It would be best . . . not to."

I have to do this. I have to get home. Emma needs me .
. .

"Okay," she said hoarsely. "Okay."

She slipped the small pack he'd allowed her off her back. He handed her a small pouch of cleanser and she noticed that when he did he took care not to touch her. He kept his gaze from her as he entered the river water to wash too.

Water played over his body in the sunlight.

Summer swallowed hard and stripped her clothes off. The water was cold and she dunked herself into it and came up gasping.

"Are you all right?" he asked, his back to her.

She was suddenly reminded of the first night they met, of her washing in this same river but way upstream, worried that all he wanted was to get an eyeful.

But he wasn't even looking at her now.

"Yeah." She cleared her throat and poured some of the spicy-smelling cleanser into her palm. "It's just freezing."

"There will be hot baths at the clanhall," he said apologetically. "And proper beds."

But we won't be sharing one.

She rubbed the cleanser between her hands and started washing her hair.

It's not like he could come and live with her on Earth, for Christ's sake! It's not like she and Ke'lar and Emma could settle into some cute little cottage and be a family.

It was him or a little girl who had no one but her mother.

Summer would never wish her daughter away; that child had brought more joy and meaning to her life—even with all the struggles of being a single mom—than she could ever have imagined. But if by some chance she had never had Emma, if she didn't have anything so precious back on Earth—

Summer's eyes were drawn to Ke'lar, to his muscled back, his black hair, his rippled brow in profile, his glowing eyes firmly turned away.

I'd stay with him. Oh, my God, I want to stay with him.

The realization held her frozen for an instant, thigh-deep in the chill water of an alien world, watching the dappled light of Hir's suns play across his broad shoulders.

And going home means I'll never see him again. I won't even remember . . .

Summer couldn't help but edge a little closer to Ke'lar when they encountered the first of his clanbrothers on the road. The men had been talking, laughing amongst themselves as they came from the direction of the enclosure, but they stopped, staring, as soon as they spotted her.

He called out to his fellow Erah, acknowledging each by name, as she and Ke'lar approached, but they didn't return his warm greeting.

They had gone silent, their glowing eyes—in shades of blue from the palest gray to sapphire dark—fixed on her, their faces slack in astonishment.

"Who are you?" one of them asked without taking his eyes off her for an instant. She had the spooky feeling that he was weighing the idea of his chances of getting away with her swung over his shoulder. "What is your namesound?"

"This is Summerelizabethmills," Ke'lar replied, making her first, middle, and last name into one long word.

Summer glanced at Ke'lar. She'd have to explain to him later how the three were really supposed to be distinct and why, but she sure didn't feel like extending this meeting any longer by starting up some conversation.

"She cannot be yours!" one of the younger ones exclaimed suddenly. He took a step closer to sniff lightly. Ke'lar tensed at her side and the young man threw a startled look at him. "She does not bear your scent."

Clearly the idea that he might be traveling with a human female he hadn't already claimed was astounding. She could also see that it was starting to sink in to the clanbrothers that she might just be fair game.

Oh, this could get ugly fast . . .

"I'm Ar'ar's mate," she said, her voice strained. "From the uh, Betari clan."

Apparently speaking just managed to rivet their attention back on her completely.

"What are you doing here?" one asked. He glanced at Ke'lar. "With our clanbrother?"

"She has come to speak to our clanfather," Ke'lar said, putting his body between her and the men who seemed rooted to the spot and blocking their way.

"I have seen Ar'ar," one of the men who had not yet spoken said. "He is a fierce warrior." His azure eyes fixed on her and his full mouth curved a bit. "But to challenge him would be worth the price."

"She is the honored mate of the Betari heir and our guest," Ke'lar said sharply. "She is deserving of the hospitality of our clanhall and its comforts. You will not offer her insult by delaying our journey." His voice lowered to a snarl. "Stand aside."

The men were startled, but his outrage—and implied threat—got them to move so that Ke'lar and Summer could pass.

Ke'lar indicated that she should go first. Ducking her head, she preceded him, and discovered she was trying to make herself a little smaller as she walked past the men.

Summer trusted Ke'lar's senses enough that she knew he would be aware if one tried to follow them but a glance back showed the men hadn't budged, still watching her with predator-like fixation.

"That was uncomfortable," she muttered when they had gone far enough along the road to be out of sight.

"That was nothing compared to what you would have encountered had you entered the capital alone," Ke'lar growled. "And there would have been none at hand to call upon clan loyalty and good manners. They would be fighting in the streets over you."

"Okay, yeah, maybe the city wasn't the best plan." She glanced back. "What did that warrior mean? That challenging Ar'ar would be worth the price."

Ke'lar's jaw hardened, his glowing gaze on the road ahead. "A warrior may challenge another for his mate."

Summer's brow creased. "What kind of challenge?"

"A battle between unarmed men. The victor takes the female."

"That's barbaric," she got out. "That's appalling!"

"Most females find it flattering, a great tribute to their desirability," he grumbled.

"And a great insult to their self-determination!" she cried. "What if the woman in question doesn't want this new guy?"

"There is the understanding that she would have voiced some interest in having him as her new mate." He gave her an impatient look. "Did you not understand that is what N'ar"—he indicated the road behind them—"was asking? He wanted you to know he would fight for you. And he wished to know if you would have him."

"Wait—" Summer frowned. "If he was asking—I can pick someone instead of Ar'ar?"

Ke'lar gave a g'hir nod. "Of course."

"No wonder Ar'ar was always showing his fangs to his clanbrothers," she murmured.

"I do not doubt it." He gave a snort. "He was trying to warn them off from flirting with you."

"*That's* how g'hir flirt?" she asked. "Hey baby, let's get a drink sometime and hey, mind if I beat the snot out of your mate?"

His rippled brow furrowed. "Only if the female already has a male who is mate-bonded to her."

"What if she doesn't?" Summer asked. "I mean, what if she's single?"

"He would court her."

"Court her how?"

He shrugged. "Dine with her, compliment her. Make a mating roar to her."

"A mating *roar*? What's—" She broke off, remembering Ar'ar coming at her in the snow, his roar so loud it made her ears ring. "Never mind. I think I know what it is." She raised an eyebrow at Ke'lar. "Hey, how come you never did that for me?"

"I did not have to," he said confidently. "*You* initiated our coupling."

Summer gave a short, shocked laugh. "Oh, sure. After you were all 'let's lay here in bed together and just talk'!"

"I offered to sleep outside the shelter, in the cave." He turned innocent, glowing eyes on her. "It was you who insisted I join you in the bed."

"*I* insisted—?" Something in his expression caught her attention and she gaped up at him. "Oh my God, you played me, didn't you? You made it all *my* idea that you sleep next to me."

He flashed a full—and unapologetic—fanged grin. "A clever hunter knows when it is best to lure the prey rather than chase it."

"You—!" She pushed at him in mock-outrage, and he caught her against him with a huffing laugh.

She shook her head, outraged and smiling up at him.

"It worked well, I think," he said huskily, and the softest of rumble-purrs started in his chest as he bent to bring his mouth to hers.

He froze and abruptly his purr broke off and he wrenched his face away.

Hurt slashed through her chest as he let her go and stepped back. "Ke'lar? What's the—" She swallowed. "Right. No touching."

"This lapse will make no difference," he growled. "It will be dismissed, as if I had helped you when you had stumbled."

"Yeah," she murmured, dragging her feet as he started again toward the clanhall.

His other clanbrothers were no less astonished by the sudden appearance of a human woman in their midst. They stared at her round-eyed as she walked past but, while they returned Ke'lar's greetings in a pretty distracted way, none sought to impede their progress through the enclosure.

The closer they came to the clanhall, of course, the more clanbrothers they met. Many of them had Ke'lar's coloring, very dark hair and blue eyes, and it was funny to think how she'd once found their alien faces so frightening. In their eyes and expressions she could read all the same emotions humans felt. Still, having dozens of strange warriors from an entirely unfamiliar clan staring at her wasn't exactly comfortable. Just their physical presence, their size and strength, was overwhelming, let alone the way they stopped whatever it was they were doing to watch her pass.

It was very, very hard not to reach out and take Ke'lar's hand in hers; not to seek refuge in his warm strength.

Ke'lar didn't have to tell her which building was the clanhall. The setup here was much like the Betari's had been. A central fountain and courtyard, the imposing multi-storied structure of the clanhall, the smaller buildings and homes that had been built out over millennia as the g'hir population grew.

The buildings here were well maintained but many of these too must be empty; there were so very many warriors and no women.

As Summer climbed the steps to the clanhall she blinked at seeing a woman waiting there—a familiar one.

A *human* one . . .

"Jenna," she breathed.

"Summer?" Jenna chocolate brown eyes were wide, her g'hir clothing as girly as you could get. "Oh my God, I can't believe it. . . Is it really you?"

Before Summer could answer, Jenna was racing down the clanhall stairs, catching her in an embrace.

"I can't believe you're here! I can't believe it's really you!" Jenna exclaimed. "Are you all right?"

"Yeah," Summer said, hugging her back. "Are you? Are you all right?"

Her childhood friend gave a smile but it was a strained one. "I'm fine."

Her brown eyes darted about, taking in Summer's and Ke'lar's clothing, the clanbrothers watching.

"Come on, let's—hey, how 'bout we go to the kitchens?" She tugged at Summer's hand to draw her along.

"I've got them making some sweet tea. I swear, girl, it tastes just like it does back home!"

"Iced tea?" Summer stared, resisting her pull. "You vanish without a trace—everyone in Brittle Bridge thinks you're dead—then I find you on an alien planet and the first thing you want to do is skip off for some *iced tea*? What do you think this is, Jenna McNally—an extraterrestrial garden party?"

"Sister, your welcoming custom must wait," Ke'lar said to Jenna, his brow furrowed. "Where is my father? And Ra'kur? I must speak to them immediately."

Just then another warrior, taller but bearing a strong resemblance to Ke'lar, emerged from the clanhall's vast entryway. Jenna's glance darted fearfully that way and Summer realized this must be Ra'kur, the alien who had kidnapped her friend all those months ago.

"Ra'kur!" Ke'lar called in relief, warmth and trust in his voice at his brother's approach. "This is Summer, of the Betari enclosure. She is in urgent need of our help."

Ra'kur glanced between them, shock flickering across his features. "Brother—"

"Why would she have need of help from you?" Ar'ar demanded as he stepped from the shadows of the Erah clanhall into the sunlight, his fangs showing. "When her own mate is here."

FIFTEEN

Ar'ar's amber eyes were molten as they fixed on her and Summer recoiled as Mirak too emerged from the Erah clanhall to stand beside his son. Ke'lar moved to stand protectively before her even as Jenna's grip tightened on Summer's hand, holding her fast, keeping her from fleeing.

"Congratulations, Ra'kur, son of the Erah," Mirak said coldly to Ke'lar's elder brother. "I was completely fooled. You had me convinced you had no idea as to her whereabouts."

"I did not," Ra'kur growled. "I told you the truth when I said I had no word of her, nor sight of her."

"And yet," Ar'ar pointed out sharply, "here my mate stands, on the very steps of your clanhall, in the company of your own brother!"

"Ra'kur did not deceive you," Ke'lar snapped. "I had no comm unit with me during my foresting, no way to contact my clan. He had no knowledge of this."

Ar'ar's fangs were fully bared. "And I am to accept your word? Trust one who would steal my mate, prey upon a female vulnerable and separated from her clan?"

"I have not stolen her!" Ke'lar insisted. "She crossed to Erah territory of her own accord."

"Before or after we met at the border between our lands, Ke'lar, son of the Erah?" Ar'ar demanded.

Ke'lar's lip curled. "You mean when you said you had crossed into our land in search of a 'fugitive clanbrother'?"

Ar'ar's gold eyes narrowed. "Would you alert an enemy that your mate was nearby, lost and defenseless?"

"Lost? Maybe." Summer squared her shoulders and shook off Jenna's hold to face Ar'ar. "Defenseless? Fucking *never*."

"Summer," Jenna began urgently. "Please, just let—"

"She has asked for the sanctuary of our clanhall," Ke'lar broke in. "I have granted it."

"Why would she be in need of sanctuary *here*?" Ar'ar's gaze went to Summer and for an instant she could have sworn she had wounded him. "For what reason?"

"She has asked for sanctuary," Ke'lar repeated, lifting his chin. "I have granted it."

"Even if she were in need of sanctuary," Ar'ar said sharply, "you do not have the authority to grant it."

"But his father does, doesn't he? So let me ask him myself." Summer put her hands on her hips. "Unless me speaking to outsiders is a problem for you, Ar'ar? Unless you have something to hide?"

"I do not know why you thought you had need to flee me, my mate. I do not understand your anger. Tell me what distresses you when we have returned to the safety of our enclosure," Ar'ar said, reaching for her. "I vow I will set it right."

Summer stepped back quickly, her gaze narrowed at Ar'ar. "I'm not going anywhere with you."

Ar'ar's glance flicked to Ke'lar. "I think our enemy has poisoned your mind to me, my mate."

"Oh, he wouldn't need to, would he? So are you going to let me speak to the Erah clanfather? Or are you going to drag me out of here kicking and screaming and show everybody what a good mate you are?"

Their little show had drawn quite a crowd of Erah clanbrothers, grumbling among themselves about how this female was being treated, something that Ar'ar and his father couldn't help but notice. There were even a couple of richly dressed female g'hir in the crowd. One, a young woman with the Erah black hair and blue eyes, seemed riveted by the exchange but the woman beside her, a little older, a blonde, had a look of haughty disdain to her, as if these goings-on were beneath her notice.

"My father would be pleased to speak with your mate," Ra'kur offered. "Since she has requested it."

Ar'ar's jaw tightened. "And since your father has not troubled himself to step outside," he pointed out with a caustic look at Ra'kur, "he makes it necessary that my mate enter the clanhall in order to speak with him."

"My apologies." Ra'kur spread his hands. "Our father is elderly."

"But wily as ever," Mirak muttered.

"Are you going let me speak to their clanfather?" Summer demanded. "Or are you afraid to?"

Ar'ar's rippled brow furrowed. "I do not fear—"

"Summer of the Betari," Ke'lar broke in, formally indicating the entrance, "in our clanfather's name, we bid you welcome to our hall."

"Hey, since you asked, yes," Summer trilled loudly, already striding past Ar'ar and his father, "I'd *love* to come in, thanks!"

The entrance to the Erah clanhall was brighter, simpler, less ornate than the Betari's, but lovely too and probably just as ancient.

"This way, please," Ra'kur said, leading them into the dining hall.

An elderly g'hir seated there stood as they entered.

"A pity you were not up to joining us outside," Mirak commented. "Feeling rested now, Rotin?"

"Yes, thank you," the clanfather of the Erah said smoothly. His glowing, pale blue eyes turned to Summer. "And who is this?"

"As if you did not know," Ar'ar grumbled.

"I'm Summer Mills and I am, uh"—she inclined her head like the g'hir did, trying to sound formal and respectful—"seeking sanctuary in your hall."

"For what reason?" Rotin asked.

"Well—" She really hadn't expected to have to give an explanation. She'd just thought she'd ask and he'd grant it. "I'm human—well, obviously—" she said in response to his faint smile. "I was kidnapped—uh, captured, from my world but I don't want to remain on Hir. I want to go back to Earth." She took a deep breath. "Right now."

"I see," Rotin said gravely. "Is this your Day of Choosing?"

"My—?" Summer's stomach clenched. "No, that's not for another eighteen days."

Rotin glanced at Ar'ar. "Has your mate mistreated you?"

Summer threw her hands out in frustration. "He kidnapped me!"

"To hunt—to capture—a mate is our way."

"I *know* that! But he took me from my—" Summer caught herself. "From my world. Without my permission and he refuses to let me return."

"Until your day of choosing," Rotin pointed out. "This is by Hir law."

"I shouldn't have to wait!" Summer insisted, fury making her voice rise. "I've made my decision—I want to go back to Earth!"

"You have that right," the clanfather agreed. "When the moon's cycle is complete."

Summer gritted her teeth. What was it with these people? Did they honestly think a few days was going to make any difference? "He kept me prisoner at the Betari enclosure."

"Prisoner!" Ar'ar's amber eyes widened. "It is your home!"

"No, it's not! Aren't you fucking *listening*?" Summer cried. "I want to go home—and home is Earth!"

"*I* am listening," Rotin said with such patient dignity that Summer felt her face flush in embarrassment. "You have asked for sanctuary in my clanhall, Mata," he reminded, using the g'hir way of addressing an honored female. "This is a very serious matter. One I must consider carefully to ascertain if there is cause to grant it."

He really did seem to be trying to help her. Summer gave a—human—nod. "I understand."

"Has Ar'ar mistreated you, Mata?" Rotin asked again.

Summer wet her lips. It would be a lie, a big whopper of one, since Ar'ar had never threatened her, never used his considerable strength to hurt her. Everything he'd done was in accordance with Hir law and custom.

But that didn't make it right.

At her silence Rotin regarded her gravely. "Then I do not see cause to grant you sanctuary here."

"Father," Ke'lar began urgently, "Summer will not *be* permitted to choose. Even if she choses to return to her world the Betari will announce that she has chosen Ar'ar!"

"You lie!" Ar'ar roared, rounding on Ke'lar.

"You are the ones who lie!" Ke'lar snarled, his fangs fully bared.

"This is my clanhall!" Rotin stepped forward. "And I will have no bloodshed within it!"

Ar'ar's fangs gleamed in the light. "Then come outside, thief. Let me spill your blood there," he taunted. "Let your lies seep away with your lifeforce!"

"My son—" Mirak placed his hand on Ar'ar's arm. The Betari heir resisted for a moment, his furious eyes fixed on Ke'lar, then allowed his father to draw him back.

Rotin turned his attention to Summer, his crinkled pale alien eyes kind but with the same lingering sadness all the g'hir carried.

"Is this true?" he asked. "Did your mate say he would not honor your choice?"

"It wasn't Ar'ar." Summer glanced at the Betari's clanfather. "It was Mirak who said that to me."

"My father would never—!"

Rotin held up a palm to Ar'ar to silence him and regarded Mirak with a raised eyebrow.

The Council member didn't even blink. "Naturally her decision on the Choosing Day will be honored. It is the law."

"That's not what you told me a few days ago!" Summer snapped, her face hot. "You told me I was staying with Ar'ar no matter what I decided!"

"I believe you misunderstood me," Mirak said coolly. "Daughter."

Summer's eyes narrowed. "Oh, man, you are some piece of work, Councilor!"

"You vow that this young woman *will* have her Day of Choosing?" Rotin asked pointedly, indicating Summer. "That your clan will honor her decision?"

"Of course." Mirak inclined his head. "You have my word."

"Then," Rotin said gravely, "I cannot lawfully grant sanctuary. I must refuse your request."

Her throat closed at the unfairness of it, at the wrongness of it. Who was *he*—who were *any* of them—to determine where she should go, what she should do?

"I can't believe this!" Summer cried, her hands clenching. "You're just going to send me back with them? No matter what I want?"

"Father," Ke'lar urged, "I implore you to reconsider! Allow her to remain with us, under our protection—"

"Ar'ar is her mate, my son," Rotin said, frowning. "He is within his rights under the law."

Like his right to Emma!

She could see it in Ke'lar's eyes, how he was on the verge of telling them about Emma. His father might be an honorable man but clearly he was one that would obey Hir law and the law declared Emma belonged to Ar'ar—and the Betari.

Quickly Summer gave the tiniest of headshakes, warning him to stay silent, and Ke'lar's jaw hardened in grim acknowledgment.

His eyes flashed blue fire as he turned his gaze to Ar'ar. "Summer stays here!"

"Summer is *mine*!" Ar'ar snarled, his fangs showing as he released her arm to confront Ke'lar. "Do you challenge me for her?"

Jenna's chocolate eyes rounded with horror. Her mate quickly drew her back, out of danger, as Ke'lar leapt forward and Ra'kur put himself protectively between Jenna and the two snarling warriors.

"He does not." Rotin sent a warning glance but his son's attention was fixed on Ar'ar.

Ke'lar roared, his fangs fully bared, his body shifting to a fighting stance as Ar'ar too readied for battle.

"This female belongs to the Betari!" his father shouted. "I forbid this challenge!"

"Take her from me, Ke'lar," Ar'ar growled. "If you can!"

Summer's heart hammered in her chest, her ears still ringing from Ke'lar's roar, her stomach rolling at what was about to happen. God knew she didn't want this but there was no other way. If Ke'lar won her in this barbaric fight, she could stay here with him. He was the only one who knew—*he* understood—about Emma, that her baby needed her, that she had to get home and fast. He would let her go back to Earth, back to her baby and—

His gaze met hers then and the blue fire in his eyes went cold as moonlight.

"No," Ke'lar growled, straightening. "As my father commands, I acknowledge your claim to this female, Ar'ar. She is yours."

Sixteen

The breath rushed out of Summer's lungs as Ke'lar inclined his head respectfully to the Betari heir.

"*What?*" Summer pushed forward. "What are you doing? You're just going to—You promised you'd—"

"There is nothing to be done," Ke'lar interrupted sharply. "This is the decision of the clanfather." He glanced at his sire. "To disobey is to defy clan directive."

"You don't mean this, you can't—" Her hands clenched and her voice rose. "You *promised*!"

"Whatever he promised," Ar'ar growled, drawing her to his side possessively, "he had no right to. You are my mate." He addressed the Erah clanfather. "Your son wronged me by keeping her from me. He has broken the truce and offended my clan. He has endangered one most precious to us."

His face grieved, Rotin addressed his younger son. "You were aware that Ar'ar sought his mate? You were aware that she was missing? That her clan feared greatly for her?"

Ke'lar blinked. "Father, she asked for my help, for *our* help—"

"Did you have any reason to believe that she had been or would be mistreated by her mate?" his father persisted.

Ke'lar's eyes were stormy.

"No," he growled finally.

"You knowingly—and unlawfully—kept a female from her mate?"

"Yes," he fairly spat.

"Then you leave me no choice, my son." Heaviness seemed to settle on Rotin's shoulders. "Ke'lar of the Erah," he intoned, "for these acts you are banished from the clanhall—"

At Summer's side Ar'ar smirked.

"Banished!" Ra'kur exclaimed, instantly stepping forward to his brother's defense. "Father, you cannot—"

"—until the snows have come twice," the clanfather finished.

There was an instant of silence.

"Hardly a lengthy punishment," Mirak growled, nettled, "for such a serious crime."

"I acknowledge the wrong done your clan," the clanfather said, his voice carrying so that everyone within the hall could hear. "My son will not be permitted within these walls again until the following gathering. But," he said, his eyes cold on his rival, "Ke'lar protected your clandaughter. He has brought what is yours safely here."

"But not—" Mirak pointed out sharply, "—brought her to us."

"Your daughter is returned, nevertheless," the clanfather said, indicating Summer at Ar'ar's side. "She is safely under her mate's protection once more and our treaty renewed."

He's not my mate!

She wanted to cry out, to rage at them all, but she knew it would do no good. There were still eighteen days to her Choosing Day, plenty of time for Ar'ar to make her his.

The two men regarded each other for a moment and the tension was palpable.

Finally Mirak gave a stiff nod.

"May the All Mother watch over you," Rotin said to Ke'lar, who stood, his nostrils flared, to receive his father's blessing, "until your banishment is at an end and you may again enter this hall."

"Be well, my brother," Ra'kur growled heavily. "Know that upon your return to us this transgression will be forgotten—and forgiven." Ra'kur put a hand on Ke'lar's shoulder. "I will await you at the very center of the clanhall, as always."

Ke'lar expression was stormy then he inclined his head toward Ra'kur. "I am grateful for it."

"Ke'lar—!" she croaked as he turned away.

"The clanfather has made his decision. I have acknowledged Ar'ar's claim to you," he said tightly without looking at her.

"You said you would *help* me." She shook her head. Was he really going to walk out of here? Was he really going to leave her? "Goddamn it, I trusted you!"

"I am a warrior of Hir and will act as one." Ke'lar's mouth thinned. "I am sorry. There is nothing more I can do for you now."

Emma!

"No, actually there *is* one more thing you can do for me, Ke'lar," Summer spat. "You can rot in hell!"

He looked at her with hard, alien eyes. "I am banished for *your* sake. I am a pariah to my clan and damned to a solitary existence for nearly two years. Think of *that* when you think to curse me."

Her eyes stung as he left the hall without even a backward glance.

"Come," Ar'ar said. "Our transport ship awaits."

"Why, you can't leave now!" Jenna moved swiftly to block their exit. "Summer and I haven't seen each other in just about forever! And besides—this is no way to send y'all home. It just wouldn't be right neighborly of us." The g'hir looked at her blankly and Jenna offered a girlish shrug. "It's a southern thing."

Summer stared at Jenna. What the hell was she doing? Sure, they'd both grown up in North Carolina, but right now her friend sounded like a deranged Scarlett O'Hara.

"What would the human custom be?" Ra'kur asked, his brow furrowing. "We would not wish to offend the Betari clanmother—nor they you, I am sure—by ignoring the customs of your homeworld."

"Well, they should stay to supper, of course! And to pass the evening in good company. The night as well if it gets too late and we all get to talking." Jenna smiled around sweetly at them all. "Summer and I played together when we were little, believe it or not. It's been a long time since we saw each other. We got us lots to catch up on."

"A feast." Rotin gave a firm nod. "To celebrate the renewal of our treaty."

Jenna spread her hands. "What do you say? After all, there's no way our clans should be enemies when your new clanmother and I are friends."

Mirak looked ready to refuse but Ar'ar spoke first. "We would be honored to feast with the Erah," he growled, inclining his head. "As I told Ke'lar when we last met, I have long wished our enmity to be at an end."

"We will remain for this human custom of being"— and here Mirak growled the English word—"'neighborly.'"

"Tell you what," Jenna began and glanced at the young g'hir woman who hovered nearby. "H'lara, why don't you go get the kitchen going on supper for everybody? Ra'kur, would you see to our honored guests while I take Summer upstairs to get cleaned up?" She gave her friend's road-worn clothes a meaningful look. "I'm sure we can find something pretty of mine that you can wear."

The g'hir exchanged puzzled looks and Jenna gave an airy wave.

"It's customary on Earth for friends to swap clothes and share outfits," she assured the men, steering Summer toward the stairs.

"I will come with you," Ar'ar said with a glance at Summer. "I would not have her lost to me again."

Jenna gave a light laugh. "I hope you aren't suggesting I would lose her on the way to getting dressed for the party?"

He hesitated, clearly not wanting to offend the next Erah clanmother.

"Tell you what," Jenna offered. "Let me help Summer get washed up and changed and we'll meet y'all back down here lickity-split, 'kay?"

"I assure you," Ra'kur offered solemnly, "your mate will not leave the clanhall while in my Jenna's company."

"I trust your intentions but Summer is my responsibility. These men," Ar'ar said, waving four Betari warriors forward, "will escort her and act as her guards." He addressed his clanbrothers. "You will accompany her everywhere. You are not to leave her alone for a moment."

"Not even in the bathtub?" Jenna asked, one hand on her hip.

Ar'ar's cheeks flushed. "You will, of course, observe decorum."

"And wait outside in the hallway while we get dressed," Jenna said pointedly. She urged Summer toward the staircase. "My quarters are three floors up and don't you worry," she said to Ar'ar over her shoulder as they started up the stairs, "unless Miss Summer here sprouts wings before we get to my rooms, she ain't going anywhere."

Jenna's quarters were gorgeous—richly furnished with a huge carved bed and complete with a balcony that ran the length of the suite, offering a sweeping view of the Erah territory. Birdsong could be heard from the forest below; in the distance the Te River curved beneath the shadow of the majestic snow-capped Zun Mountains.

Somewhere in those mountains lay the cave that had sheltered her and Ke'lar during the storm as it millennia ago had sheltered ancient g'hir . . .

He left me! He left Emma too, for all that nonsense about thinking of her as his daughter. He followed his clanfather's orders like—like a—

Summer swallowed hard. *A g'hir.*

Damn it, what did I expect anyway? That he'd really put me over his clan? That he could ever love me like a human man could?

She and Jenna hadn't talked on the way here. Something about having four towering alien warriors marching behind them inhibited conversation.

Jenna wasn't kidding about leaving them outside either. She shut the big heavy door firmly right in those warriors' faces and as soon as it was closed Jenna grabbed her in a big hug.

"Thank the All Mother you're all right!"

"The 'All Mother'?" Summer echoed, untangling herself from Jenna's embrace to stare at her.

Jenna laughed. "Sorry! Just used to saying it these days, I guess."

"Right," Summer murmured. "How long have you been here?"

"Since January. And now it's, uh—"

A troubled look crossed her friend's face.

Jenna didn't know the date back home.

"It's December," Summer said quietly. "December seventeenth."

Jenna glanced toward the balcony, out at the warm, spring afternoon on Hir. "Guess I must've lost track of time . . ."

"And gone all belle of the county," Summer pointed out. "What was all that down home crap? I'm surprised you didn't try to lead the reel."

Jenna gave a faint smile. "Guess I get it from Pap. He used to get all folksy when he was trying to charm people. Always worked too, he could charm a snake right out of its skin."

"Yeah," Summer said, shifting her weight. "I'm sorry I didn't get to the funeral. This winter's the first time I've been back to Brittle Bridge since before—Anyway, I know how close you and your grandfather were. Losing him had to be hard."

"It was." A sheen of tears showed in her friend's chocolate brown eyes for a moment, then her gaze focused on Summer. "God, it really has been since forever since I've seen you. How long has it been? Four years?"

"Five," Summer corrected. "But finishing college, and you know . . ."

"The Sweet Tooth," Jenna agreed. "And after Pap got sick, selling the bakery and moving home, taking care of him . . ." She waved her hand. "Never mind all that now. Are you okay? I mean . . . no one's hurt you?"

"Hurt—? Nobody's raped me if that's what you're asking," Summer said, frowning. "But no, Jenna, I would say I am decidedly *not* okay." Her glance went over her childhood friend. She looked healthy, a little heavier than she had been the last time she'd seen her, 'course it *had* been a while, but Jenna had never been so . . . positively glowing. "You seem all right though."

"I'm great." Jenna face melted into a smile. "And Ra'kur is—"

"Wait—" Summer shook her head. "You mean you like it here? You actually *want* to be on Hir?"

"Come here." Jenna caught her hand, tugging her along. "You need to meet somebody."

The bedroom was large, unmistakably feminine with furnishings fit for a princess. In an elaborate hand-carved crib lay a sleeping baby, perhaps a few months old, with warm brown hair and a daintily rippled forehead.

Oh. My. God.

"This is Anna," Jenna murmured, looking lovingly down at the infant.

"She's *yours*?" Summer blurted stupidly. "Yours and uh . . ."

"Ra'kur's," Jenna supplied and when she spoke his name she did it with the g'hir roll to it.

The baby responded to her mother's voice by pursing her lips but didn't wake up.

"Congratulations," Summer said faintly, her hand going to her solar plexus.

Jenna lightly smoothed away one of the baby's curls then indicated the doorway. Summer left the room on wooden legs, waiting as Jenna eased the door to the nursery closed behind them.

"I know this is all upsetting—" Jenna began.

"Upsetting?" Summer broke in. "I mean, Ar'ar kept going on and on about us having children—they all did— like they were sure it was going to happen, but I guess I just—" Her knees seemed to give out and she sank down onto one of the room's plush chairs. "I just didn't think it was possible. I didn't think that g'hir and humans could *actually* reproduce, but if you—"

"And Hope." Jenna sat across from her. "She and R'har are expecting a baby now."

Summer's brow creased. "Who the hell is Hope?"

"My friend." Jenna waved it away. "You don't know her."

"How many of us are there here?" Summer demanded. "How many women?"

"You're the third."

"But there's going to be more?"

Jenna closed her eyes briefly. "Yes."

"Did you—" She didn't want to ask this, she *really* didn't. "Have you been helping them, Jenna? Helping the g'hir do this to us?"

"Once they knew about me," Jenna said roughly, "there was no stopping them. When Ra'kur brought me here, when they knew there were females that were compatible—"

"Jenna," Summer broke in. "You've got to help me! Help me get home!"

Jenna hesitated. "What's happening here is very delicate, Summer. The clanfather has already denied you sanctuary and—"

"I meant what I said about Mirak! He told me I would be staying with Ar'ar no matter what I decide."

Jenna's mouth tightened. "Oh, I believe you. I know what kind of man Mirak is."

"Then let me stay here! If not sanctuary, maybe as your guest—"

"You could . . . if the Choosing Day had passed." She shook her head. "Think of it as a human honeymoon. You wouldn't up and go to a girlfriend's house in the middle of it."

"*Please.*" Summer clasped Jenna's hand. "I need your help! I need to get home!"

Jenna wet her lips, her chocolate eyes hesitant, and Summer's hopes rose.

Then Jenna shook her head. "Try to understand, the Erah have no way to keep you in our territory—not without facing a very bloody clan war." Jenna squeezed her hand as she delivered the devastating words. "Legally you have to wait until your Choosing Day."

Summer's throat tightened. Jenna wouldn't—or maybe *couldn't*—help her.

She was on her own here.

But she hadn't seen Jenna since before she'd taken up with Dean, Jenna had been so busy with her bakery, with her grandfather's illness—

She doesn't know about Emma. She can't or she would have asked about my baby right off. . .

And I'm sure as fuck not going to risk telling her now.

"That's what everyone keeps saying." Summer pulled her hand out of Jenna's grasp and stood wearily. "Look, I took a bath in the river a few hours ago but I sure wouldn't mind splashing water on my face and some clean clothes."

"Oh, I knew that dress would match your eyes," Jenna said from her place in the living room as Summer came out to join her. She was seated, her baby in her arms, nursing. "Turn around. Let me see."

Sighing inwardly, Summer held out the skirt of the sky blue dress and turned so her friend could see the back of the floor-length gown. She had brushed her hair smooth and Jenna had found delicate little crystal decorated silk slippers for her too.

"What about jewelry?" Jenna offered.

"No jewelry, thanks." What was she supposed to be dressing up for anyway? To be marched back to the Betari enclosure for a life sentence?

"But you have to have some!" Jenna protested.

Summer folded her arms. "Hey, have you seen my friend Jenna anywhere? You know, the girl who wore denim overalls all summer for *years*?"

"Go back into my dressing room," Jenna insisted. "Open the top drawer and take the dark blue jewelry set. There's a necklace, bracelets, earrings—put them all on and let me see."

"Jenna—"

"Let me see, for heaven's sake!"

"Fine," Summer muttered, stomping out of the living area and heading through Jenna's suite to her dressing room. Pulling just the top drawer open revealed jewels to rival those she'd taken from the Betari, jewels that remained, still wrapped, in the pack she'd left in the corner of this room when she'd come in to change.

Not that she wanted to wear the Betari jewels any more than she wanted to wear Jenna's . . .

"Happy?" Summer asked as she rejoined Jenna in the living room. She held her arms out, the bracelets sparkling in the afternoon sunlight streaming in from the balcony, the necklace heavy with jewels around her neck.

"What about the earrings?"

"Marie Antoinette wore smaller earrings! Those things weigh a ton and I really don't need my ears hurting on top of everything."

"Well, I guess that'll have to do then," Jenna sighed.

"Well, thanks," Summer grumbled. "I'm having a great day too."

"I didn't mean it that way." Jenna stood, holding her baby with one hand as she closed her top with the other. "You look wonderful."

Watching her, Summer couldn't help but smile a little. "Ah, Mommy dexterity. You could probably breastfeed, swing a hula hoop on your left foot, and recite the—"

Just then Jenna's infant daughter—Anna—looked her way and Summer broke off.

She was a gorgeous baby, with cherubic fat cheeks, pink little mouth, and chubby fists; her barely rippled forehead made her look cute rather than beastly.

Emma's eyes were blue too.

But Anna's glowed the same vibrant shade as her g'hir father's—and Ke'lar's.

"I think she's beautiful," Jenna said sharply.

"She is," Summer said hoarsely. "She really is, Jenna."

The sincerity in her voice seemed to soften her friend but caught her attention too.

"You two were alone for days," Jenna said bluntly. "Did something happen between you and Ke'lar?"

"No." Summer met her gaze squarely. "Nothing."

Jenna's brown eyes narrowed. "Summer Mills, you are worst liar in three counties."

Summer gave a short laugh. "And now this quadrant of the galaxy."

Jenna chuckled too then her smile faded. "Ke'lar . . . the way he looked at you I thought—"

Summer's throat tightened. "Then we were both wrong." She looked at her friend, at the tender way she held her baby. "So . . . you really love him? Ra'kur?"

"Yes," Jenna said fiercely. "I do."

"Then I'm happy for you."

She meant it too.

Jenna wet her lips. "Summer, listen, I know what you think but Ra'kur—"

Whatever her friend wanted her to know about her g'hir mate was cut off by a sharp knock. Before Jenna could even respond, Ar'ar was opening the door and stepping inside.

Annoyance flashed over her friend's face at the rudeness, at the unapologetic intrusion.

But hey, that's a g'hir for you . . .

The four Betari warriors, Ar'ar's clanbrothers, still stood guard outside Jenna's quarters and they exchanged a look with Ar'ar as he shut the door behind him in silent assurance that they wouldn't be going anywhere.

"Ar'ar," Jenna said, shifting the baby to her hip, her tone pleasant as if he hadn't just barged into her quarters without invitation. "We were just about to go downstairs."

"This is your daughter?" Ar'ar asked, his eyes fixed on the child as he approached.

"Yes," Jenna said, proud as any momma would be.

"May the All Mother bless us too with a child so healthy, so lovely," Ar'ar growled fervently. He glanced at Summer then addressed Jenna again. "And may She bless you with many more offspring."

"Thank you," Jenna said formally.

"The feast will begin soon," he said. "I have come to escort my mate to your hall."

"Thank goodness," Jenna said cheerfully. "I'm starving, y'all! Back home we have something called pancakes. Usually they're eaten for breakfast—first meal, that is—and so I was thinking for in the morning—"

"We are grateful for your hospitality"—Ar'ar's glance flicked to Summer—"but we will not remain the night. I am eager to take my mate home."

"Oh," Jenna murmured then brightened. "Well, we should get downstairs then."

"I will speak with my mate first," Ar'ar said firmly. "Alone."

Jenna looked like she was scrambling for some excuse but this wasn't Jenna's battle, it was hers.

"Go ahead," Summer said, swallowing back her own trepidation. "I'll see you in a couple minutes."

Jenna hesitated. "Just a couple, okay?" She looked at Ar'ar. "It's the human custom that no one begins the meal until everyone is assembled." She gave him a tight smile. "Now, don't you keep us waiting, you hear?"

"I'll let you know if I see any Yankees coming to burn the place," Summer promised, with a wry look toward the balcony and the alien forest beyond.

Despite the joke, Jenna sent her a worried look, pausing at the ornate door to shift the baby's weight onto her hip. Summer sent her friend a confident smile she wasn't feeling at all and Jenna gave a nod, then shut the door behind her.

But now she was alone with Ar'ar.

And from the molten yellow gaze that fixed on her, that *wasn't* a good thing.

SEVENTEEN

"I searched for you," Ar'ar growled, his fangs showing. "For days I searched and I feared for you."

Summer lifted her chin. "I find that a little hard to believe."

"That I searched for you?" he demanded, outraged. "I crossed and re-crossed our territory a dozen times seeking you!"

"That you were worried about me. If you cared about me, you'd care about what I want."

"You are my mate. You are my responsibility!"

"I am not anyone's responsibility—I'm not anyone's period—except my own."

His jaw worked for a moment. "You slipped from our bed in the middle of the night—"

"*Your* bed," she corrected. "*My* bed is back on Earth, remember?"

His nostrils flared. "I was a fool to trust you. A fool to believe you might come to care for me."

Yeah, that's going around.

"I have tried to be a good mate to you. To make you happy," he continued.

Summer folded her arms. "What part of ripping me out of my life and holding me prisoner on an alien planet do you think would make me all holly-jolly, anyway?"

Ar'ar, all seven feet of solid warrior muscle, glowered down at her. "My capture was intended to honor you, a tribute to your beauty. I tried to keep you safe within the enclosure you will someday rule as clanmother. I sought you day and night when you vanished, fearful of your safety. I have gifted you all I have and you spurn my offerings at every opportunity!"

Somewhere in those narrowed glowing eyes she saw the hurt—the deep hurt—that she'd caused him.

"But I don't want to be here, Ar'ar," she said, her tone softening a little. "I don't want to be your mate."

"Then that is what I must address . . ." he murmured, stepping a little closer, the softest of rumble-purrs starting in his chest as he pulled her against him.

Summer's mouth parted as his purr sent waves of pleasure through her.

"Wait . . ." she got out as he gently cupped her cheek. "What are you doing?"

"What I should have done long before this." His rumble-purr deepened as he bent his head, brushing his nose up one side of hers and down the other. "What is it called again? A kiss?"

His mouth touched hers, lightly, experimentally. His purr kept her frozen in place, fearful if she did move it would only be to wrap her arms around his neck and pull him closer.

He breathed in deeply. "I can scent your arousal. Shall I be gentle with you? Or would you have me put your back to the wall? Hold you open while my cock pleasures you?"

Summer squeezed her eyes shut. "Stop it."

"Why?" he rumbled. "I know speaking of it has roused you more."

His fingers traced her back and buttocks and she shivered at the sensations it brought.

I have to distract him or I'm really not going to want to stop!

"You really want to do this here?" she gasped. "At the Erah's clanhouse?"

"Perhaps we both do," he rumbled, his cock hard against her belly as his fangs brushed the sensitive skin of her throat.

"I think you're enjoying this," Summer got out. "Enjoying playing with me."

"I am not playing," Ar'ar murmured tightly, his soft rumble-purr fading enough for Summer to catch her breath, for her head to clear a little.

"We have a responsibility to our clan, Summer, and it is long past time we were mate-bound." He caught her chin to brush another light kiss against her mouth, his amber eyes burning as he let her go. "I promise, tonight, when we return to our enclosure, to *our* bed, we will both find pleasure . . ."

Summer pushed her hair away from her flushed face with a shaking hand and took a moment to steady herself against the balcony wall. The suns had nearly set, the Brothers turning the sky magnificent shades of pink and orange and golden yellow.

Ar'ar must have turned up the heat on that rumble-purr of his somehow because she sure didn't remember having this much trouble controlling herself last time he'd tried to seduce her.

She turned her burning face toward the evening breeze, grateful that Ar'ar had left her alone in Jenna's quarters; thankful he was allowing her these few spare minutes to compose herself here in the twilight.

And Ar'ar *was* as eager for it as he'd made her. He seemed just as out of sorts as she felt when he left so he probably needed time to cool off as much as she did.

Unfortunately, he'd had it together enough to leave the guards outside the door.

Credit where credit was due: he was absolutely smoking hot. 'Course her problem with Ar'ar had never been his body, and if her experience with Ke'lar was any indication of typical g'hir male prowess, Ar'ar was going to see to it she had a long night—many long nights—of amazing sex ahead of her.

Man, and you know your life is fucked up when that's a bad thing . . .

She didn't love Ar'ar, probably never could, but she sensed somewhere in that muscled chest he had a true and loving heart. In another life—before Emma—she, like Jenna, might have found some happiness here. Maybe not with Ar'ar but with—

Summer gripped the balcony railing. Ke'lar, like Dean, had run out on her just when she'd needed him most.

Emma was only three, so very, very little, and her early memories would be hazy.

And if I never get back to Earth—

Summer put her palm to her forehead, trying to think, trying to draw on a bit more of Paw-Paw's heritage, summon just *one* more crazy-like-a-fox plan.

The little blaster was still in her pack but she wouldn't stand a chance against four warriors. Even if she killed them—and she didn't think she could—she wouldn't get far.

Jenna's quarters were only three floors up but there were no decorative carvings within reach to aid her escape. The old tie-the-bed-sheets-together thing wouldn't work; the next balcony was about thirty feet down and desperate didn't mean fucking *suicidal*.

Ar'ar wasn't going let her out of his sight unguarded again—that was for sure. Having seen how gorgeous Jenna's half-human half-g'hir daughter was, the deep longing in his amber eyes was undeniable. She didn't have to be told how determined Ar'ar was now to have a baby of his—*their*—own.

Her eyes stung.

Dear God, Emma's going to forget me. Will anyone ever even show her pictures of me—of her and me together? Will she ever know how much her momma loved her?

Half of Brittle Bridge thought Jenna McNally was dead and rotting in the woods, the other half thought she'd just met some guy and took off, leaving her and Pap's half-packed house to rot.

Was that what people back home would think about her too? What would people say to Emma? What would her daughter believe as she grew up without a mother?

Summer swallowed hard, looking out over the alien landscape, out to the vast green forests into which Ke'lar had vanished.

Will she think I just took off and forgot about her? Left for some man or fell to drinking and drugs? Will she hate me?

Or will my baby spend her whole life thinking I'm dead even if nobody knows it for sure?

And who would take care of Emma, who would raise her? Dean sure as hell would do a crappy job of parenting— if he even took it on. Summer doubted very much that he would.

After all, he wasn't—had never been—the responsible type.

Dean's momma, Marthe, loved Emma, always sending her little things, dresses she'd sewn for the child herself, toys and ribbons for her hair. Despite her heartache, Summer smiled faintly, remembering how Emma hated having anything in her hair. Summer could scarcely get her to keep the ribbons in long enough to take a picture to email to Marthe.

Summer's smile faded. Marthe was struggling with a list of health problems a mile long. She might love her granddaughter but she might not have the strength—or the time—to raise her.

Uncle Lester was kindly to them, her and Emma both, always had been, but he'd never married and had no kids of his own. She could hardly see him jumping up to raise a grandniece, either.

He just walked away! Ke'lar just left me with Ar'ar and left Emma alone!

Her fingers clenched. She couldn't think about him now; she could cry a river for her broken heart when she knew Emma was safe.

When she'd first seen Jenna she'd instantly thought the two of them could escape together, but Jenna was happy here—or maybe just brainwashed into thinking she was. Her friend might help her, or she might be too afraid, but either way Summer was going to get herself home.

A whole room full of people were waiting for her downstairs and she'd give almost anything to hide here in Jenna's rooms. But if she didn't go down soon Ar'ar would probably just come back up and get her.

She was a little surprised he hadn't already.

Summer drew a deep breath and let go of the balcony wall. Squaring her shoulders, she turned toward the door of Jenna's quarters, toward the guards who would be her new constant companions.

I won't let them intimidate me. I won't let them break me and I promise, baby, I won't ever give up.

She was the only real parent Emma had. She had to get back before the Day of Choosing, before Sunday afternoon. Even if she had to start over, even if she had to endure the Betari enclosure again, outwit Mirak, trick Ar'ar. There would be another chance at escape, she'd *make* one if she had to, and this time she wouldn't be stupid enough to trust someone like—

She gasped, instinctively throwing her arms up protectively as a blur dropped down to land in front of her.

He straightened and Summer, her hand pressed to her rapidly thumping heart, blinked up at Ke'lar.

His glowing glance went over her. "Are you all right?"

"Am I—? You scared the crap out of me!" she hissed. "Where did you even come from? And what the hell are you doing here anyway?"

"From there," he said, indicating the balcony above.

Summer glanced up and to the right to a terrace twenty feet above her head.

"And I am here"—his fangs flashed in a grin—"to steal you."

EIGHTEEN

Summer stared. "What?"

"*Steal* you. I am taking you unlawfully from your acknowledged mate." With a g'hir's astonishingly quick, silent movements Ke'lar yanked the inner curtains closed, shut the balcony doors, and effortlessly placed one of the huge chairs to block them. He caught her hand, gently tugging her toward the balcony wall. "I am new to crime so you may wish to make it easy for me."

"*You're* going to help me? You really think I'm going to trust you again?" she demanded, ludicrously trying to get her hand out of his grip since as soon as she broke his hold his g'hir reflexes let him catch her fingers again. "Goddamn it, Ke'lar, stop that!"

"I am trying to save you the trouble of another escape," he returned, catching a firm but gentle hold of her wrist this time. "After all, I cannot have you leaping from balcony to balcony." His glance went over her. "Your dress is entirely unsuitable to the task."

Joking? He was *joking*?

"You left me here!" She was so happy to see him she could throw her arms around him, so mad she could burst into tears. "You left me with Ar'ar!"

"I could not fight him," Ke'lar said, serious now. "If I had won, my clan would insist you remain the whole moon cycle, till your Choosing Day. If I had lost, you would have to return with Ar'ar."

"So you just took off?" she demanded with a wave toward the forest.

"I retreated so I could rescue you and return you to your homeworld."

Summer blinked. "You have a way to get me back to Earth?"

"If you will cooperate! And if," he growled, "we are not caught by the Betari, or my own clan, or the entire g'hir—" Ke'lar went stock-still. "His scent is on you." He sniffed again, more deeply this time. "His scent is all over you!" His brows rushed together. "He roused you!"

Summer's cheeks burned. "Don't be ridiculous."

His face was like a thundercloud.

Hell, Jenna's right; I am a lousy liar.

"It's none of your business," she mumbled, trying uselessly to pull her wrist from his grip as she decided to go on the offensive. "You're the one that left me here with him!"

"Not my business!" he growled. "And I did not leave you at all!"

"You walked away!"

"From the dining hall! Not from you! Do you . . ." His shoulders were tense, his eyes guarded. "Do you want him?"

"No! It's not—" She threw her free hand out in frustration. "Haven't you ever been turned on by someone, even if you didn't even really like them?"

"No," he growled. His fangs bared. "You desire him!"

"Desiring someone isn't the same as loving them, Ke'lar! *That's* the only thing that matters!"

His breath caught and he searched her face.

"What?" Her brow creased. "Why are you looking at me like that?"

"You love me?" he rumbled and his whole face softened. "You love me."

"Hey, I didn't say . . ." Summer trailed off because now he was grinning.

And he was right.

"Oh, goddamn it," she muttered.

He caught her against him to brush his nose against hers then tilted his head and brought his mouth to hers for deep, slow kiss.

He cupped her chin to look into her eyes. "I love you, my sweet Summer." He searched her gaze and his brow creased again. "You do not believe me."

"I don't know what to believe. I want to believe you." Summer swallowed hard. "I've just gotten used to not having anyone be there for me, on having to depend just on myself. And, then you were there, just when I needed you, every time I needed you." Her eyes stung. "Until . . ."

"I never left you. I would never—could never—leave you." He took her hand and placed it over his heart; she felt its steady, strong beat beneath her palm. "Even when we are apart, you are here. You alone and no other, for always." He gave a faint smile. "It is in your eyes, my mate, you believe me now."

"Man, I should never take up playing cards," she said, ducking her head. "How did you even know I'd be here to rescue? This clanhall is huge."

"Jenna was going to share her clothing with you," he reminded. "Naturally she would take you to her rooms."

"Naturally," she echoed. Of course he would have overheard Jenna say that, even after he'd left the room. "How were you sure could get here from there?" she asked, indicating the balcony he'd jumped from.

"I grew up in this clanhall. But come, it is time to take you away from Hir." His fangs showed for an instant. "And from Ar'ar."

"I don't see how we're going to get anywhere. There are guards outside the door," she warned. "Betari clanbrothers who won't be happy to see you and certainly aren't going to let me leave."

"We are not going that way."

"Oh, please don't say . . ." She glanced over the balcony and her stomach clenched. It was an awfully long drop. "You want to climb down from here?"

"Of course not. We are going to climb up."

"Up?" she squeaked, twisting her neck to look that way. "You mean back up to the balcony you jumped from?"

"No, to the roof."

Summer wet her lips. "You're kidding, right?"

"Hundreds of my clanbrothers await below," he pointed out. "As do Mirak, a dozen Betari warriors, and"— here his lip curled— "Ar'ar. We cannot go that way. We would not be an hour in the forest before they caught us. No," he said firmly. "We must go to the roof."

"And then what?" Summer asked. "Hang out on the roof and hope no one thinks to look for us there?"

"There is a transport landing on the roof of our clanhall." He was already eyeing the side of the building as if deciding the best way to tackle the climb. For a moment a shadow covered his features. "I hope I will not have to fight my own clanbrothers."

"You'd . . . do that? You'd fight your own kind—your own clan—for me?"

"For you—" His glowing eyes met hers. "And for our daughter, Emma."

Our daughter . . .

"Oh," Summer murmured, her throat tight.

"Are you ready?"

"Ke'lar . . . there's no way that I'm going to be able to climb up there."

"I know that. I will carry you."

"Carry—!"

Before she could get the words out he'd swung her over his shoulder. And then he was leaping upward onto the balcony ledge and she was hanging down, dangling over a fifty-foot drop.

"Ohmygod!"

Summer squeezed her eyes shut and, finding that no better, opened them again.

"Ke'lar," she whimpered, morbidly wondering whether she actually had time to faint during the fall.

"This is an easy climb but you must try not to distract me." She heard the smile in his voice as his hand lovingly patted her bottom. "If that is possible."

She could feel his muscles working as he began the climb—one-handed—finding handholds and footholds where she would have sworn none existed. He couldn't climb with his body flush against the building either, not with her swung over his shoulder. He had to climb sideways, pitting his strength against the force of gravity and the awkwardness of the unbalanced load on his shoulder.

It was the longest, most agonizing wait of her life and she'd been in labor with Emma for thirty-six hours. She was too terrified to move and she had nothing to hold onto. She didn't dare grab him and her nails dug into her palms as she struggled against the scream building in her throat.

Ke'lar climbed without pause up the side of the clanhall, not even pausing to catch his breath. Too afraid that he'd drop her or more likely, lose his grip and plunge them both to their deaths below, she didn't utter another sound.

Then he was over the roof wall, and he let her go so abruptly that her knees gave out and she landed hard on her backside.

Summer's breath was shuddering in her chest and she couldn't have stood if she'd wanted to, not with all the blood having rushed to her head during the climb, the terror of the ascent itself.

Ke'lar had already dropped into a fighter's stance, his brilliant eyes searching the roof in the evening light for others of his enclosure, clanbrothers he would battle to reach the transport.

After a moment he straightened. "We are alone."

Summer's fingers spread wide, the clanhall's ancient stone roof still warm under her palms from the day's heat. She bent her head, trying not to be sick.

He crouched at her side, his eyes eerily bright in the fading light. "Are you all right?"

"I guess . . . I was wrong about," she gasped, "being over . . . my fear of heights."

"Darkness, heights." He gave a quick, teasing smile. "You humans must spend a lot of time on the ground, during the day."

"Yup," she agreed, really very impressed with herself for not throwing up. "That's actually how I intend to spend the rest of my life. In fact, if I ever hit the lottery, my penthouse is going to be located on the ground floor." She shook her head—a little. "I can't believe you did that. I can't believe you actually got us up here. With *one* hand."

He gave a light laugh. "My brother and I used to challenge each other to reach the top first. I won nearly every time. But it has been a long while since I made this climb. It was a game for us as children."

Summer's head came up, trying to gauge if he was kidding or not. "They let you do that? Let a bunch of kids climb up the side of a building?"

Ke'lar's smile faded. "I imagine our mothers would have not have."

He stood, taking her hands to raise her up with him. Her knees were shaking but she was able to walk under her own power as they crossed to the transport vessel.

She'd ridden in one of their transports only once before, when Ar'ar had brought her directly from the space-dock to the Betari enclosure. Capable of great speeds, these transports weren't capable of space flight and were used exclusively for journeys inside the atmosphere.

And if it really was unoccupied . . .

Ke'lar went up the short ramp first, his posture tense and alert, but the cabin was empty. He slid into the pilot's seat, already activating the door controls to seal the vessel and powering up the transport.

Her glance darted about the landing pad as she took the co-pilot's seat. "Someone just happened to leave a transport vessel unattended up here?"

"This vessel should not be unattended, the roof unguarded, especially with members of an enemy clan about," he agreed. "This is Ra'kur's doing. That is what he meant when he said he would 'await me at the center of the clanhall.' He was telling me to go to the roof. It is the boast we would make to one another before we made the climb."

She blinked. "You mean Ra'kur arranged this to help us escape?"

"As Jenna has the Betari occupied with a feast that involves much noise and the confusing comings and goings of many Erah clanbrothers to cover my return."

Summer shook her head. "That's what she must have wanted to tell me, that Ra'kur was going to—And I was so mad at her for not even trying to help!"

He gave her throat a meaningful glance. "Clearly she did not want to send you off empty-handed."

Summer's hand went to the jewels at her throat. "Well, damn it, I guess I *should* have taken the earrings when she told me to."

"Do not worry." He nodded to a small box left conspicuously near the control panel. "I think we will find a number of credits have been made available to us as well." Ke'lar threw her a grin as the transport finished powering up, already using the controls to lift the vessel from the landing pad. "And I would say that we have just escaped."

"Why would they do all this?" she asked. "Why would they think you'd even come back for me after you'd been banished?"

"Ra'kur knows me well enough that he could read in my eyes what the Betari could not—that you are my mate and I would never leave you." He gave a huffing laugh as the trees below became a blur. "And besides, I was never the most obedient of clanbrothers."

"Where *are* we going anyway?"

"Be'lyn City. There I will secure a ship to return you to Earth."

"But . . ." She frowned. "I thought Earth's location was secret. That it was kept that way so warriors couldn't just go there whenever they pleased."

"It is," he agreed. "But it appears that encrypted into this transport vessel my brother has also provided the coordinates of your world . . ."

NINETEEN

"Finally!"

Summer stood as soon as the transport door opened and Ke'lar stepped onboard. The window tinting kept anyone from peering inside to see her but being stuck in here while he ventured into Be'lyn City had her gritting her teeth.

"I'm getting really tired of being left behind so I can be 'safe' while you run off someplace. In fact," she said, hands on her hips, "this is the last time you get to do that."

"Even this late hour," Ke'lar said with a pointed look out at the lights of Hir's capital city as the door shut behind him, "would not keep you from being noticed by the warriors who inhabit this city. I do not mind fighting for you, my mate, but even I cannot hope to vanquish so many, all determined to have a human female for his own."

"Well, I can't just stay here!" she exclaimed, with a gesture out at the public landing area where the transport was parked.

"No, you cannot," he agreed and shook out the bundle he was carrying.

"A cloak?" she asked. "How does that make me look like less like a female? I mean, me being a woman is the problem, right?"

"No one will ever believe you are a male, my Summer, even if I dressed you in warrior clothes." He offered a faint smile. "I am not the only bloodhound here and you smell far too sweet."

"Right," she muttered, her face warming. "So much for disguising me."

"At least we will attempt to disguise you as a g'hir female, instead of a human one."

She shrugged into the cloak. "You think this will do it?"

"Possibly," he allowed.

He pulled up the cloak's hood and regarded her with a critical eye. "It would do better if you were not so short."

"I'm five-nine," she objected. "That's really tall for a human woman."

"But short for a g'hir." He yanked the hood further forward to hide her face completely. "Perhaps they will think you are still an adolescent." He shook his head. "You are too beautiful, my Summer."

"Wow," she said, unable to hold back a grin. "No one's ever said that to me before."

"You will have warriors fighting in the streets for you if they see your human beauty."

"How long are we going to be in the city anyway?" she asked worriedly. "I'm sure everyone's noticed I'm not at the Erah clanhall by now. They must be tearing the place apart looking for me."

A deeply troubled look crossed his face. "The Betari will be furious; my father will be facing a war with them."

Summer chewed her lip, thinking of Jenna and her new baby. "You think Ar'ar and his father will attack your enclosure?"

"Not if they believe you might still be within it," he growled quietly. "But it is possible that our transport was observed leaving. For their sakes, to prevent a war, I hope that my father and Ra'kur have laid all the blame to me and convinced the Betari they are willing to join in the search for us. We cannot risk the Betari—or my own clan—finding us if we hope to make it to your world."

"So what's the plan?"

"I believe I can secure us a ship to take us to Earth but I must see the owner in person. We will travel to the center of the city and I will do my best to persuade the ship master." He activated the door control to open it then knelt before the transport's controls and opened a panel beneath. "But before we go—"

He pushed something inside and snapped the panel shut. There was a loud pop and a flash from inside that made Summer jump and all the power in the transport cut off.

"What did you do?"

He stood. "I have shorted out the transport's main computer." He met her gaze. "And erased the coordinates to Earth."

She raised her eyebrows. "But you memorized them first, right?"

"We will need a ship to know for sure," he said with a smile. He took her hand and his expression grew serious. "Stay close to me. Usually a female will not venture out to even the most respectable of neighborhoods without a half-dozen warriors from her clan, and this one is far from the most respectable."

She gave a nod and followed him out.

"A moment," he said when they were standing on the landing area platform. "I would leave this as inconspicuous as possible."

While Ke'lar hefted the heavy door and forced it shut, Summer looked toward the spires in the center of the capital, rising high into the sky.

"Summer?"

"I wish I could see the city," she murmured. "It must be amazing."

"Perhaps once it was." He adjusted her hood again. "Little one, you must not speak."

"Not speak?" Summer's brow creased. "Why the hell—Oh, right. Because I'm speaking English. Because anyone would know I was human just by hearing me talk."

Funny how she'd forgotten that. How those growls and snarls were starting to sound natural, to sound normal, how she'd gotten used to hearing them and the translation in her head too.

"The ship master's home is not far from here," he said and she noticed that his free hand already hovered by his blaster. "And the sooner you are indoors again, the better."

Summer was careful to keep her face hidden, looking out from under the hood to see, clutching the garment to her from the inside so no one would see that she was far too fair to be g'hir.

The city had an air of hopelessness to it and seemed too empty for a metropolis this size. It was clean, much better maintained that any city on Earth, but the warriors here were narrowed-eyed men, some of them clearly drunk, and Ke'lar sped her past more than one brawl.

It was a tense trip to the city's center. It was full night and the streets well-lit but Ke'lar wasn't kidding about her drawing attention. Even cloaked, her face covered, she drew the interest of every passing male. It wasn't her attractiveness—hell, what could they see of her under the voluminous cloak?—it was that she seemed to be the only woman around.

Certainly she didn't spot any others—accompanied by a half-score of warriors or not.

A few of the warriors were bold enough to step in her path but even those few were warned off by the viciousness of Ke'lar snarls, his bared fangs and ready weapon. She bit the inside of her cheek at every encounter, frightened she would give herself away as human and double their interest in her.

And I was just going to show up here alone with a pack of jewels! Ke'lar was right, I wouldn't have made it ten feet without one of these guys trying to capture me.

She was trembling by the time they reached their destination, a building near the center of the city, set back from the empty street and fronted by a very neglected front yard. The houses beside it seemed to be abandoned and the whole area rundown and forlorn.

Ke'lar stood before the security panel and thankfully whoever was in the house recognized him because the gate opened.

"That was pretty awful," she said as soon as they were safely inside. There was no one about to hear her just then but she kept her hood up and her voice low.

Ke'lar threw a narrowed look back the way they'd come. "Not nearly as bad as I expected. We were fortunate."

"Who is this guy anyway?" Summer asked worriedly as they reached the door. "Is he really going to give you a ship?"

"She," he corrected.

The door opened and Summer reared back, away from the large insectoid creature standing there.

Ke'lar caught her, frowning at her. "This is Ezzari, the ship owner I told you about."

Summer turned toward the creature that regarded her with enormous multifaceted eyes. She wore an elaborately beaded dress over her dark gray exoskeleton and seemed to be looking back at Summer in equal astonishment.

"A human!" she exclaimed—or rather buzzed.

Summer blinked. This creature wasn't speaking English any more than Ke'lar was but Summer could understand the buzzing as words.

"You did not say you had a human!" Ezzari continued, looking her up and down. "I have never seen one."

"May we come inside?" Ke'lar asked, throwing a look over his shoulder. "No one must see her."

"Of course!" she buzzed. "Forgive me!"

She stepped back to allow them entrance and only Ke'lar's pressure on her back got Summer's feet moving. Ezzari shut the door behind them, content, it seemed, to stand just inside and stare at her.

"Is that your natural coloring?" the creature asked.

"Yeah," Summer stammered. With platinum hair she got that question a lot. "It's all mine."

The creature tilted her head. "Then all humans are this pale?"

"I thought you were—No, not all of us. But what— what are—"

"She is a xenari," Ke'lar said with a puzzled how-could-you-not-know-that look.

"Oh," Summer said faintly. "I didn't—I mean I thought there were only humans and g'hir . . . and the Zerar. I didn't realize there were other intelligent species too."

"The xenari are allies of the g'hir," Ke'lar assured. "They have been great help in defending us against the Zerar's incursions. They are an honorable people and great friends to ours."

"Thank you." Ezzari inclined her large head but her buzz sounded amused. "But I do not think you have come to my home when the Sisters are so high in the sky with a disguised human in tow to pay homage to my species."

"I have come to ask a favor," Ke'lar admitted.

The xenari glanced at Summer. "If you have a human consort your clan would provide all you could wish and more." Her head tilted. "So I am thinking that she is not yours, Erah warrior."

"She *is* mine," he said, his fangs showing.

"Then what do you need of me?" Ezzari asked. "If you already possess what the males of your species all clamor for?"

"I need a ship. A xenari ship. Tonight."

"Since you cannot make use of any g'hir vessel?" The xenari regarded him with curious eyes. "An expensive favor since you will need xenari exit codes to leave orbit. So you need the ship and my help to disguise you as a xenari vessel leaving the system?"

Ke'lar's jaw twitched. "Yes."

"And what do you offer me in exchange?"

"What do you want?" Summer asked sharply. Despite the bug eyes and the buzzing language Summer was starting to feel like she was standing on a used car lot in Alexandria instead of an alien world.

The xenari turned her big bug eyes on Summer. "Perhaps I do not want for anything, human."

"Yes, you do." She hated buying cars and had learned the hard way about getting screwed over. "Or you wouldn't still be talking to us. You'd have thrown us right out into the street."

Ezzari stared at her then suddenly started making a weird chirping sound.

It took Summer a moment to realize the xenari was laughing.

"These humans are delightful!" she said. "Even if they are primitives."

Summer's eyes narrowed. *What I wouldn't give for a can of Raid . . .*

"Ezzari," Ke'lar prompted, no doubt noticing how Summer's nostrils had flared. "The ship?"

"Yes, yes." The xenari waved an appendage. "What will you give in exchange for such an . . . *expensive* . . . favor?"

Ke'lar indicated the jewels Summer wore and named a sum that made Ezzari's appendages flutter a bit.

But she sure recovered fast. "I am not saying I do not appreciate the merit of your offer but . . ." She looked around her dismal quarters. "It is hardly enough to make me comfortable."

Summer gritted her teeth. "And just what would it take to make you 'comfortable'?"

The xenari turned her huge black eyes on Summer. "The location of your world is a valuable and much desired commodity, human. Yes," she buzzed. "The sale of *that* information to a few select g'hir would make me very wealthy indeed . . ."

The breath exploded out of Summer's chest. "Absolutely fucking not!"

Ezzari gave her as haughty a look as an insectoid could. "If you wish *my* help—"

"Ezzari—" Ke'lar began but Summer broke in.

"Come on," she urged, grabbing his arm. "Let's go talk to that other guy again. It's pretty far but at least *he's* willing to be reasonable."

Ke'lar's gaze searched hers for an instant. "I am sorry to have made you walk such a distance," he rumbled, catching on. "I have dealt with this honored xenari before."

He sighed. "But if it is your wish, we will return to the other ship master and accept his offer instead."

Ezzari was startled. "Other—?"

Summer opened the door and paused at the threshold to give the xenari an arch look. "Hey, sorry, obviously Ke'lar really would rather work with you but . . ." She lifted one shoulder and pulled her hood up.

"It is regrettable," Ke'lar agreed. "I think highly of you, Ezzari, and knowing your present difficulties I wished those funds to be yours."

"A moment please!" The xenari scrambled to follow after them into the courtyard. "Ke'lar—my friend! I did not mean that we could not *negotiate* . . ."

TWENTY

Summer held her breath as Ke'lar transmitted the xenari's codes, wondering if Ezzari had managed to screw them over after all. Vast, terrifying g'hir warships patrolled the space around their homeworld to protect against any Zerar attack but they would just as easily stop a g'hir fugitive and the human woman he'd taken from her clan.

After an agonizingly long moment the Hironian station sent the signal allowing them to pass through the battleships that orbited this world. Ke'lar piloted the ship past them, only the slight tremble in his fingers betraying his anxiety.

"Well done, my Summer," Ke'lar said approvingly as soon as they were clear.

"You're the one flying the ship," she pointed out.

"I meant with Ezzari." He gave a huffing chuckle. "I have never witnessed such maneuvering."

"The only reason I got away with it at all is because she'd never seen a human before," Summer said dryly. "Anyone else would see right off I was lying through my teeth."

The xenari ship was not at all like a g'hir ship. All delicate controls and fine shapes, this ship was far better suited to slender insectoid digits, not broad powerful warrior hands.

But Ke'lar was handling the ship beautifully.

"The chairs are pretty comfortable," Summer commented, settling back into the co-pilot's seat.

"The padding protects their exoskeletons during space travel."

"Well, it's pretty nice under a human butt too." Summer glanced back at the main part of the ship. "Do you think there's anything we can eat onboard? I'm starving."

"I requested the ship be stocked with g'hir foodstuffs," he assured gently. "You will not starve, little one."

So freaking literal. Just like—

She swallowed hard.

Just like Emma.

Summer undid the safety straps of her chair and stood. "I'm going to see what's back there."

She found the galley easily enough, and even recognized some of the food there. She grabbed a piece of cali fruit, munching while she searched through the more substantial selections.

"There is kartlet," Ke'lar suggested, joining her. "It is not of my hunting but I would be pleased to prepare it for you."

"I *can* cook, you know," she said, fingering the cali in her hand. "Kinda . . . if it's Earth stuff."

"There is nothing more I can do until we reach the jump point and the ship is set to bring us there." He offered a smile. "And I like to cook."

"Roasted, right? You said that's your specialty."

He chuckled. "I had hoped to impress you."

"You did," she said softly.

He was as efficient in the kitchen of a spaceship as he was in the forest of his own world and he soon had their meal ready.

Summer inhaled deeply as he placed the plate in front of her at the ship's table. The furniture was affixed to the floor and Ke'lar gave her a proud look as he took a seat across from her.

At the first taste she closed her eyes in appreciation. "Oh, man, this is amazing."

He grinned. "I am very glad it pleases you."

Apparently he was as hungry as she because he cleaned his plate, and a second helping before she finished her first.

"Seriously," she said, savoring her last bite of kartlet. "You should have been a chef instead of a warrior."

He gave a huffing chuckle. "My father would have been scandalized."

She bit her lip. "I'll bet he's pretty scandalized now, Ke'lar . . ." She wrapped her hands around her water cup. "What will happen when you return home?"

"I do not know," he rumbled. "And I do not care. Once you are safe—our daughter is safe—what happens to me is unimportant."

"Of course it's important! Everyone is furious with you."

"Not as angry as you when you thought I'd left you to Ar'rar." He tilted his head, his vibrant eyes crinkled with humor. "Do you still wish me suffering in the underworld?"

She gave a faint smile. "No, I take back the 'rot in hell' thing. And you didn't answer my question. Will they banish you permanently for taking me home?"

"I think they will be far angrier that I have returned you with your memories intact. By doing so I have broken Hir law and endangered all g'hir who follow me to Earth. Humans on your world are to have no knowledge of us." He gave a rueful smile. "I am not sorry for *that* either."

"My memories aren't worth sending you back to a life of misery," she said hoarsely.

He cupped her cheek. "I could not bear for you to forget me. To forget that you once loved me. To remember that I will always love you."

Summer's vision swam. "How long do we have?"

"Not long," he rumbled.

She entwined her fingers with his and stood, leading him to the bedroom. It too was meant for xenari, less a bed than a large padded floor.

His bright gaze was pained. "Summer . . ."

"I know," she whispered hoarsely.

He nodded—a human gesture. His nose brushed hers in a g'hir kiss, and then he cupped her chin to touch his mouth to hers tenderly.

She wound her arms around his neck, pulling him closer, relishing the taste of him, breathing in his spicy scent. She shivered as his purr started, soft and deep. He flicked his tongue against the inner part of her lip, his rumbling sending heat curling between her thighs.

He made short work of her gown, a rush of air raising goose bumps on her skin as the fabric slid away.

His gaze was fevered, his purr vibrating through her. "Are you cold?"

Mute with need, she shook her head.

Ke'lar gave a faint smile, pulling at his own clothing, bare in moments. "Good."

His fingers brushed her breastbone and his hands moved lower. She gasped at the sensation as he traced her nipples, his hands dipping to her waist. He bent his knees, taking her with him to the softness of the floor.

He coaxed her thighs open and she shivered as he ran his fingers down the inside of her thighs.

"I have longed to do this," he said huskily, then his lips were tracing the path his fingers had followed. Summer's breath drew in sharply as his mouth found her clit, his hands cupping her buttocks to hold her.

Her hands were threading through his black hair, the flicks of his tongue and the growling-purring rumble sending tingling fire racing between her legs. She arched against him, gasping, as she came, and then Ke'lar was spreading her wider, sliding easily into her, filling her to the hilt with his slick hot cock.

Ke'lar's brilliant gaze held hers as he rocked inside her.

His hips picked up speed. "My Summer . . ."

"I love you," she managed a moment before she contracted hard around him.

His purr thrummed through her and he moved faster, deeper, drumming against her with a g'hir's speed. His fangs flashed then he was pulsing hard inside her.

He raised his head then to meet her gaze.

Tears stung her eyes. "I don't want to lose you."

"You cannot," he promised, brushing away the wetness with his thumbs. "I am yours, my mate, always. I will love you for all my life, and into the next."

He touched his forehead to hers and started to move again, slower this time, savoring every stroke. Summer shut her eyes as his rumble-purr vibrated through her again . . .

Sometime later Summer awoke. She rolled over, reaching for Ke'lar, and found only emptiness.

She half sat up, her hand still stretched toward where he had lain.

I'm going to do this for the rest of my life. I'll reach for him, look for him, and the place beside me, where he should be, will always be empty . . .

Summer dressed in the blue gown and slippers again, the only clothes she had with her. The ship was very quiet.

She found him in the cockpit. He would have heard her coming with that g'hir hearing of his but he didn't turn around, his gaze toward the vast black emptiness of space framed by the ship's front windows.

"We are clear of the Hironian system," he said quietly. "I can initiate the jump any time."

Summer's throat tightened. "Okay."

He waited until she was seated in the co-pilot's chair, until she was strapped in.

His fingers moved over the controls. "Initiating jump in three . . . two . . . one."

She drew her breath in sharply as a blinding burst of light appeared and vanished again, leaving the stars in completely different places, and a wondrous sight filling the viewport windows.

It was beautiful, hanging in the blackness of space like some exquisite blue jewel, so isolated, so vulnerable.

"Earth . . ." she whispered.

"You are home, my Summer," he rumbled hoarsely, and the world blurred at the anguish in his voice.

TWENTY-ONE

"The house looks okay," Summer said, chewing her lip for a moment and pulling the cloak tighter around her.

The sky was an ominous gray and it looked like more snow was on the way but her uncle's cabin looked as it always did—a little rundown, the porch in need of painting, but quaintly nestled in the woods and a mile in every direction from the nearest neighbor.

"You are shivering."

"Yeah. December. Smoky Mountains. Pretty fucking cold."

Ke'lar's eyes were troubled. "I should have secured you more suitable clothing for this weather."

She reached out, her fingers intertwining with his. His hand was warm, strong—as always.

"I wasn't complaining. I was actually trying to be funny." She gave a half smile. "Though I'm really sorry those boots you made got left behind on Hir. They rocked."

He smiled faintly. "I wish there was time to make you others."

And we're almost out of time, aren't we?

He could never return here; the briefest visit would endanger him and not even Beya awaited him on Hir now. He would return as a criminal on his world, alone and hated, without even the unconditional comfort of the multari's steadfast presence.

Ke'lar was making the greatest sacrifice a warrior of Hir could, to be separated from his bound mate, for her sake and the sake of a child he had never met, yet considered his own . . .

All I want to do is cry till I don't have a tear left but I can't make this harder for him. I have to honor his courage; I have to match it— he deserves that from me at least.

Summer swallowed hard and wrenched her gaze from his and back to Uncle Lester's cabin.

Her car, covered in snow, was still parked outside. The lights inside the cabin were on, and shifting a bit she could see the TV still on as well. If someone—or even the police—had come by the cabin they wouldn't have left everything on like that, would they? They would have towed her car, checked it for evidence or something.

"Well," she murmured, "everything looks just like it did when I left it."

"You do not sound certain."

"I won't be certain till I get inside," she admitted. "But no one has even cleared the snow off the steps. I don't see any sign anyone's here—or has been here. Let me take a look. I'll be right back."

He caught her before she'd taken more than a single step. "I will go and ascertain if it is safe."

So beloved to her now, his brilliant eyes were alert as they scanned the cabin and the area, his rippled brow lowered a bit, the showing fangs a dead giveaway he was anticipating danger.

"I think it's better if I go," she said. "If Uncle Lester's come home early, you won't have to lift a finger. He'll take one look at you and have a heart attack."

His glowing eyes turned to her. "I will not let you go alone."

Summer sighed inwardly. At this rate they'd be here till nightfall.

"Fine, we'll just go together, okay? But I go first and if there are any humans around, *don't* let them see you."

Her feet, still in slippers, were half-frozen by the time they made it to the door. It wasn't locked.

"Hello?" she called but silence answered.

The Christmas cards she'd been addressing were still spread across the table. Her mug still stood beside them, the once-hot chocolate inside now dried up and nasty looking.

Ke'lar's nose wrinkled in disgust. "What is that stench?"

"That's what you get when nobody takes the trash out for almost two weeks." She pulled her cloak off and flung it across Uncle Lester's comfortable but ugly green patterned sofa. She grabbed the remote from the coffee table and shut the TV off. "But no one's here," she said and pushed a few of the windows open. Better cold air than that old trash smell. "No one's *been* here either."

Summer held her breath as she bagged up the trash. She went out the back door and threw the bag into one of the cans. Set on wheels to be moved to the road for trash collection, they hadn't been touched either.

"This is a very primitive shelter," Ke'lar commented as she scrubbed her hands at the sink. The heat was still on—thankfully or the pipes might have busted—but the fire she'd gone out to the shed to fetch wood for had long since burned out.

She grabbed a towel to dry her hands. "Says the man who suggested we live in a cave."

They grinned at each other for a moment then the smiles faded.

She was home, in time.

And he should leave this world—now—return to his own before there was any chance he was discovered here.

Get back to the ship that waited in the nearby woods, cloaked from view by holo-reflectors that made it invisible to the human eye, and lift off immediately.

Ke'lar looked away first. "Can you track where Emma is?"

"I have been meaning to get her ear tagged," Summer joked, reaching for her bag, still hanging where she'd left it over the back of the dining room chair. "But I think I should start with my cell phone."

Ten days and forty calls, but only two from Dean. One where he didn't leave a message and the second confirming he was dropping Emma off today as planned.

"I should change," she said, indicating the blue gown she still wore. "Looks like I owe Jenna a dress." She looked at the wet slippers she wore. "And some shoes."

"I will see she is compensated," he rumbled.

When you get home.

"I repacked our things to carry them better for the walk to the clanhall and . . . I have something for you," he said, uncharacteristically clumsy when he reached into his pocket to draw it out. "Something someday—" His throat worked. "For you to give to our daughter."

A lump formed in her throat when she saw the carved comb in his hand, the one that had been his mother's.

She took it from him. "Ke'lar . . ."

He met her gaze and in those glowing pained eyes she saw she didn't have to say what she was feeling. He understood perfectly.

He reached for her and then she was in his arms, his mouth against hers, the cinnamon scent of him warm and soothing. He brushed his nose against hers, slowly up one side, down the other, a tender g'hir kiss, then his mouth touched hers and she wished this kiss could last forever.

But none ever could and she leaned into his strength, suddenly finding that all of hers had gone.

He touched his forehead to hers. "My own sweet Summer."

"Ke'lar," she murmured. "My mate . . ."

Suddenly he lifted his head, looking toward the cabin's front windows.

"What is it?" she asked, looking that way, but she couldn't see anything, hear anything, outside.

"I am not sure," he murmured. "It is unpleasant sounding." He sniffed and his expression went taut. "It smells like your land transport. The smell is getting stronger. It is coming this way."

Dean.

Even if it wasn't her ex, it was someone. Someone who couldn't be allowed to see an alien warrior.

"No, wait." She dropped the comb on the table to reach out to him, to catch him before he could go. "I'm not ready. Please, not yet . . ."

He cupped her cheek. "I wish I could express to you what it is for a g'hir male to be bound to a mate. My people have poems, songs, stories, and through them I thought I understood, but I did not, I *could* not. Truly it is not something a male can understand until he knows it. It is more than love, deeper than loyalty, greater to me than even the All Mother. I would do anything for you, my Summer." His glowing eyes were tormented. "Even let you go."

She could hear the car now too and her tears welled up. "I can't do this. I can't be without you."

He placed her hand over his heart. "You will never be without me. I am yours. For always. No matter how many stars separate us."

"It might be nothing. Maybe it's somebody I can send away. Don't go yet," she begged. "Just a little more time. An hour. A minute. Anything."

"A lifetime would scarcely be enough." He gently brushed the wetness from her cheek. "We do not cry as humans do but know, my mate, I will keen for you all my days."

His glance darted toward the door, toward the crunch of footsteps in the snow. She felt the barest brush of his mouth against her lips, and then with a g'hir's speed and a warrior's stealth he was through the back door, silently closing it before she could blink.

She took a stumbling step after him. "Wait . . ."

Behind her a heavy knock fairly rattled the front windows.

"Sum!" Dean called through the door. "Come on, girl! I ain't got all day!"

Blinking away her tears, she turned that way, toward Dean's hammering, her fingers numb as they wrapped around the doorknob.

Dean was no longer handsome, not like he had been in college when he'd been a blond baseball player, a square-jawed All-Star with an easy smile, confident he'd make the majors someday. When he'd hurt his shoulder, after they were married and Emma was on the way, the life just seemed to drain out of him. He was drinking more these days, or maybe it was just finally catching up to him; it showed with the puffiness in his face, the gut he was starting to get.

"Where the hell you been?" he demanded. "I done called you about a million times." He scowled, apparently forgetting that everyone had caller ID now; she knew exactly how many times he had called. "You'd think a person be by the phone day and night worrying about their child."

That he had hardly visited his daughter in three and a half years, that it sometimes took Summer three weeks to get him on the phone only to have him tell her he didn't have time to talk about "kid stuff," went right out of her head.

Because there, in his arms, a tumble of white-blond curls and rounded pink cheeks, sound asleep in her Hello Kitty pajamas, was Emma.

With a cry Summer reached for her daughter, ignoring Dean's surprised grunt as she swept her baby right out of his arms. She closed her eyes, cradling Emma against her, breathing in her scent, feeling Emma's soft, downy hair against her cheek.

"Baby," she murmured. "Momma's home, sweetheart. Momma's home."

Emma didn't even stir. Thanks to all the time in daycare, the child could sleep through an earthquake.

One unfamiliar with how g'hir moved might have dismissed it, might have thought that quick movement among the snowy branches a bird or small animal, but Summer, turning her head that way, just caught a flash of glowing blue eyes on her, on Emma, making sure they were both safe.

Then he was gone.

TWENTY-TWO

Her vision blurred and she looked down at Emma.

"She's so beautiful," Summer murmured thickly. "I can't believe I forgot how beautiful she is."

Dean was looking at her askance.

Right. Act normal; this is just a normal co-parenting kid hand-off 'cause nothing weird has happened at all.

"What the hell you all dressed up for?" he asked. "You look like the blond chick from *Frozen*."

Summer glanced down, dismayed to see she was still wearing Jenna's dress and the jeweled slippers.

Perfectly normal.

"Christmas party," Summer mumbled, laying Emma on Uncle Lester's green patterned sofa. He kept the blanket that Granny Crawford crocheted across the back and Summer pulled it down to tuck around Emma. "Sorry. My cell was busted. I, uh, dropped it in the toilet."

"That was pretty fucking careless." He let the storm door shut behind him and leaned Emma's small suitcase against the wall. "You ought to be more responsible."

"Well, you know me." Summer smoothed Emma's hair back. The little girl's face was speckled with what looked like that neon orange powdered cheese from Cheetos and she wondered when the child had last had a decent meal. "Anyway, they had to send me a new one. I just got it half an hour ago. How did the visit go? She and Marthe have a good time?"

He looked troubled. "She got bad news. The cancer's back."

Summer bit her lip. "I'm sorry, Dean. What are the doctors saying?"

He gave a shrug but it was far from careless. "That she probably won't make it to spring."

Summer's glance went to the beautifully carved comb on the dining table. "It's real hard to lose . . . someone you love."

"I forgot," he said. "Yours died a while back, didn't she?"

Her mother had died just before they'd met but that was just like Dean, not to notice something that didn't impact his comfort directly—like the needs and grief of other people.

"Yes," she said instead. "But I'm sorry about Marthe. She's always been good to me, good to Emma."

"She was glad to see her."

"I'm glad she could."

"Yeah, well . . ."

He shifted his weight again and it occurred to Summer that this might be the longest and most meaningful conversation they'd had since before she'd gotten pregnant with Emma.

Her brow creased. "Something wrong?"

Dean cleared his throat, looked at her and then away. "Chrissie and I are getting married."

Summer had been so focused on Emma she hadn't even noticed the woman waiting in the car.

Chrissie looked enough like her that they could be sisters. Same platinum hair, same fair tone to their skin, but this woman had a hard look to her. A partying girl where Summer had always been more a homebody. A girl up for anything, a wild one, happy to stay out half the night doing shots then throw her tank top off and run topless through the bar's parking lot just for the attention. The kind of girl Dean always wanted Summer to be, only to be disappointed to discover she was anything but.

"Oh," Summer said, surprised that he'd even think she'd care after all the misery he'd put her through. "Congratulations."

That she hadn't flown instantly into a jealous rage at the news seemed to melt the tension right out of his shoulders.

"I bet your momma's excited about you get married again," Summer said, just to say something. "I bet she's all about doing up the wedding."

He looked away, reaching into the pocket of his jeans. "We don't want to tire her out. We're just going to head out west. Get married in Vegas. Listen, I just—here."

He shoved some papers at her, folded into quarters to fit in his front pocket, the edges worn.

"What's this?" Summer asked, her frown deepening, already opening the papers to look at them.

Her mouth parted.

"I got it notarized and everything. Should be good to go."

"Why?" she got out, looking right at Dean's signature scrawled on the paperwork that waived his parental rights to Emma. "Why after all—why *now*?"

He glanced out the window, out at Chrissie sitting outside in the Hyundai. She was half-kneeling, the rearview mirror skewed so she could see herself to fix her makeup, apparently completely unaware that the passenger side sunshield would have a lighted mirror just for that purpose.

"Chrissie . . . Look, she just don't want to be a mom."

She stared. Your boyfriend having his kid once in a blue moon could hardly be called being a *mom*.

"I tried to call you," he grumbled.

Summer scanned the paperwork, her heart pounding, trying to check it before he vanished again.

It looked all right. Everything looked in order.

"No," she breathed. "It's okay."

Her grip tightened on the agreement as if he might snatch it back. Chrissie was regarding her reflection with a critical eye, turning her heavily made up face this way and that.

"You know this means you don't get no child support or nothing." His tone was halfway between surly and triumphant. "Not anymore."

With Dean bouncing from job to job, taking one crap job after another and getting fired when he didn't up and quit, the support the state forced him to pay was less than three hundred dollars a month. *And* he was late paying every damn time. The time and trouble it took to file the paperwork with the family court and have her lawyer remind him they could get a bench warrant for failure to pay, plus all the time and worrying herself sick he wouldn't take proper care of Emma when he did take her wasn't worth a million times that.

She gave a nod. "I got it covered."

He paused at the door to the cabin. "She'll be okay, right?" He glanced at his daughter, asleep on the sofa, her soft golden curls and rounded baby cheeks. "Even if she don't have a daddy."

"She'll be fine."

Summer pushed the storm door open in a not-so-subtle hint that he should get going. He took his time about it too, this boy who, no matter how old he got, would never really be a man, crossing to his car and getting in.

He said something to Chrissie and she gave Summer a catlike smug look as she settled into her seat. He fixed the rearview mirror she'd skewed and put his arm on the back of her seat, looking over his shoulder as he backed up, going fast enough to kick up a bunch of snow and ice.

"You look like a princess, Momma," Emma murmured, her big blue eyes sleepy.

Summer smiled through tears and shut the door, sitting beside Emma on the sofa to smooth her hair back. "I missed you so much, sweetie."

"I missed you too, Momma. Where's Dean?"

"You mean Daddy?"

"He said I can't call him Daddy no more." Emma rubbed one eye with a chubby fist. "It makes Chrissie mad."

"Oh. He's gone home."

Summer turned her face toward the window. It was starting to snow.

"Daddy's gone home . . ."

Emma was blinking up at her.

"Come on, baby," Summer said quickly, wrapping the blanket around her daughter and scooping her up.

"Momma?" Emma asked as Summer ran with her through the back door, her slippered feet crunching in the snow.

"It's all right," Summer panted, balancing Emma on her right hip, her daughter's little arms tight around her neck. "Everything's all right."

"Why we out in the woods, Momma?"

Don't be gone! Oh, God, please, don't be gone!

Summer was out of breath, fighting the drifts, the cold air burning in her lungs as she ran.

Willow Danes

"Ke'lar!"

TWENTY-THREE

Every step away from her was more difficult than the last. It was as if Summer's world itself pulled at his feet, dragging on his limbs to slow Ke'lar's progress, to make the parting ever more painful.

He could understand now why so many warriors had simply stopped caring if they lived when the Scourge had taken their mates. Why it was better to die in a challenge over one than to survive it and live without her . . .

By force of will alone he kept going, one boot sinking into the snow after another, closer to the ship, to Hir, half a galaxy away from her and the child.

He had not gotten a good look at her, Summer's child—*his* child—the human male blocked much of his view. He could see the top of her head, the shimmering gold of her hair, the curve of her cheek, but more importantly he had seen the love that lit Summer's face when she gazed upon the girl . . .

Weeks ago he had gone into the forest to demand the All Mother reveal the purpose for his life—and She had.

To be their provider, their protector, was the reason for his existence. His chest ached with wanting to stay, to share in their lives. But it was impossible. To remain here would make him more burden than warrior.

Still, to go, to leave them here on this uncivilized world, unprotected, roiled his stomach, an act in defiance of every instinct he had.

He would never see the face of the child he sacrificed all to protect, he would never see his Summer again, and he clenched his fist to keep the keen from rising in his throat.

There would be time enough to mourn their loss when he had done all he could to keep them safe.

No other human must see him. His very presence here in this forest, so near his mate and child, endangered them.

His fingers felt clumsy as he keyed the control to open the ship's door. The ship was warm and bright, in utter contrast to the fading light outside, the clouds heavy with snow, but he took no pleasure in its comforts. Only disgrace and banishment awaited him on Hir but until the Goddess took him, he was Summer's mate and he would wear that honor proudly, be a warrior worthy of her. He would face them all without shame, without regret; all he had done had been for her.

You are well worth the price indeed, my mate.

He fell heavily into the pilot's seat, looking dully out at the woods. Snow was beginning to fall, the flakes drifting through the air, and soon even their last steps together would be wiped away.

It was as if he left his lifeforce here, with her, as if his body and heart would forever be separated by the emptiness of space. Ke'lar closed his eyes briefly, his fingers resting on the ship's controls as the vessel powered up.

May the All Mother stand in my stead and protect you always, my Summer, my child . . .

Then he keyed in the commands to lift the ship for the return to Hir.

TWENTY-FOUR

"Momma?"

"Ke'lar!"

Summer's glance darted about, her quick breath visible in the cold. She'd run out here without a coat, intent on following the faint tracks she and Ke'lar had left, her long dress dragging behind her in the snow.

She couldn't see anything but woods and drifts, and the falling flakes were making it harder. She was no g'hir warrior, no hunter. The trail to the ship had disappeared, or he'd covered it when he'd backtracked.

The ship was cloaked, equipped with advanced technology that allowed it to blend so perfectly into the surroundings she could be standing right next to it and miss it entirely.

Unless it wasn't here to miss anymore.

No, no, please . . .

Summer's nose was running, her eyes stinging from the icy wind, the thin crocheted blanket not nearly enough to keep Emma warm in the dead of a Smoky Mountain winter and they were both shivering.

"Momma?"

"Hold on, baby." She scanned the ground as she walked, the snow halfway to her knees in places, looking for more footprints, for some hint which way to go. Why hadn't she paid more attention?

How do I find him if I can't see the ship!

"Ke'lar!"

Her cry echoed through the woods but there was no response, the woods as white and clear and empty as ever.

The ship was right here! Wasn't it? Or maybe farther down, farther from the road—

The light was fading fast as the snowfall picked up. Summer spun around, her gaze darting around the woods, turning so she could see in every direction, searching the quiet winter forest.

If he were here he would have heard her calling him. She wouldn't have had to call out to him at all; he was a g'hir warrior. He would have heard her coming, trudging through the snow.

If he were here . . .

He wasn't safe here. We both knew that. He had to leave.

"Why are you crying, Mommy? Are you hurt?"

"I—" Summer swallowed hard. "I lost something, baby."

Emma nestled closer. "I'm cold."

"I am too, sweetie," Summer whispered, her teeth chattering. Emma was heavy, even carried on her hip like this, but she wasn't even wearing shoes, just socks, so she couldn't put her down.

Emma was shivering and her own feet in Jenna's damn slippers felt frozen. It was going to get dark soon; she couldn't keep Emma out here like this.

"Let's get you home," Summer said numbly, turning that way. The way back was harder going. The snow seemed harder packed, with a crust of ice she had to break through with every step. There were drifts, some very deep, and Summer kept her head down, careful where she stepped.

Emma gasped, her tiny arms tightening around Summer's neck in fright, and she quickly followed her daughter's stare.

His face was softened by the fading winter light, strands of his long black hair were lifted by the wind, his glowing eyes a vibrant blue as they met hers. Standing here, in the woods, the snow swirling around him, he seemed not alien at all but some magical creature.

"Ke'lar!"

Summer stumbled toward him, half-afraid he was an illusion, a dream she'd conjured up that would vanish before she could reach him.

But his hands were the same warm, strong ones they had always been and they caught her as gently now as they had when she'd first begged him for help on Hir.

"Why are you here in the cold and snow?" he asked. "What has happened?"

It was so like that first meeting that Summer, her tears overflowing, started to laugh.

"How come your eyes look like that?" Emma asked.

Ke'lar's throat worked for a moment as he beheld the child he considered to be his own. "Emma . . ."

He reached out to her then hesitated, his gaze anxious, but he would have little experience with any child and none with a human one.

"It's okay," Summer assured.

"She is so like you, my mate." He touched the girl's cheek with just the tips of his fingers, as if fearful she was too fragile even for that light caress, and next to Emma he seemed a giant indeed. "She is lovely beyond words."

Emma regarded him with wide blue eyes and he addressed her.

"I am not human. I am g'hir," Ke'lar rumbled, speaking very softly. "That is why my eyes are different."

"He's growling, Momma!" Emma cried. "Is he going to bite me?"

"She cannot understand me." Ke'lar's shoulders slumped, utterly crestfallen. "She is afraid of me."

"Emma, this is Ke'lar. He can understand what you say but you can't understand him yet. I promise, though, he'll always protect you. He will always keep you safe."

Her daughter pondered that for a moment. "Like Beast?"

Ke'lar's rippled brow creased. "A beast?"

Summer bit the inside of her cheek. Ke'lar was gorgeous. "She means Beast from *Beauty and the Beast*—it's a movie, one for kids. He's big and has fangs too but he's nice to Belle. Emma loves that movie."

He gave a g'hir nod even though it was clear he wasn't really following. "She is shivering," he said. "As are you. Why are you here? What has happened?"

"I was looking for you. I—" She tilted her head toward Emma. "We want to come back with you."

He went still. "What?" he whispered hoarsely.

"We want to come back with you," she repeated. "Emma and I. To Hir."

He wasn't taking this the way she thought he would. In fact, he didn't look happy about it at all.

"Don't you—" Summer wet her lips. "Don't you want us to?"

His throat worked and he glanced at Emma. "We must get her inside, we must get you both warm. Come—" He reached for the girl and surprisingly Emma went right to him. He held her easily, as if she weighed nothing at all, as if he could carry her forever. "We will return to your shelter."

Summer got her and Emma into clean, warm clothes as soon as they got back to the cabin. While her sheepskin boots didn't compare to the ones she'd left behind at the Erah clanhouse, after running through the snow in dancing slippers, they were positively toasty.

Emma was hungry, of course. Finding out that Dean had handed her a bag of junk food from the gas station when they filled up rather than take the time to stop and get her a real meal had Summer's blood boiling so she put off Emma's bath for after supper.

She'd been gone ten days so the milk was a loss but she had plenty on hand at the cabin that was still edible. She decided to make Emma's favorite—spaghetti and meatballs—while Emma, with all the seriousness of a cultural ambassador, queued up the movie so Ke'lar could see who Belle was.

Summer had just put the water onto the stove to heat and managed to catch the look on Ke'lar face as Emma, an expert at using the remote at age three, scrambled onto the sofa to cuddle next to him.

G'hir didn't tear up but his expression showed that with Emma tucking the blanket around them both and leaning against him, he would be if he could.

Summer set the table as Emma told Ke'lar all about the movie he was already watching. He listened patiently to her as she talked about Belle and Gaston and gave a solemn human-style nod when she assured him that the Beast wouldn't really hurt Belle's father.

He dwarfed Uncle Lester's dining table and twirling the pasta proved such a challenge for him that Emma insisted Summer cut his spaghetti too. Emma talked a lot about her Granny Marthe, about watching TV and such, but it seemed that she hadn't seen a whole lot of Dean during the visit.

Emma didn't seem bothered by it but then again she'd seen so little of Dean in her short life she didn't have any expectations of him either.

Ke'lar ate all Summer put on his plate, and seconds too, but he wasn't saying much.

In fact, he wasn't saying anything at all . . .

Summer chewed at the inside of her cheek as she gave Emma a quick bath. She struggled against the impulse to open the bathroom door and peek out to see if he was still there in the living room where she'd left him. In fact, she rushed Emma, who always liked to linger and play in the water, and got her bath done in record time.

She dried her daughter's hair and watched Emma brush her teeth. As soon as she was dressed in clean pajamas she went racing out to the living room to Ke'lar.

His face lit with a smile when he saw them, but it was a strained one.

"*This*," Emma began, settling in beside him again and starting the movie where they'd left off before supper, "is where Belle goes to Beast's castle, but don't be scared, okay?"

He gave another human style nod. He was careful around Emma, even while eating, not to show his fangs if he could help it.

Summer perched on the sofa with them. Ke'lar seemed to be watching the movie but his continued silence made her stomach clench.

Belle and Beast were in the middle of their waltz when Summer glanced down at Emma and smiled.

"She's asleep," she whispered.

"I know," he rumbled softly, his glowing eyes on the child who snuggled with such complete trust next to him.

Mrs. Potts was just finishing her song as Summer picked up the remote to shut the movie off.

"I should put her to bed," she said into the sudden, awkward silence.

"Let me," he said when Summer bent to take Emma. His growl was low so as not to wake the child, a little pleading, as if this was his only chance to carry her.

His last chance to see her.

Summer's throat tightened and she gave a nod.

He stood, holding Emma carefully as he would a tiny bird, to carry her to her bed. He was so tall he had to duck under the doorway, waiting as Summer turned the sheets down.

He placed Emma gently on the bed and Summer tucked the blankets around her. Summer smoothed back one of Emma's curls, her fingers touching her daughter's soft rounded cheek for a moment.

Ke'lar hovered just inside the doorway, his face ragged, then he turned abruptly, gone from the room with a g'hir's speed.

Summer ran after him, scarcely remembering to shut the bedroom door in her rush.

When she reached the living room she saw he hadn't left, vanishing into the night, as she'd feared but his back was to her, his shoulders tense.

"Ke'lar?"

"I should never have let her see me," he growled. "I should have not have lingered here."

Summer folded her arms, holding them tightly against the ache in her ribs. "Look, if you don't want me—if you don't want to be saddled with a kid—just say so, damn it. It's not like it's the first, or even the *third* time, I've heard it."

"Want you?" He turned, his glowing eyes wild. "I want for nothing else than you." His glance went toward the bedroom where Emma slept. "Than our daughter. But I cannot stay here on Earth."

Summer reached for him but something in his expression made her hesitate.

"I know that. We'll go with you. To Hir."

"No," he growled.

She blinked. "You said you wanted us—"

"I do. More than anything. But you hated my world, hated being a g'hir's mate." His hands clenched at his sides. "I will not grasp my own happiness at the cost of yours."

"I didn't hate Hir . . . Okay," she admitted, shutting her eyes briefly. "I did hate it there . . . at first. But things are different now." She took a step closer. "If we were together, you and me and Emma . . ."

"You are willing to live there with me, on Hir, raise Emma there?" he asked sharply. "She has a father—a *human* father—here."

Summer grabbed the papers from where she'd left them on the dining room buffet and shoved them at him. "Do you know what this is? This is an agreement—signed by Dean—that waives all parental rights to Emma."

His glowing eyes blinked. "I do not understand what that means."

"It means that he's given her up." Summer laid the papers down. "That he didn't want to be her parent anymore, be responsible for her anymore."

Ke'lar's head reared back. "That is not possible. Why would he do such a thing?"

"Because it's the heart that makes a dad so really, Ke'lar, he isn't her father. *You* are. You were willing to do whatever it takes for her. And I'm willing to do whatever it takes for us to be together—all of us—because we're a family." She gave a short laugh. "Just one that's going to live on an alien world."

"Emma . . ." He swallowed. "She will grow up among the g'hir. Not among the humans."

"Jenna's daughter, Anna, is half-human and that other woman—Heather or whatever—she's human and expecting a baby, that's another half-human. Emma will grow up on another world but she'll be loved." She wet her lips. "Won't she?"

"Yes," Ke'lar said instantly. "She will be adored—protected—by all of my enclosure." He searched her eyes. "Are you sure?"

"I'm sure that I can't be without you. I'm sure that you will love Emma like a father should. We're a family. We can be happy—together."

He took her hands in his. "I do not regret bringing you home, seeing our child safe, but I am a warrior. I always intended to return, to face them all—my clan, my father, Ar'ar—to stand before them to answer for this crime as a man of honor. But when I stole you from your lawful mate, when I brought you home to Earth—it was not with the thought that you would ever wish to return."

"Wait." She stared. "Are you saying I *can't* go back?"

He shut his eyes for a moment. "You can return."

"You mean return as Ar'ar's mate," she said for him.

His grip tightened on her hands. "I will fight him," he growled and his jaw worked for a moment. "But if I do not win you will belong to Ar'ar again. And he will have another moon cycle to convince you to stay. You and Emma."

"Boy, you guys are really stuck on that whole moon cycle thing, aren't you?" she grumbled.

"It is our way," he reminded. "If you are to come with me to my clan's enclosure, if we are to live honorably, this must be done by Hir law."

Summer chewed her lip for a moment. "Couldn't we go somewhere else? Just go live in the city or someplace no one knows us?"

He gave a faint smile at that. "A g'hir warrior with a beautiful golden human mate and child? There is no place on Hir or even on our colonies where we would not soon have renown. The Betari would come to take you back." He shook his head. "This must be done if we are to be together. I must challenge Ar'ar for you—and win."

TWENTY-FIVE

"Momma!" Emma cried, pointing. "Look how big Belle is!"

Summer glanced at the ship's holoprojector playing a decidedly two-dimensional but very large recording of Emma's favorite movie as she joined them in the ship's main living section.

"Nice resolution," Summer commented, wondering how he'd managed to rig the xenari system to play the film at all. "Please tell me you didn't reroute life support to do that."

Ke'lar gave her a half chiding, half-relieved look and stood. "I was worried for you, my Summer. You are late."

"I was just up at the cabin," she reminded.

They'd both agreed that it would be best for him to remain hidden within the ship while Summer settled things enough that she could leave. Summer knew he delighted in having Emma with him and he positively doted on her. He'd insisted she be put under when the translation chip was implanted so she would feel no fear or discomfort, and waking up to find she could finally understand him just convinced Emma that he could do magic. He enjoyed his time becoming acquainted with his daughter, but he was still a g'hir warrior and anxiety gnawed at him when his mate had to venture out to what he considered a dangerous and primitive world without him. "And it was worth it to finish up today."

"Then you have concluded—" Ke'lar glanced back at Emma still singing along with Lumière. "Everything?"

"My lawyer pulled some strings at the family court and got everything signed before the holiday break," she confirmed quietly.

He let his breath out. "Then by Earth law, too, she is my child."

Not exactly true since Ke'lar hadn't—*couldn't*—adopt her here but having Dean's paperwork filed with the court and signed by a human judge satisfied his g'hir sensibilities.

"And"—her voice brightened as she lifted the container she held—"I brought something to help us celebrate." She set the container on the table and lifted the top with a flourish. "Lemon pie."

He inhaled deeply and a fanged smile lit his face at the sight of his new favorite dessert. "When did you make this?"

"Oh, believe me, the lemon pie was the easy part, it was everything else that took the whole day. Let's see—" She pulled plates and some of the weirdly shaped forks and a slicing knife from the xenari galley as she counted things off. "My lawyer also has power of attorney to sell the Alexandria house and its contents to put in a trust. Sarah Jane bought my car." Summer sliced the pie and placed the pieces on plates, topping them with homemade whipped cream and candied lemon peel. "I resigned from my job. Hmm," she said, licking some of the filling off her thumb. "Of course my boss wrote back and implied that he had always intended to make me Director of Marketing in the new year, which is a bunch of bull; he's just being catty."

Emma appeared at her side. "Can I have pie in there while I watch the movie?"

Summer said no at the same time Ke'lar said yes.

Then she had two sets of blue eyes, one human, one glowing, looking at her pleadingly.

"Oh, fine." Summer gave a sigh and handed the girl a slice. "Go ahead."

She handed Ke'lar a plate with an extra large slice of pie as Emma ran to her place in the living area. Not that it would matter—she knew he'd wind up finishing the rest of the pie off—but it looked nicer to serve it to him sliced and topped each time.

"I called the daycare," she continued. "Told them Emma won't be coming back after the holidays. They were pretty nice about it, though. They even refunded the new year's registration fee."

She couldn't help grinning at the rumbling sound of happiness that he made as he took his first bite of the pie.

"It's love that makes it so good. Well, actually," she amended, spearing a bite from her own slice, "love and gobs of fat and sugar."

He gave a huffed laugh. "And your uncle?"

"Yes, I got hold of him—finally! Real estate agents *live* on the phone so he doesn't carry his cell on vacation but I got him at his place in Florida. 'Course I had to call him at six this morning to do it, which he wasn't thrilled about. But he was happy for me and my new boyfriend, the anthropologist—"

He raised an eyebrow. "Anthropologist?"

"—and that Emma and I were off to exotic places with him to explore cave paintings and such. You know," she said proudly, "that whole thing with Ezzari might have really helped. I think Uncle Lester actually bought it. And I just finished cleaning and closing up the cabin . . . that's all of it."

He scraped the plate, finishing the last of his pie, and put the plate down.

"I can take you home," he rumbled softly, his eyes warm on her. His brow creased. "You are worried."

"What's to worry about?" She put down her half-eaten pie, brushing her hands on her jeans. "Just your clan, and the Ruling Council and the Betari clan and Ar'ar . . ."

He took her hands in his. "Nothing will take you and our daughter away from me," he promised. "Nothing."

"I know," she said, leaning against him. His arms went around her; with her cheek against his chest she could hear his heart beating strongly.

But even you can't fight them all . . .

"If you keep looking back at her like that you're going to crash this thing," Summer chided, the forest of Hir speeding by below.

"The proximity detector is engaged. I cannot crash." Ke'lar faced front again, his fingers never leaving the transport's controls. "And I want to be sure Emma is strapped in properly."

"You strapped her in yourself," Summer reminded. "She's fine."

She really was too. With a child's innocence, Emma simply accepted that that carpets could fly, candles could sing, and glowing-eyed men could show up one winter night and whisk them both off into the sky.

Emma had been dazzled by the stars, accepting spaceflight as easily as she would a plane ride. She had Ke'lar so wrapped around her tiny finger Summer was surprised he hadn't just turned over the ship's controls to her.

"Do they know we're coming?" Summer asked quietly. She'd actually been surprised that they hadn't been arrested at spacedock, that they'd been permitted to reach the capital city at all.

"My father has long since ordered my return to the clanhall. He sent the message as soon as we were known to be missing." His fingers moved calmly over the controls. "I have acknowledged his command. They will be expecting us to arrive shortly."

Summer's stomach clenched and she looked out over Hir's forests as they sped toward the Erah enclosure.

"This is really a beautiful world. Your clanhall is amazing. Emma's lucky she'll get to grow up there. No clanhall climbing though." She threw him a mock-warning glance. "Not till she's eight."

He smiled faintly. "Perhaps nine."

"How much longer?" Emma demanded. "I want to see the castle!"

"What castle, baby?" Summer asked.

"The castle!"

"But what—oh. No, sugar, it's a *clanhall*, not a castle."

"Daddy said 'castle,'" Emma insisted.

She had taken to calling him that almost immediately. A shrink would probably blather on about grieving the parental bond and attachment and whatnot, but Summer figured none of them ever had an alien warrior in co-parenting sessions so what the hell did they know?

"No, he didn't." Summer frowned at Ke'lar. "Did you say 'castle'?"

He gave a sheepish half shrug. "They are not so different."

Summer shook her head a little at him fondly. "We'll be at the castle soon, honey."

She was trying to hide her anxiety from Emma, from Ke'lar too, but the journey was far too short and her stomach clenched when the clanhall came into view.

It didn't help that the entire Erah enclosure seemed to have turned out for their arrival, standing in grim-faced formal assembly as Ke'lar landed the transport.

Mirak was there too, waiting for them.

As was Ar'ar.

"I will not fail you," Ke'lar rumbled, meeting her eyes squarely.

Summer's throat tightened. She was far more worried about him getting hurt.

"I know you won't." That was quite a crowd of g'hir waiting for them and this situation was tense enough. She gave a nod. "Okay," she said, unfastening the safety straps that held her to the seat, then undoing Emma's. "Let's go."

"Is this the castle, Momma?"

"Sure is," Summer agreed, taking her daughter's hand. "So we have to mind our manners, okay?"

Ke'lar hit the control to open the door and extend the ramp and the bright light of Hir's suns filled the transport's cabin. He went first and every eye was on him until she and Emma emerged behind him.

A ripple ran through the crowd.

Ar'ar, his expression thunderstruck, stepped forward to stare at Summer and Emma beside her.

Standing with Ra'kur and the other Erah clanbrothers on the steps of the clanhall, Jenna's mouth parted in shocked understanding, her gaze too riveted on Emma.

On the steps near Jenna waited a handful of females as well, possibly all the g'hir women of the Erah enclosure. Two were white-haired, one bent with age, and one was the dark-haired young woman she'd seen before when she and

Ke'lar had first arrived at the clanhall, but beside her stood another woman accompanied by—

"Are they princesses?" Emma said excitedly, her attention fixed, of course, on the two little girls. "Their eyes glow too but they have hair like mine!"

The eldest looked to be about seven, her sister perhaps four or five. Obviously beloved, they stood sedately beside their mother, their rounded, soft faces pink with health as they stared back at Emma. Their hair was blond, like their mother's, but darker than Emma's, more gold than white blond, and entirely *un*like her daughter these two had hair that was braided and beribboned.

Summer wondered wryly how their mother got the girls to sit still for all that styling when she could barely manage to get Emma to sit still long enough to have her hair combed. Emma wore jean overalls but these girls wore miniature versions of g'hir ladies' gowns and jewels sparkled on their fingers and throats.

Emma waved. The eldest girl stared but the younger one smiled, showing dainty little fangs, and waved back. Her mother tugged at her hand in silent rebuke and swept Summer's attire with a disapproving gaze.

I should have worn Jenna's dress! I look like a goddamn lumberjack.

In fact, realizing she was out in Hir's spring weather but had dressed for winter in North Carolina in sheepskin boots and a sweater made her want to slap her hand over her eyes.

Ke'lar strode to where his father waited and Summer and Emma followed. Rotin seemed to have aged five years in the short time since Summer had seen the Erah clanfather.

Ke'lar inclined his head to his father. "I have obeyed you and returned."

"After five days' absence!" Mirak burst out. "After shameless thievery of my son's mate!"

Rotin bared his fangs. "This is an Erah matter."

"Hardly," Mirak spat.

"This—" Ar'ar began, his throat working. "This is your child, Summer?"

Ke'lar was right next to them but Summer couldn't help drawing Emma a little closer to her. "Yes."

He shook his head a little, his glowing amber eyes wide. "Why did you not tell me?"

"*Two* daughters of the Betari have been kept from their clan by the criminal acts of your son!" Mirak snarled, rounding on Rotin. "And you say this is not our concern?"

"Summer is *my* mate," Ke'lar growled. "Emma is *my* daughter."

"By what right do you claim them?" Mirak scoffed. "None! You stole this female—"

"I admit what I have done!" Ke'lar's voice rang out. "I took the lawful mate of another without offering challenge as a warrior should. I journeyed to a world forbidden to any who do not have the Council's sanction. But I do not regret what I have done! I brought a mother to her child and—no matter what laws I have broken—I have done what is right!"

Summer threw him a proud look.

You tell 'em, honey!

He addressed Ar'ar. "By what right do you claim her?" he demanded. "No female is to be taken from her offspring. That is the law. Your capture of her was forbidden!"

Ar'ar's fangs bared. "I did not know she had a child! How could I have? She never told me."

"But *he* captured her honorably," Mirak broke in. "So Ar'ar's claim is the lawful one. The child is here now and she too belongs to my son. I insist these females be returned to their true clan—the Betari!"

"Mommy?"

Emma could understand their language now but all the roaring was frightening her. Summer's own ears were ringing from it.

She swung Emma up to hold her on her hip. "It's okay, sweetie," she murmured, stroking her back. "You're safe. I promise."

"Summer should never have been taken, never forced from her young one." In the wake of understanding his son's actions, the life and color had returned to Rotin's face and he faced his old enemy confidently. "And so Ar'ar has lost all claim on her. She is Ke'lar's."

"Your son is not a warrior!" Mirak's fangs bared fully. "He is a criminal!"

"He sought only to remedy the wrongs done by *your* son!" Rotin roared back.

"My son will prove himself the warrior deserving of *our* clansisters," Mirak spat. "By killing this thief!"

"I will fight," Ke'lar growled. "For the mate and child that are mine."

Rotin gave his son a short, proud nod. "Do you see? My son will fight as an honorable warrior should."

"As will mine," Mirak snapped. "And we will see this matter decided now."

With a grim look at Summer, and Emma in her arms, Ar'ar followed his father, and the Betari clanbrothers as well.

People were moving about, changing places, clearing room for the coming fight. The g'hir woman was already leading her children away.

Jenna crossed quickly to Summer. She smiled at Emma but her face was tight with tension. "Hi, I'm Jenna. What's your name?"

"Emma."

"Hi, Emma," she said. "If it's okay with your mom I'd really like to take you inside to meet my little girl, Anna."

Emma's eyes widened. "Inside the castle?"

"The—? Uh, yeah," Jenna said, nodding. "The castle."

"Is it okay, Mommy?"

Ke'lar caught her eye and gave a firm nod.

We sure don't want her watching this. Actually, I'm not sure I want to watch this either . . .

"Yup," Summer said with false cheerfulness and put Emma down. "You go inside with Miss Jenna and I'll come see you after, okay?"

Emma's brow creased. "After what?"

"After your visit," Ke'lar said smoothly. He crouched down but Emma still had to look up to meet his eye. "You will like the new baby."

"Oh," Emma said, disappointed. "She's just a baby?"

"For now," Ke'lar agreed. "But someday soon she will be old enough to be your playmate." He smiled ruefully. "Remember always that I love you, Emma."

She threw her arms around his neck for a hug. "I love you too, Daddy."

He patted her back, his face taut, but when she pulled away he gave her another smile and stood. "You must go with our clansister Jenna. She can make icy tea."

"Iced tea," Emma corrected. She looked up at Jenna. "I like lemonade."

Jenna gave a nod. "I'm sure I can wrangle up something."

"You be good, okay?" Summer knelt to hug her. "I'll come get you soon."

"How long?" Emma demanded.

Summer glanced to where Ke'lar stood a few paces away in grim conversation with Ra'kur and their father. She smoothed her daughter's hair. "Not long."

"Have you ever been inside a castle before?" Jenna took Emma's hand to lead her away. "This one is really, really old . . ."

"Do you wish to go with her?" Ke'lar asked seriously as he came to stand at her side.

"No, I'll stay here with you."

He hesitated. "This may be difficult for you to watch. The end is often . . . ugly."

Summer glanced at Ar'ar. "I actually don't want either one of you to get hurt."

"He was your mate," Ke'lar rumbled quietly. "Would you like to speak to him before we begin?"

"No," Summer said with a sigh. "I'll speak to him afterwards."

"Afterwards?" His brow furrowed. "That will not be possible if I win."

Summer raised her eyebrows. "You mean if you win I can't even talk to him anymore?"

"Of course not," Ke'lar said, surprised. "He will be dead."

Her breath stopped. "What?"

"That is how the winner is declared," Ke'lar growled with a narrowed look across the courtyard at Ar'ar. "When only one of us still lives."

TWENTY-SIX

Summer felt the blood drain from her face. "This is a fight to the death?"

"Of course."

"You never—Why the fuck didn't you say so?"

He gave her a puzzled look. "I just did."

"No, I mean—" She passed her hand over her eyes. *So. Fucking. Literal.* "I meant, why didn't you tell me *before* you agreed to do this?" His brow creased but before he could say anything she held her palm up. "You know what? It doesn't matter. You aren't doing it."

"You are my mate. She is our child." His fangs flashed. "I *will* fight for you."

"Ke'lar—" She folded her arms. "I am not just going to stand here and watch you die!"

He gave a short huff. "I did not realize you had such confidence in my skills."

"You aren't doing this," she insisted. "I won't let you!"

He searched her eyes for a moment.

"I think you say this because you are human," he said slowly. "Perhaps this is how as a human you would show you care for me. But I am g'hir and we are on my world." Ke'lar took her hand. "If I die, remember you have only the moon's cycle with Ar'ar. I have secured my father's promise and Ra'kur's they will be present for your Choosing Day. You will have your choice."

Her throat tightened. "*You're* my choice, Ke'lar."

He cupped her cheek in his palm. "And I fight to prove I am worthy of you."

"Are you ready, brother?" Ra'kur asked, joining them.

"In a moment," Ke'lar agreed and began unfastening the jacket of his warrior clothing.

"What are you doing?" Summer exclaimed. "You guys don't fight naked do you?"

Ke'lar froze and the looks the men gave her were priceless. If this hadn't been so horrifying, so deadly serious, it would have been funny.

Ra'kur recovered first. "Weapons are forbidden," he explained. "A warrior fights bare chested to show he has none hidden on him."

"My child, Emma—" Ke'lar rumbled with an anxious glance at Ra'kur, handing over his jacket to a waiting clanbrother.

"My mate will keep her inside," Ra'kur assured. "Far from the windows and balconies until we come for her. She will not see. It is just as well," he rumbled. "I do not wish Jenna to witness this either."

"You aren't making me feel any better here, you know," Summer said, wrapping her arms around herself.

"A challenge of this kind is no small thing, nor to be lightly undertaken," Ra'kur said, a little sharply. "They are a relic from the time when the clans began but the number of these battles has increased since the Scourge. The enclosures have actively tried to discourage them but to little avail. There are too many warriors and too few females and we have all witnessed such battles. There are no rules but to kill your opponent. These challenges are fierce, and bloody." Ra'kur's face was grim. "It takes a great deal of damage for one g'hir warrior to kill another."

Summer's gaze snapped to Ke'lar. "I don't think—I don't want you to—"

"I *will* fight for you," he snarled, his fangs showing. "I will not let you and Emma go to another. I will die first!"

Oh my God, he means that.

"I changed my mind." Summer wet her lips. "I want to talk to Ar'ar."

Ra'kur scowled in disapproval and Ke'lar went still.

"That is your right," he agreed, but she could see it hurt him.

"Okay." She gave a nod. "Okay."

"It is inappropriate that I go with you"—he glanced toward the other side of the courtyard—"if you wish to speak to your mate."

"He's *not* my mate, you are," Summer said thickly. "But—just maybe—I can convince *him* of that."

"The challenge will begin shortly," Ra'kur growled. "If you wish to speak to"—he glanced to where the Betari had gathered, to where Ar'ar stood shirtless, his molten gaze on her—"Ar'ar, you should do so now."

"I'll be right back," she said to Ke'lar.

Summer could feel every eye on her as she crossed the courtyard and she wondered if she were breaking some death-battle etiquette or something.

Certainly the Betari weren't happy to see her.

"Daughter," Mirak greeted her with narrowed eyes and heavy sarcasm. "How honored we are you have seen fit to stand with us."

"I need to speak to Ar'ar," she said. "Alone."

The Betari warriors shifted in their places, looking to their clanfather, but Ar'ar spoke first.

"Leave us."

The men inclined their heads and after a moment, Mirak, with a bitter look at her, gave them some privacy.

"I will kill him," Ar'ar said without preamble. "I am the mightier warrior. The better fighter."

Summer's eyes stung. What if Ar'ar was right? Was her happiness worth Ke'lar's life?

"I love him. Doesn't that matter to you?"

"The Zerar took the luxury of love from us when they unleashed their plague on my people," he growled. "Now it is about which of the g'hir are deserving enough—*strong enough*—to survive. The Betari must be among those who do."

"Ar'ar, if there is one thing my time on Hir has taught me," Summer said tightly, "it's that surviving isn't *living*. And your people have known enough killing."

Ar'ar looked to the far side of the courtyard where the Erah stood, where Ke'lar stood, waiting for this battle to begin.

"Do you think me a monster? My heart is sick with what will result from this challenge," he rumbled. "All that will be lost."

"Then don't fight it," Summer pleaded. "You don't have to. What if I agreed to go with you? What if—"

"No. The matter must be settled here, today. There can be no doubt to whom you belong." His fangs bared. "And when I kill their clanbrother the Erah will hate us even more. It will not be long before our enclosures are at war."

She shook her head. "I'm not worth a war, Ar'ar."

"Why did you run from me?" he demanded sharply. "Why did you not tell me of the child? She is a daughter of mine—of the Betari!"

She closed her eyes briefly. "Because I had to get back to Earth to protect her. Me not being there when she was returned from a visit to her grandmother would have put Emma in great danger. I know," she hurried to say at his frown, "you don't understand. That something like that would never happen on Hir, but believe me, getting back to Earth—*fast*—was the only way to keep her safe."

He searched her face.

"I believe you," he rumbled at last. "I believe that you acted to protect our child. What I do not understand is why you did not trust me to protect her."

"I think you would have—the g'hir way. You would have gone and tried to find Emma . . . if you'd known about her."

"I will be a good mate to you, Summer," he growled softly. "I am strong. I will protect our daughter . . . and all the offspring that follow her."

Summer chewed the inside of her cheek. "Please don't do this."

His nostrils flared. "I do not have any choice."

"We always have choices," Summer said hoarsely.

He looked away, his face hard and set now. "Not if the Betari are to survive."

It was clear that she wasn't doing any good here, that she didn't have any more chance of talking him out of this than she did Ke'lar.

Ke'lar was watching her warily, his expression guarded as she approached. "Is there something you wish to tell me, Summer?"

"Yeah." She nodded. "Don't die."

"I dare not." He gave a faint smile. "The All Mother has given me too much to live for and She will be much vexed if I am not here to appreciate it."

She rested her hands on his chest, feeling the strong steady beat of his heart. "I love you."

"And I love you . . ." he rumbled and brushed his nose against hers, then pressed a kiss to her mouth. "My sweet Summer . . ."

From the other side of the courtyard, Ar'ar came forward. Mirak and the other clanbrothers took up a place near Rotin but the Erah clanfather did not even acknowledge his rival.

"It is time," Ke'lar said, waving his brother forward. "Ra'kur will keep you safe until this is ended."

Ra'kur's hand was at her elbow, seeking to draw her away, but she couldn't make her feet move. "Ke'lar . . ."

His glowing blue gaze was steady. "I will not fail you."

"No . . ." she whispered but Ra'kur's hold was less gentle now, pulling her back, away from the combatants.

The men faced each other as Ra'kur hauled her up the clanhall steps.

"Wait!" Summer pleaded, pulling against Ra'kur's hold. In the courtyard Ar'ar was already falling into a fighter's posture. "Let me talk to them again!"

"Ar'ar!" Ke'lar roared, taking position before his opponent, his fangs fully bared. "I challenge you for the female, Summer. Will you fight me for her?"

"Let me—"

Ra'kur's grip tightened against her struggles. "Be still," he hissed. "Or I will take you into the clanhall!"

Ar'ar glanced her way then, his yellow gaze burning, his face savage, terrifying.

"No," Ar'ar growled and straightened from his battle stance. "I will not."

TWENTY-SEVEN

"You . . ." Ke'lar rumbled into the collective stunned silence, his brow furrowed, his body still tense as if suspecting a trick. "You concede?"

"Fight, Ar'ar!" Mirak urged, regarding his son in astonishment. "She is yours!"

Ar'ar shook his head. "No, she is not. We never mated. She did not surrender to it because she longed to return home, although I did not know why then, and I did not—" His throat worked for a moment. "Because I long for another."

"Another?" Summer echoed, pulling free of Ra'kur's hold. "You mean . . . you don't want me?"

"I . . . desired you," Ar'ar rumbled, his cheeks flushing, as she came to stand before him in the courtyard, and Summer suddenly realized it wasn't *her* he was embarrassed to admit that in front of. "Very much. Your human beauty is astonishing but you are not . . ." His eyes were drawn to the clanhall steps, to the young black-haired Erah woman standing there who now blushed becomingly.

Ar'ar swallowed. "H'lara and I met at the wedding ceremony at the Yir enclosure during the last gathering. I have thought of little else since. . ."

The g'hir woman, H'lara, stepped forward, pushing past her astonished clanbrothers.

"And I have made my choice!" she called out in trembling defiance to the shocked crowd, to the wide-eyed

Erah clanfather. "I will have no other than Ar'ar as my mate!"

Ar'ar's face fairly glowed with joy. "H'lara . . ."

As if suddenly remembering why he was standing here shirtless, that Ke'lar still waited to tear him to pieces, Ar'ar quickly inclined his head to his opponent. "I cede all claim to this female, Summer," he said formally. "She is yours."

Ke'lar blinked and then he straightened, his fangs flashing in a wide grin.

"Wait—" Summer looked around at Ke'lar. "Did I just get ditched g'hir-style?"

He spread his hands, his glowing blue eyes crinkling with humor. "I was ready to fight for you."

"I can't believe . . . all this time you were in love with her?" Summer asked, indicating H'lara.

A look of consternation came over Ar'ar's face. "You are a worthy female. I had hoped to be a good mate to you." Ar'ar's rippled brow creased. "If I had met you before H'lara—"

Summer held her hand up. "No, just stop right there. Believe me," she assured with a glance at Ke'lar, "I'm really okay with this but . . . Okay, why did you capture me if you really loved her? Why go to Earth at all?"

Ar'ar hesitated. "It is a great honor to be chosen to hunt a mate on your world."

Summer glanced at Mirak. "And you didn't want to disappoint your father?"

"Ar'ar . . ." Mirak frowned at his son. "Why did you not tell me?"

"She is of the Erah clan, Father," Ar'ar said tightly. "Our enemies, as you have said time and again. You taught me hatred of them before my milk teeth had come in." His gaze went to H'lara, the longing in his eyes so evident it was painful. "And with so many suitors, I did not dare to hope that . . . But when we were last here, when Summer sought sanctuary, we spoke again and . . ."

"My son—" Rotin prompted.

Ke'lar glanced at his father then cleared his throat. "Of course. Ar'ar, I accept your . . ." He paused, looking as if searching for the right word. ". . . decision."

"You concur that the matter is settled?" Rotin asked Mirak.

"It is settled," Mirak agreed. "And," he added with a look at his son, "we are honored to welcome your clansister, H'lara, as the Betari's next clanmother."

"Thank you, Father," Ar'ar breathed. "And thank you, Summer," he rumbled. "For reminding me that there are some things we must never let anyone, even the Zerar, take from us."

I did?

"Oh . . . sure." She gave a nod. "You're welcome."

His brow creased. "Are you offended that I lack the fire to fight for you? I would not have you and I be enemies."

"No!" Summer said instantly. "I'm happy for you! And . . . her. And me. And that Ke'lar doesn't have to fight you. And nobody has to die. In fact—go." She pushed him toward H'lara. "Go be happy."

He threw her a grateful look and lost no time crossing to where the g'hir woman eagerly awaited him.

"I suppose . . ." Mirak met Summer's eyes hesitantly, discomfiture so out of character for the Betari's forceful clanfather. "I was wrong to try to force a match between you and my son."

"You suppose?" Summer echoed.

"I . . . apologize," Mirak said as if choking on the words a bit. "I regret any pain I caused you, Summer of the Erah."

"Pain?" she wondered. "Oh! You mean threatening to keep me captive, married against my will?" She gave an airy wave. "I can't believe you'd even mention such a little thing!"

"Think of me what you will," he growled, serious in the face of her sarcasm. "But to live out a life alone, for a g'hir warrior, is a pain you cannot imagine. To save our son—*her* son"—his amber eyes had a pained look remembering one he lost long ago to the Scourge—"from that solitary existence—to give him the hope and joy he deserves—I would do what I did again . . . and more."

"And since our clans are going to be pals," she said with a pointed look at Ar'ar and his soon-to-be mate, "you want my forgiveness?"

Mirak tilted his head. "Would you do it for your child? Your Emma?"

She and Ke'lar exchanged a look.

"You got me there." Summer heaved a sigh. "And I hate to say it but—yeah, I would." She glanced to where Ar'ar and H'lara were already brushing noses. "I'm happy for him. . . for both of them."

"You are gracious, Mata." He cleared his throat. "The clanmother's jewels—"

"Right," Summer said with a nod. "They're in the pack I brought from your enclosure. I'm sure Jenna still has it. I'll get them to you before you go."

He looked at Ke'lar. "I hope she will be happy with you, and that you will value her as she deserves."

"Wow," Summer said, surprised. "I think you really mean that."

"I do. And before you return those jewels, I would have you choose one for yourself." Mirak inclined his head to her. "As a gesture of our friendship. Now, if you will excuse me, I should greet Ar'ar's intended, the Betari's new clanmother."

"That was generous of him," Ke'lar said. "To offer you such a gift of goodwill."

"True, but if he were really thoughtful he would have left them alone for five minutes, for God's sake," Summer muttered, watching him walk to the pair. "How that man ever got to be a Council member with *that* level of tact and sensitivity, I'll never understand."

"I am only glad the matter is decided," Ke'lar rumbled.

"Oh, that's right, I'm all yours—" She grinned. "By default."

"I would have won, my mate," Ke'lar mock-grumbled, pulling her close. "No one would doubt you are mine."

"Oh, believe me . . ." Summer slid her arms around his waist and lifted her face to brush a kiss against his mouth. "Nobody's *ever* going to doubt that."

EPILOGUE

Emma's brow creased as she looked between Summer and Ke'lar. "She'll be like Anna?"

"Yes," Ke'lar rumbled solemnly, crouching down to get as close to eye level with her as he could with his height. "This baby will be like Jenna's daughter, Anna. Half-g'hir and half-human."

The exam room of Be'lyn's medical center was comfortably homey and Summer didn't want to put this news off any longer. She'd insisted they waited till they were sure, till every test the healers could run showed the baby she carried was healthy, before they told Emma.

"But she'll still be my sister," Emma said.

"Your half-sister," Summer corrected.

Her daughter's face took on a look of obstinacy, her little jaw hardening in stubbornness, and Summer sighed inwardly.

Gets it from Dean.

"Don't care if she's half-g'hir." Emma fixed them both with a stern look. "She's gonna be my *whole* sister."

Ke'lar's mouth twitched, his fangs showing for an instant, but he swiftly controlled his smile.

Man, he's going to repeat that *to anyone who'll listen . . .*

"Hmmm." Summer shifted, pressing her lips together.

Ke'lar looked up immediately. "Summer?"

Doctor Ki'san was just coming back into the exam room and his gaze went immediately to the display over her head. "The nausea has worsened?"

Her stomach was roiling, and it was a moment before she could speak.

"You know," she gasped then took a few slow breaths to continue, "with Emma I had morning sickness maybe *once* but this . . ."

"Mommy?" Emma piped. "Are you okay?"

She wanted to assure her daughter, explain that it sometimes was something you had to get through when you were growing a baby, but right now all she could do was manage to hang onto the exam table and force out a pleading: "Ke'lar?"

"We must wait outside, Emma," he said, swiftly scooping their daughter up. "So the doctor can help your mother feel better."

Summer threw him a grateful look as he hustled the little girl out.

"And you are certain the sickness is normal for humans?" Doctor Ki'san asked.

"Absolutely. 'Course this is a little on the high side," Summer got out. "And it usually doesn't last so long."

The doctor touched a few controls to adjust the display then gave a nod. "I see no reason not to administer a mild anti-nausea injection."

"Hmmm . . . If you value your shoes you might want to hurry . . ."

The injection didn't even hurt and was instantly followed by blessed relief as her stomach settled right down.

"Thank you!" Summer breathed. "I'm actually hungry again."

He gave a huffed laugh. "I am pleased I could ease your discomfort. There is an oral version of the medication that we should start you on, to prevent a return of this symptom."

"And it's safe for human—I mean, half-human babies?" she asked, laying her hand on the slight curve of her belly.

"I would not have administered it if it were not," he assured. "I have studied all the data to be had on humans, as well as the new generation of g'hir."

"Lucky for me," Summer said, sliding off the exam table. "Can I get out of here now? I mean not that I don't like you, Doctor . . ."

"I understand." Ki'san threw her a smile. "No one enjoys being a patient. Least of all physicians. But yes," he agreed, indicating the door. "If you feel up to it you may return to your enclosure. Please contact me if these symptoms return—or if there are any new ones. Otherwise I will see you in a half moon cycle for your next checkup."

It was none of her business but—

"Why are you studying humans?" Summer asked when he joined her in the hall. "I mean, are we just a particular interest of yours?"

"Yes," Doctor Ki'san said. "But actually I will soon have the opportunity to see your world. I am looking forward to it."

Summer blinked. "You're going to Earth? To find a mate? I thought only warriors were allowed—"

"No," he said with a quick, embarrassed smile. "I have not been permitted to compete for that opportunity."

"Oh," Summer said. "So why are you going?"

"As a physician only. The Council has decided someone with advanced medical training should accompany the warriors who venture to your world."

"Because of my daughter." Summer's glance was drawn to Emma and Ke'lar, who was keeping her entertained by pointing out the city sights visible from the medical center's windows. "Because of me."

"Partly," Doctor Ki'san agreed. "But Jenna of the Erah nearly died before she reached Hir. I am also going to be on hand in case of such an emergency." He hesitated. "I thought it might relieve your mind if you knew that no other woman captured would be separated from her offspring."

"Because you'll run a scan on them after they've been captured," Summer concluded. "To make sure they haven't given birth."

"And I will be on hand to erase their memories so that they can be returned to their lives immediately, without disruption."

"Okay, but . . ." Summer cleared her throat. "Won't that be awkward as hell? Just you and a warrior and his mate?"

"Two warriors this time. And it will be a larger ship with private quarters. Unless a medical emergency occurs I doubt I will encounter any of them. But I am an adequate pilot," he allowed. "I am sure ship's operations will fall to me when we leave Earth."

"They're sending two warriors this time? Why?" She shook her head. "Never mind. Stupid question. Because the whole human-g'hir repopulation plan is working so well."

Ki'san tilted his head. "You are happy here, are you not?"

Summer looked down the hall at Ke'lar, at Emma in his arms, felt the flutter of the baby inside her. "Yes," she said fiercely. "Yes, I am."

Maybe other women would be happy to find themselves a warrior too—happy as she was, and Jenna and her new friend, Hope.

But just in case, I'm personally going to visit each and every one and make sure that when her *Choosing Day comes she really gets her choice heard.*

Summer looked back at Ki'san. "I come from a really beautiful world, a really precious one."

"And one that must protected, at all costs." He gave a wistful smile. "I doubt I will do more than step outside the ship for a moment or two, but I will cherish that little time I have on your world."

"Is everything all right?" Ke'lar asked, concerned by her long talk with the doctor.

"Yup," she assured. "Everything's fine. Come on, you two," Summer said and smiling, caught both his and Emma's hands in her own. "Let's go home."

WARRIORS OF HIR SERIES
BOOK ONE

Willow Danes

CAPTURED
WARRIORS OF HIR

Jenna McNally is tending to the heartrending task of clearing out her grandfather's cabin when she's knocked off her feet by the impact of a nearby plane crash. She races into the snowy North Carolina woods to help and discovers that this is no plane that's crashed.

Ra'kur's people have been brought to the brink of extinction by war. After years spent searching for a compatible mate to bond with, an enemy attack lands him on a backward, primitive planet and right to the very female he has been seeking. And a Hir warrior's first task in claiming a mate is to capture her . . .

WARRIORS OF HIR SERIES
BOOK TWO

Hope MacGowan is a city girl but reeling from a break-up on top of a layoff has her determined to have a weekend away in the North Carolina mountains—even if all her friends have bailed at the last minute. Hope's life is one big train-wreck and getting kidnapped by a tall, blond alien—even a gorgeous one—sure isn't helping.

R'har crossed the galaxy to seek a mate on this newly discovered world and this delicate red-haired female is everything he's dreamed of—except happy to find herself mated to him. R'har knows in his heart he's her true mate, even if he's not human. But taking her doesn't mean he can keep her and somehow he has to convince Hope to choose him before time runs out . . .

Her family's fortune can buy Tara Douglas anything—
except more time. Determined to make peace with her fate,
she's come to the house her great-grandfather built in the
Smoky Mountains to spend the time she has left. But for
once Tara becomes the healer when she finds wreckage of
an otherworldly vessel, and a badly injured man whose
glowing eyes see right into her soul . . .

When Ki'san volunteered to journey to Earth he never
imagined he would find himself dying there. A physician
from a vanishing race, he knows his people's law allows
only a chosen few to hunt the females of this planet as
mates. Ki'san's mere presence on Tara's world endangers
them both but the crash that leaves him clinging to life also
brings him a female like none he could have imagined, one
he cannot help but love . . .

Acknowledgments

My deepest gratitude and thanks to my editor, Erin McCabe. Her support and encouragement make this book possible. Erin, you are the best!

Many thanks to Christine LePorte for her warm support and sharp eye.

Thanks to my cover designer Steven James Catizone for his talent and, as always, his patience.

Thank you to everyone who supported and encouraged me and, most of all, to my family.

Willow Danes

Willow Danes loves all genres of Romance but especially Sci-fi, Paranormal and Historical.

Science Fiction (Warriors of Hir Series)
> *Captured*
> *Taken*
> *Stolen*
> *Hidden*